Praise for *One*

"I couldn't p...

—S... author of *The Power of a Pra... oman*

"*One Sunday* touched my heart in a deep way that many of us who have looked for love in the wrong places can relate to. This refreshing tale, told with honesty and humor, gives a transparent view of a hurting woman in search of love, healing, and clear direction to her true God-given destiny. It is a wonderful translation of the human condition . . . the created looking for the Creator."

—Rebecca Nichols Alonzo,
speaker and author of *The Devil in Pew Number Seven*

"Carrie's story is very real and compelling. The incredible impact of Christ upon her life that is felt in these pages is not fiction, but an authentic testimony of amazing grace. This book is a great gift of hope to anyone who doubts that God cares about their pain."

—Dr. Rice Broocks, cofounder of Every Nation Churches and Ministries,
bishop of Bethel World Outreach Church in Nashville,
and author of *The Purple Book*

"*One Sunday* is a novel that takes hold of you. Carrie Gerlach Cecil gives a vivid depiction of the life of Alice Ferguson. This humorous journey paved with rocky roads takes you from dark to darker. Yet, in a realistic way, a beacon of light shines through, which leads to a brighter day. In short, it a story of hope, in spite of hopeless situations."

—Debbie Winans-Lowe, gospel music artist

"The message of this Christian novel: Jesus loves everyone, and no one is beyond forgiveness."

—*Kirkus Reviews*

ONE SUNDAY

CARRIE GERLACH CECIL

HOWARD BOOKS

A Division of Simon & Schuster, Inc.

New York   Nashville   London   Toronto   Sydney   New Delhi

Howard Books
A Division of Simon & Schuster, Inc.
1230 Avenue of the Americas
New York, NY 10020

Copyright © 2013 by Anachel Communications, Inc.

All rights reserved, including the right to reproduce this book
or portions thereof in any form whatsoever. For information,
address Howard Books Subsidiary Rights Department,
1230 Avenue of the Americas, New York, NY 10020.

First Howard Books trade paperback edition February 2013

HOWARD and colophon are trademarks of Simon & Schuster, Inc.

"Alabaster Box," words and music by Janice Sjostrand, © 2004 Little Pooky's Music
(administered by PurePsalms Music, Inc.), originally recorded by CeCe Winans on
Alabaster Box (PureSprings Gospel). Reprinted by permission.

Permission to quote from the interview between Jody Powell and David Alsbrook has been
graciously granted by the Jimmy Carter Presidential Library and Museum.

For information about special discounts for bulk purchases,
please contact Simon & Schuster Special Sales at 1-866-506-1949
or business@simonandschuster.com.

The Simon & Schuster Speakers Bureau can bring authors to your
live event. For more information or to book an event, contact the
Simon & Schuster Speakers Bureau at 1-866-248-3049 or
visit our website at www.simonspeakers.com.

Manufactured in the United States of America

10 9 8 7 6 5 4 3 2 1

Library of Congress Cataloging-in-Publication Data

Cecil, Carrie Gerlach.
  One Sunday / Carrie Gerlach Cecil.
    p. cm.
  I. Title.
  PS3603.E337O54 2013
  813'.6—dc23
                                                2012029504

ISBN 978-1-4516-6476-8
ISBN 978-1-4516-6477-5 (ebook)

This book is dedicated to You, Jesus, because of all You did and continue to do in my life.

For those who believe they are too screwed up for God to accept, forgive, renew, and love them. Remember, some of Jesus' most loyal followers were forgiven murderers, prostitutes, adulterers, and crazy people. He champions the humble underdog, and He is just waiting for you.

If you set a candle in a perfect pot, you will see only a tiny bit of light. If you set a candle in a cracked pot, the light shines out of all of the jagged holes. This book is for all of my cracked pots; it's time to let your light shine!

Your devoted prayer warrior
and partner in the cracked-pot club,
Carrie

Acknowledgments

With love and special thanks:

- To Chuck, who loves me through it all and in spite of it all. Thank you for being a Godly, faithful man, husband, and father. Thank you for still holding my hand and praying with me in the mornings. I wouldn't want to do this life without you.

- To Charli, who brings joy, laughter, innocence, surprise, and relevance to my life every day. Thank you for letting me be your mom.

- For my spiritual parents, Pastor Tim and Le'Chelle Johnson. Without your family, this story would not have taken place. Thank you for every ounce of Jesus, prayer, hope, understanding, and home-cooked food you poured into me. Through your Godly guidance, supervision, and encouragement, I am forever changed.

- To my mother, Sandy, who always saw the light in me no matter how dark it got.

- To my brother, Jeff, for being my first true friend and continuing to grow with me.

- To Dad and Betty, for your humor and supporting my transformation.

- To my longtime friend and associate Jennifer Erin Hermes (JJ), thank you for always being my first read. Thank you for seeing my vision and hearing my voice. Your incredible ideas, energy, edits, creativity, support, and constant cheering are blessings in my life.

- To my pastors: Dr. Rice Broocks and Jody; James and Debbie Winans Lowe; and Bruce and Carol Fidler. Thank you for continuing to walk my husband and me through this miracle called life. Your teaching, support, belief, and unwavering devotion to Jesus have helped me grow into a true woman of faith.

- To my publisher, Jonathan Merkh, who pulled this story from me over a good Pinot Noir and despite my trepidation. You may easily be one of the most interesting men I know.

- For my patient and meticulous editors, Beth Adams, Amanda Demastus, Holly Halverson, and Jaime Costas, and the entire creative and sales team at Howard Books.

- To my business manager, Janet Bess, a wonderful woman of Christ, and for Alan Nevins and the boys at Renaissance.

- To Dr. Nicole Schlechter for delivering my most precious gift during an NFL playoff game, when you weren't on call and had a big pot of chili cooking. Thank you for being a wonderful doctor, friend, and editor!

- To the entire pastoral, worship, and service team at Bethel World Outreach Center. My gratitude is immeasurable. No matter where this life takes me, Bethel will forever be a place I will call home.

- To my sisters in Christ: Flor Martinez, Kelly Putty, Stormie Omartian, Joyce Meyes, Priscilla Shirer, Jaime Jamgochian, Anny Donewald, Rebecca Alonzo, Mama Winans and her fabulous daughters, as well as so many other ladies in ministry who have showed me how to follow my God-given purpose and talents.

- To my football family in the NFL: From the coaches, front office, players, and folks who work tirelessly to make the game happen, as well as their wives, husbands, children, and families who bleed the game—you are an amazing tribe! Thank you for always letting me stand and scream on third down.

- To Mim Drew, who long ago gave me a book entitled *Traveling Mercies* by Anne Lamott, which gave me the courage to break out of the normal when it comes to writing about faith.

Foreword

When the hand that is dealt you in life is harsh—especially if you are too young to be able to do anything about it—you learn to play by your own rules for survival. And if the people in your life who are supposed to love you do loveless and hurtful things that scar your soul and deeply disappoint you, there comes a time when you see clearly that if you don't save yourself, no one else is going to do it. So you steel your mind and insulate your heart so that no one can penetrate the wall you have carefully erected for self-protection. But all this does is take you far from where you should be.

I know this because I have been there and done that. That's why Carrie Cecil's novel resonated with me. The specifics of her situation were not the same as mine, but the consequences were all too familiar.

However, that is not the only reason I couldn't put this book down. I have known Carrie for years. We were neighbors until her husband was offered a position in another city and they moved out of the state. I have known the pastor, Tim, and his wife, Le'Chelle—whom Carrie bases her characters on—for years as well, until they, too, moved to another state in order to start a new church. In fact, they lived across the street from me and are two of the kindest and most loving people I have ever met. I know you too will come to admire them as you read Carrie's fictionalized depictions of them in this story. All that to say, I bear witness to the truth of her character's experience.

Carrie knows personally of what she writes in this book of redemption. As a young woman with a heartbreaking past who had hardened her heart against God, she could be reached only by the powerful presence of His love as it manifested through people who are consistent examples of it. That kind of love is persistent, yet patient. It is uncompromising, yet unconditional. It is gentle, yet powerful enough to break down any wall. It is unfailing. Who doesn't want or need that in their lives?

Some of Carrie's storylines are not pretty, but she would be less than honest were she to not show the desperate condition that comes as a result of a life lived far outside of God's purpose. What other way is there for us to fathom how far redemption reaches down to lift someone up if we don't understand the depth of their fall? Carrie's novel encourages us to not give up on people—no matter how resistant they are to the truth—for no one can resist the love of God extended toward them for too long. And we never know whom God will use to break down those walls.

—Stormie Omartian

Stormie Omartian is the bestselling author (more than 23 million books sold) of The Power of a Praying™ series, which includes *The Power of a Praying™ Wife, The Power of a Praying™ Husband, The Power of a Praying™ Parent, The Power of a Praying™ Woman,* and *Just Enough Light for the Step I'm On.*

Foreword

It is stirring that *One Sunday*, a novel about reconciliation and forgiveness, would be set in the South, where ethnic tensions can still be high between people because of the color of their skin. God's tapestry is a mix of beautiful colors from a variety of walks of life, and thus the setting, storylines, and connections in the book—albeit fictional—are very familiar, and are a perfect landscape to portray a modern-day tale of hope and grace.

When my wife, Le'Chelle, and I met Carrie Cecil, she began throwing curveball questions at us like "You believe Noah honestly got all those animals on the boat?" and "You truthfully think the Devil exists?" We knew that we were in for a long ride and needed to prepare our hearts, minds, and kitchen for anything. Our relationship with Carrie convinced me that God has a great sense of humor. What Carrie doesn't know is that it was a refreshing, authentic, crazy, and oftentimes hysterical question-filled journey for us. Seeing her willing to explore the simple truth that God is real, and witnessing Him become a certainty in her life, has been one of the highlights of our lives. She is a spiritual daughter to us. It was an honor to witness God's plans unfold and see Carrie's gifts and purposes come together to write this novel. Prepare to have your life touched in a deep and meaningful way and, depending on how open your heart is, to be transformed by the God that we all know loves and came to restore us all.

—Tim Johnson, Senior Pastor,
Orlando World Outreach Center

—————————

Tim Johnson graduated from Penn State University with All-American honors. He was drafted into the NFL, where he played for the Pittsburgh Steelers, Washington Redskins, and Cincinnati Bengals. He was the senior pastor at Bethel World Outreach Center, a large multicultural, multi-congregational church. In 2006, Tim and his wife, Le'Chelle, were inspired to launch Orlando World Outreach Center in Orlando, Florida.

Although this novel is fiction, I believe we write what we know: I know the feeling of brokenness, and I know a big black man and his family who showed me a way to put my little white jagged pieces back together.

ONE
SUNDAY

1

On My Porch

May 2005: *Nice to meet you, Husband. My name is Alice. It's official. I have willingly followed you to the South and fallen into your rabbit hole.*

I drowsily watch my sports-doctor husband, Burton, as he prepares for work at the hospital. He buttons up his crisp, white Brooks Brothers shirt and tucks it into his navy trousers. He's escaping under the camouflage of early-morning darkness. It's so early. I believe even the sun would be grumpy for being awakened this early. I'm certainly not giddy.

Repositioning my large body, I rub my feet up and down the sheets because I like the way they feel like warm butter against my toes. I am lying in our four-poster bed, tugging at the chocolate-brown chenille blanket to better cover myself up. When Burton leans down and kisses me good-bye, I hold my breath, trying not to repulse him. He's had an opportunity to brush with Crest, and my mouth tastes like the poop fairy has visited it.

"You gonna to be okay?" His Southern charm lazily rolls off his tongue, yet he manages to sound authentically concerned.

"I'm fine . . . Go." I wave him off with a sleepy smile the way I imagine I would if we were an old married couple. But we are anything but that.

We were married eight days ago after living in sin for just over five months. The ceremony was private, held beneath a gazebo covered in ivy and next to a lake on his parents' two-hundred-year-old vacation plantation. An overly large, bald, perspiring, African-American minister, whom I could barely understand due to my current condition, made it official. Amid the preacher's Bible flailing and the elongated syllables at the end of every vow he preached, the sweltering Tennessee humidity—already in full boil despite its only being early May—and the distraction of mosquitoes attempting to suck my sweet blood, I was lucky to still be vertical.

Although this legalized religious ceremony may or may not have been my idea, I couldn't help but daydream about lying in the sand in Malibu, gulping a Grey Goose vodka on the rocks with a lemon twist, and popping a Xanax to take the edge off. I just nodded halfheartedly at phrases like *Till death do y'all part* as I had been nodding for the past ten years at Jose, my car-wash guy in Los Angeles. Jose, who was from El Salvador, would ramble on and on about his family while he detailed my Navigator. I should have won an Oscar for how convincingly I would nod as if I heard him, as if I cared about what he was saying.

Once again, I was kinda listening, kinda not. Only this was my wedding, which should give an indication of my laissez-faire ideology regarding commitment.

The memories of my wedding fade in and out. They're not the

typical scenes you'd watch in a Lifetime movie but more akin to something out of a Coen brothers' film like *Fargo*. We were quite the motley crew. A black woman named LeChelle, whom I'd known for what seemed like only a second or two, was my maid of honor. She held my elbow to ensure that I didn't fall over or possibly make a break to escape. She sure beat Annabelle, Burton's judgmental, snickering, and recently divorced socialite sister, who kept rolling her eyes and making sucking noises with her monster veneer teeth. A doctor friend of Burton's, whose name I cannot recall, was his best man, and I had only one guest from my side of the family: my gay business partner, Amos, who wore a superb Armani ensemble and held my white rosebud bouquet.

I do distinctly remember the wave of nausea that hit me when my groom's plump father, Burton Banister II, clad in a pale-blue-and-white seersucker suit, wiped sweat off his comb-over and drooled a piece of a chewed unlit cigar onto the ground. I swear a little vomit came up my gastrointestinal tract and into my mouth.

I remember that Burton's mother hid her disappointment in me under a large-brimmed white hat with a yellow sunflower on it that matched the trim on her tan linen-and-lace suit. June-Rae was clenching her jaw so tight that her red lip liner seeped into the creases of her frown lines and made her look like a mean jack-o'-lantern.

LeChelle, Annabelle, Dr. What's His Name, Burton Banister II, June-Rae, and Amos were our witnesses, I suppose, so no one else would have to be.

Here's the really horrifying thing, though. It isn't 1956. It's 2005! But change is slow to come to the South, if it comes at all. For instance, good Southern boys are not supposed to have a baby out of wedlock with a Los Angeles tramp. The Banisters had such high hopes for their only son. He was supposed to finally settle down with a homogenous, white-bread Southern girl. Subtract the shotgun and add some generational land and money and, well, we got ourselves a hoedown.

But back to what really mattered: I looked fabulous. I wore a fantastic off-white, Empire-waisted Vera Wang dress that accented everything I wanted to show off and beautifully concealed everything I didn't. My swollen breasts were on proud display for all to see. They left no question unanswered about the extent of my lustful ambition and the shame it had cast on the pristine Banister lineage. It was a great dress.

Now, eight days later, the wedding is the least of my worries. I have a husband. And a supernice one at that. After kissing me good-bye, Burton stands back up and pauses.

I tried not to show my discomfort as he stared at me. "Take a picture, it'll last longer," I teased.

"You take care of our baby, okay?" he says, placing his hand below my baby bump, rubbing it with care over my Superwoman PJs. "You sure you're gonna be all right? I can get Jed to fill in for me this trip."

"I'm not even dilated. *Go.* Save a hockey player or an NFL football player's life. 'Tis the season for off-season surgeries. I don't need a babysitter. I'll be fine."

I want to scream that I've been taking care of myself since I was fourteen. But I just blink lovingly as even now, when I am as huge as a house, his puppy-dog hazel eyes make me melt. Being a nasty hormonal nightmare isn't an option. I just smile. Wave and smile.

I understand that *sexy* and the name *Burton* do not traditionally fit together, but I will tell you: Burton is fine-looking to the bone. At six foot three, he has brown hair cut like Cary Grant's in *An Affair to Remember*. He is an old soul. A good, bourbon-drinking, forty-two-year-old sports doctor who swaggers like Dean Martin, minus the cigarette.

My husband.

Husband. Husband. Husband. The word cartwheels around and around in my brain. It doesn't feel real. How can any of this be plausible?

My husband, I am convinced, is from another era, an era when men still call women, not text them, when they want to ask you to go to dinner. An era when men open the car door for their best girl, pay the check, and still love their mothers even when their mothers are overbearing, judgmental cows. He is a sporty, smart Southern Baptist who believes that God has some greater plan, but like many other men has fallen prey to a woman like me. He graduated from Ole Miss just like his daddy did before him, and his granddaddy before him.

Burton is a family name, and in the South, family does mean something. Even if that family is as crazy and mean as a pit of poisonous snakes. Family means everything, which is why I suppose he chose to marry me: I was carrying his unborn baby girl. That made me family. For better or for worse.

On this particular bleary-eyed morning, Burton is off to make his rounds at the hospital. He is always off to something at this hour. When I moved here in the chill of winter, he was always off to another professional hockey or football game. I don't hold it against him or the gig. I love a hard-hitting sack of a quarterback, a half-court shot at the buzzer during March Madness, and *"Gentlemen, start your engines!"* at a NASCAR race. Call me a competitive junkie, but I like them in prime time, not before dawn. Later, it was another road trip and another surgery. The reasons for these painful 5:45 a.m. departure times are all starting to meld.

According to his corporate biography on the Baptist Hospital website, Burton is one of the leading sports doctors in the country. I have landed one of Nashville's most eligible bachelors without even trying, and believe me it hasn't gone unnoticed or ungossiped about, or left me unscathed. However, the cackling neighborhood hens had better beware. This isn't my first rodeo. I've been up against women before who place their hands over their mouths while whispering unsavory comments and drawing their assumptions out of the gutter. In fact, I've been material for women like them my whole life. The only difference is, where I'm from there were no pleases, thank-yous, or good manners to mask their bad behavior.

So, ladies, let's be clear: I am your friendly neighborhood harlot with an illegitimate offspring to prove it. It wouldn't be worth it if Burton weren't so yummy. He's intelligent and accomplished, sure, but he's also a hunka-hunka burning love. He has a great smile. His strong jawline is the perfect frame for his gleaming, white teeth, which are neatly aligned from years of braces. He also has broad shoulders and, my personal favorite, a firm, juicy tush.

He's smokin'.

To be perfectly honest, that's all I really know about him. Which, I suppose, is exactly the type of shallow observation that landed me here, barefoot and pregnant, in some handsome Southern stranger's rabbit hole.

I suppose, too, that I deserve to be tethered to a man I barely know by the unborn child in my belly. I did, after all, sleep with him the first night we met.

Ahhh, the night we met. I close my eyes and imagine I can inhale the salty sea air, and go back to that night in California . . .

Almost nine months earlier: It's Burton's green eyes that lead me to the open, striped four-ball on the pool table. It's a summer night and I'm at a party in Bel Air. The place and the party are courtesy of NFL bad boy Chad Johnson, otherwise known as

Chad Ochocinco. Fred Flintstone and Barney Rubble mill about his rented house. Guests take in the sparkling lights of Westwood from the second-story deck and outdoor infinity pool. Everyone is gyrating to the techno music courtesy of a hired DJ.

Any Friday night in Los Angeles can seem like a costume party, but this *is* a costume party. I'm dressed as Alice from *Alice in Wonderland*. Art imitates life, so my costume isn't quite that simple. I'm Alice after being hit by a car. My blue dress is torn and bloodied. There are black tread marks on the white apron. I have glued surprisingly realistic fake blood and gashes onto my cheek and arms. My white tights are ripped from the trauma. Some Alices in short skirts try to be sexy. I am not one of those Alices. I am the inside-out Alice who is demented and broken, with all her wounds showing.

Everywhere I look, I see A-listers flitting about. First, there's the who's who of Angeleno pro athletes: Laker players Kobe, Lamar, and Luke Walton; Dodger closer Eric Gagne; a very pregnant Britney Spears and her husband, Kevin Federline. Charlie Sheen, Jessica Simpson, Jennifer Aniston, Clooney, and producer Jerry Bruckheimer are making the rounds, and finally, we have the decoration beauties: six-foot, long-legged *Sports Illustrated* models and happy-ending ladies who were hired to make the night more fun for dorky CAA talent-agent types.

The wigs, false eyelashes, and elaborate costumes would confuse the casual party guests, but I am a tabloid reporter who has been trained for almost a decade to see through all the fakeness. I know who is here and I am on the clock.

I can't help but feel a tinge of pride as I note fear in the eyes of celebrities when they see me now—fear and trepidation. After launching Trashville, my twenty-four-hour website dedicated to digging in the Dumpster of Tinseltown, celebrities have grown to both loathe and love me. More than anything, LA has become a celeb society and an industry that needs me. And I am more than happy to serve it. I was born to play the role of tabloid reporter and, after playing it at *National Celebrity News* magazine for five years, I've become the very best. I can cut to the jugular of gossip stories before my competitors can say, *Would you like to comment?* During the hunt for my next image kill, I can hear this town cheering and egging me on, beating the drums even as they pretend to look away. I am the celebrity-hunting femme fatale.

I have so much sour juice and dirty evidence in my vault of shame, at this point in my career I can make or break almost anyone in Hollywood. At thirty-eight I have made it to the top, and I don't care that I had to climb a pile of bloody glass to get there. I wear my scars like Girl Scout badges of honor.

Celebrities pretend to hate the paparazzi and tabloids, but it is their hired publicists who are texting tips to our team at Trashville, telling them where Lindsay Lohan and Paris Hilton are going to be dropping their drugs and undies on the floor every night. This is why I'm usually invited to parties. They want the publicity and love looking shocked for the camera. Why oh why? The facade satisfies our bloodlust and we are all too happy to don our masks and play along.

I have wandered into the entertainment room, when I lock eyes with Burton. He is wearing hospital scrubs. It's clearly a last-minute costume. He had come to Los Angeles on Friday morning to speak at a medical conference in Marina del Rey with Neal Spartelli, a sports doctor who specializes in fixing jacked-up shoulders. Neal is dressed as Groucho Marx. He heads up an orthopedic clinic in Los Angeles and scored his invitation because he operated on Chad last season.

Chad is talking about himself in third person. He's dressed as some type of vampire thing and is promoting a new reality football show. I'm here tonight because Chad needs free publicity and

Trashville needs real scoops on his guests, which I will get after they snort a line of cocaine or two and get overly chatty and sweaty.

Burton and I are partners playing a game of eight ball on the pool table. We are paired up against Chad and his date, and it is my turn to shoot. I have taken my time chalking up my stick, looking puzzled and purposely missing my first couple of shots.

I coquettishly lead Mr. Johnson to increase his wager with Burton, my unwitting partner in the short con. I hit the four ball in the side pocket followed by the six and the two, but it isn't until I drain the eight ball that Ochocinco realizes I've hustled him in his own house.

Oh goody, goody. Shame on me.

More satisfying than taking Mr. NFL's benjamins—which I scoop up and tuck into my Louis Vuitton purse—is watching the true surprise and delight on Burton's face.

Burton isn't from LA. He doesn't know me. He's never clicked on my links at Trashville. He doesn't know the dangers or the pleasures of being friends with a tabloid editor. He just sees a five-foot-six, fairly decent-looking, sandy-blond-haired, blue-eyed gal, whose hips, booty, and boobs are equally curvy and real. I'm not freakishly LA skinny and I work hard to keep my muffin top soft, but not flabby. I'm a firm believer in women looking like real women, with hips, hourglass silhouettes, and laugh lines. I like food too much to barf it up and I hate doing the lunges I do to keep my bottom at its current address. I have mastered the craft of male conversation by perfecting my act of understanding the trifecta of things men care about—box scores, movie quotes, and political folly—all while licking the salt off a tequila shooter. Mostly, I'm not book smart, but life smart, which in this business is the key to survival.

It is only one night at the St. Regis hotel. One long, sweaty night that involves Patrón, Jack Daniel's, and for me, a Vicodin or two.

I can't help but get the feeling that Burton isn't the one-night kind of guy. Case in point: He kisses me for hours before ever touching another one of my body parts. He dims the lights and lets the moonlight flood the room with Andrea Bocelli belting out "Con te partirò." It is, for what it is, romantic. And I need it. Boy, do I need it.

He has a way of taking care of me, even on this first date. I use the word *date* loosely. He covers me with a blanket when he thinks I am asleep. He orders me coffee and pancakes with bacon for breakfast. He does this long before my head starts pounding from that last shot at 3:15 a.m.

He was and still is thoughtful and endearing, two concepts in a man that were foreign to me.

Flash forward to today. As sweet and glamorous as my life seems replaying in my head, I have been forced for the most part to throw my career, my friends, and my pseudo-powerful existence down the swirling porcelain flusher. Those parties in the Hollywood Hills, premieres at Paramount Studios, steak dinners at Dan Tana's, trunk shows at Lisa Kline, and A-list celebrity-laden farmers' markets in Santa Monica on Saturday mornings are now temporarily (note to self: the word *temporarily*!) behind me—and not because I chose to let them go.

How I got here is a blur. It's a bad version of a weird, dream-infused movie like Tim Burton's *Charlie and the Chocolate Factory*. I have no idea if this is reality or if I'm living in someone else's subconscious. It's a dream that began with my hurling at the smell of salmon lox on a toasted onion bagel at my office on Sunset Boulevard, then a blurred blue plus sign on an EPT, further blurred

into the blood test confirming that Burton's baby was indeed growing in my belly. Through my careless practice of not insisting on a
condom, I am now imprisoned in the land of *y'all*s.

I can barely remember being in my Thanksgiving-decorated
corner office with my business partner, Amos. Designer jeans, cotton tee, and Fred Segal blazer dripping off his tall, lanky frame, he
was holding me up as I leaned on him from wooziness. The door
was shut and our people were scurrying around outside trying to
make a midday deadline about celebrities on the move.

"I'm almost forty. This is possibly my last chance to ever have
a child, not that I ever really wanted one," I say, then gag. Amos
extends me a tissue when I'm done dry heaving in the trash can. "I
have no husband, and I've had no boyfriend—present company
excluded—for over two years. I'm way past the start date when
women shoot gallons of filler into their cheeks and lips. I'm totally
wrecked."

"You're beautiful." He tries to sound convincing, "Except for
that little bit of barf on your gray cashmere hoodie. Happy gobble-
gobble, Baby Thanksgiving!"

"Gross!" I bang my head on my desk as Amos tries to dab my
sweater clean.

My only true male relationship of substance up to this time
has been with Amos, a Mormon queen from Utah. We met at
NCN and he laid down the money his parents gave him to get
married *to a girl* to help fund Trashville. He had been a fantastic
publicist turned assistant editor, then was promoted to editor and
is now an even better copublisher, business partner, and friend.
He knows everyone, and everyone knows and loves him. We are
the good cop/bad cop of electronic tabloid publishing and I'm,
shockingly, the bad one. Okay, it's not such a stretch.

"You don't have to keep it." He winces as if he thinks I will hit
him with a stick.

"Not an option," I say emphatically. "It's not politics or God or anything. It's just not an option." What I should really say is that I understand the unbearable consequences of losing a life meant to be held in your arms, but I have no energy to share that with anyone, not even Amos.

While Amos runs off to fetch me an apple juice with crushed ice, I type out an email to Burton:

Happy Holidays. Hope the Titans are winning. FYI, I'm with child. We are all good. No worries.

And hit send.

I feel he has the right to know that he's going to have a kid somewhere in the world. I owe him that, at least. And I want nothing from him.

Honestly, nothing.

I don't want his money or his involvement at all. This kid is, like my life up to this point, something I can handle on my own. Most people don't get second chances like this, but I'm getting a second chance to make up for my past and I'm taking it.

Well, honestly I figure Amos and I can raise it. He'll be my baby's surrogate father figure. Better a well-dressed dad with a flair for shopping and cooking than no dad at all—or the dad that I had.

I am capable of predicting with 98-percent accuracy the next move of every Hollywood mover and shaker, but I never anticipated that upon receiving that email, Burton would leave the operating room immediately after surgery and be on the next taxi-flight-taxi trajectory directly into my living room.

That Los Angeles fall day he and I cover all obvious questions and answers and discuss DNA testing. The latter is totally needless, but I want it more for his sanity than my own. I haven't had an actual intimate encounter with another person since last summer when I woke up with a B-list actor after a long, hot night in his Malibu beach house. Burton offers all the appropriate financial and emotional suggestions that a man offers a woman who is pregnant with his child. He even suggests prayer, which I politely decline. I do agree to let him be a part of our child's life if he wants to do that—which he does. But honestly everything at this point is negotiable. Before he clumsily kisses my cheek and walks out of my house, he asks if I would consider moving to Nashville with him, which, as fairy-tale-like as it sounds, makes me shudder.

It's ironic how the punishment for my sinful behavior of a one-night stand at a swanky hotel is a pregnancy punctuated by barf, high blood pressure, and high risk to my health and that of my unborn child. Seven or so weeks after Burton and I sat in my living room, my womb and my life got tossed into a *"you're going to die unless . . ."* pressure cooker. Here are my choices: One, stay in LA and die. Two, move to the South and feel like I'm dying. Thus, I've been sentenced to the South, where my husband—wow, that's still so weird to say—and his medical staff can monitor my health and support my every move. I've been grounded with no travel, no work as it adds too much stress and spikes my heart rate—and basically, no fun.

Amos is now broadcasting Trashville on the web solo. He's posting headlines and scandalous celebrity photos and cracking the whip on our minions. He's managing Trashville without me, and while I'm boohooing about it, I know I had no choice. If I were to leave my work-baby to anyone, it would be Amos—at least for now. I look at it as a pregnancy sabbatical.

But I will be back. I've come too far to give it all up for a kid and pretend family in a pretend land.

For now I'm serving my time in a Tennessee cottontail lair behind electronic gates with a guardhouse bigger than most guest cabanas in Beverly Hills. The entrance to my rabbit hole is magnificently shaded by magnolia trees. Their boughs drape over the cursive marble lettering of LAUREL BROOKE on the iron sign that announces the community's status to all those looky-loos who drive by.

Well, if I'm sentenced to do time here, at least my surroundings are pretty. I will admit this much: I do really love the scenery of the South. Water spouts high into the air from a three-tiered fountain, sparkling when it lands in the green murky pond that surrounds it. Two swans paddle around the fountain's muddy edge, giving prestige to this highly developed community.

I hate those swans. They make a beeline for me every time my 175-pound, blubbery body ambles near their mating area. They are vicious and territorial. They try to intimidate me with their thick, white, dirt-stained necks outstretched and wings batting like those of prehistoric predators. It works on unsuspecting passersby but not on me, not anymore. I made the mistake last week of walking on the path by one of the swans that was out of the pond. It looked harmless and beautiful until its neck overextended like ET's and it spread its massive wings and started running toward me. It was terrifying. I've never been afraid of barking dogs or runaway galloping horses, but that charging, menacing swan scared the living daylights out of me. I scurried up the hill away from it and tripped on a tree branch and scraped my palms and knees. I swear that bird stood there squawking, mocking me.

The swan wasn't so lucky yesterday. I am proud to report that I came prepared. I will not be bullied by anything with feathers and a brain the size of a peanut. I walked the same path where I had fallen down, and there it stood, like an outlaw on a dusty street waiting to have an old-fashioned gunfight. I stared it down and gave it a chance to mosey on into the lake, but again it mocked me and stretched its neck, let loose its large white wings, and lunged for me. My heart beat faster and faster as it charged until I put my arm out in front of me and showed it my Mace canister and . . . it stopped.

Not so fast, buddy-boy.

I had my finger on the trigger, ready to take my place back at the top of the food chain, and then something caught my eye.

Eggs. Six enormous eggs in the marsh in a weird-looking nest.

It's not a mean mugger bird; it's a momma bird.

I started to back-step slowly as if to say, *Sorry, I didn't understand*. Or *I know how you feel*. But she just kept her wings out, signaling me to *keep on going, fat lady*.

It gave me a whole new appreciation for those birds.

Minus the rabid momma fowl, there is a richness to these luxurious rolling green acres, peppered with seven-thousand-square-foot estates; hundred-year-old oaks; weeping cherry trees; scarlet maples; and rows of tangerine, yellow, and purple tulips lining the golf-cart paths. The flowers get replanted and replenished as the seasons change.

New-world McMansion security and old-world charm have been sewn together to create a suburban utopia. Everything is manicured to perfection. I can't help but wonder what a ragtag like me is doing here.

"Good mornin'!" A ponytailed, tennis skirt–wearing woman waves at me as she zips by in her golf cart. I manage a smile as I inwardly grimace and wonder if it's the Adderall that makes them all so thin and perky and able to play tennis in this heat.

To be honest, I could use some of that Adderall to shrink my bloat. I'm actually too enlarged and pregnant to slip into any rabbit hole. It is at this moment, slowly walking the paved walkway, that I realize I have fallen deep and I am trapped!

This is a backward place where churches, not Starbucks, have been erected on every corner. My husband, whom I barely know, works late at the hospital and is on the road every weekend, which practically guarantees I never will know him.

I sit down on my porch to get my breath, and reality begins to really set in. I am alone, sober, huge, depressed, and dangerously close to kicking the bucket. I don't recognize the last five months of my life. I miss Trashville and I miss being single and free. I am longing for anything and everything but what I currently have. Sure, there are pockets of relief. But they are times I can count on my fingers and toes. I'm in a state of what seems like constant desperation, and I'm slowly going insane.

My only friends, and I use that term very loosely, are our neighbor Tim and his wife, LeChelle. He senses my dissatisfaction. My wanderlust. My lostness. My frustration.

Tim, a forty-four-year-old African-American, is a former NFL defensive lineman who is now an imposing 250-pound evangelical pastor. He's a retired football Bernie Mac whose stand-up shtick is the Bible.

He jogs past me in an old Florida State T-shirt as I not-so-invisibly sit on my porch perusing a stack of *Us Weekly, People,* and *In Touch* magazines. "How you doin', baby girl?" he calls out to me from the mailbox.

I love that he calls me *baby girl*. Love, love, love it. It's like some ethnic thing I didn't get growing up next to a Circle K in the heat of Tucson. It's endearing and makes me feel organically included in his heritage. "Oh, I'm just peachy," I answer with enough sarcasm to fill my Lincoln Navigator. "What's up with you, preacher man?"

He places his hands on his large thighs, trying to catch his breath. His legs are more fleshy than muscular these days. The evening breeze is cooling the heat of the day, but that doesn't stop beads of sweat from pouring through the razor stubble on his big brown head and onto the pavement.

"I can see you're filling up with some good word." He smiles at my magazines.

"I read it for the pictures," I say, holding up an *In Touch* with Jennifer Aniston half-naked on the cover.

"You hungry? LeChelle's makin' friiiiiied chicken, biscuits, and gravy," he says.

That is all it takes for me to unanchor my buttocks from the cushioned rocking chair and lurch forward. He had me at *fried*. He knows that after a few months of being here, following sixteen years of starving on a strict diet of lettuce cups filled with air and celery in Los Angeles, I can be easily convinced to cancel my solo reservation at the bitter porch pity-party for one with the promise of food—real food.

2

The Invitation

As I discovered months ago, the Jacksons live next door to Burton and me, or rather Burton, as I'm just a squatter. I remember that day on my porch when they first lured me with food. When I smelled Tim's wife's cooking floating in the air and met their kid clan of exuberant chaos, I remember thinking: *Their house is full of life. The type of life I have never known.*

I rest for a minute on the chaise lounge in our bedroom. I set down my blood pressure machine on my nightstand and wait for my heartbeats to register. It's a twice-a-day ritual. It's been like this since the twentieth week of my pregnancy, when I first realized I was sick and my sickness was putting my baby and me in danger. My sickness with this child is what sentenced me to the South.

I knew something was amiss the first time my head started thumping uncontrollably. It was eerily similar to when I'd taken two hits of ecstasy on New Year's Eve at the Millennium Hotel in New York. My blood pressure raced. My vision became fuzzy and rolled like a tide. Even heavy squinting and buckets of meds didn't make it stop.

Good news came with my generally awful diagnosis: some, not all, of my weight gain, my newfound flappy-arm wings, my freakishly unquenchable thirst, and my exceedingly high blood pressure was due to gestational hypertension. The awful part is that gestational hypertension could be fatal for both the bun in my oven and me. This condition has to be monitored—constantly. From the proteins in my pee to my heartbeats . . . I measure, measure, and measure some more.

So here I sit . . . *tick, tick, tick* . . . making sure I'm not dying . . . at least not today. Hence my decision to accept Burton's offer and move to the Southland. I need his medical expertise to survive this pregnancy and I need a place to go, and home to my family is not an option.

Once I see my blood pressure is okay, I leave. I have no energy to waddle down my driveway and waddle back up the Jacksons' for food or for appropriate front-door salutations or appearances. Instead I've taken to cutting across our adjoining greenery. I've been making my way to the Jacksons' backyard regularly these past few months. I plod over the small grassy hill and cut through a gap in the bushes that separate our yards. It's not far but it feels like a summer hike to the pregnant version of me.

Spring has sprung into early summer and the trees are in full blossom. Tim's wife, and my favorite new chef, LeChelle, has curated a floral garden, and the budding blooms are releasing a sweet, fresh scent.

Their six-thousand-square-foot home sits atop a long cobblestone driveway. It is a house paid for by herniated discs, blown-out knees, and six trips to the Pro Bowl. Tim's hard-earned NFL money is now put to good use for what he calls "God." I don't think he makes a dime in his new born-again role. Their home is like a real-life *Run's House* on MTV, where Run from the rap group Run-D.M.C. has turned from rapper to reverend. Only in the Jackson house, instead of gold and platinum albums on the walls, there are framed football jerseys and helmets on display.

I love the style of their house. The gray-and-white two-story chateau has brown, tan, black, and gray slate bordering the foundation, garage, and front patio deck. Their lush, sloped yard overwhelms my sense of sight and smell. Mammoth cream and lilac Japanese cherry trees release sweet scents into the air. The cherry trees are deliberately positioned next to maples. The pale colors of the former contrast with the bright Crayola colors of the latter.

Lines of pear-shaped bushes create hedgerows to frame the yard behind nature's fortress. Thorn-studded red rosebushes, sun-kissed tangerine perennials, purple asters, red-petaled chrysanthemums with yellow centers, and tall, lavender blazing stars are arranged perfectly in beds around their mailbox. Even more flowers are nestled in large crescent-moon shapes along the steps leading up to the oiled oak and wrought-iron-cased twelve-foot-tall front door. It is a grand sight.

Their wooden window frames are accented with a rich Swiss-almond-white trim that matches the doors of their four-car garage and the archway that leads to the freestanding guesthouse that doubles as Tim's office. This house is probably valued at a little over a million and a half dollars in Tennessee; in my old hood of Hollywood it would run upward of six million. It's massive and excessive, but it's not over-the-top in a neighborhood filled with small modern-day castles owned by the likes of Alan Jackson and Kenny Chesney.

I can smell something frying from a hundred feet away. I swear on a stack of Neiman Marcus catalogs that I have the pregnancy superpower of smell. I can smell things I have no desire to smell. In the grocery store, it's the bad cologne two aisles over. At home, it's the aging meat in the refrigerator. In the neighborhood, it's the cigarette smoke residue left on my mail from the postal carrier.

Thankfully, while those things smell way worse than normal, things like LeChelle's cooking smell way better. Mmmmmmm. It's a double-edged sword, though. It is making me eat for eight even though there are only two of us.

As a bonus, my extra weight makes my body feel constantly hot and slathered in sweat. I am wearing a long, flowing, black sleeveless cotton dress and still, all of my body parts are touching each other. There's lots of rubbing and sticking. Even wearing flip-flops is uncomfortable for my stuffed-sausage toes.

Three more weeks: I'm in the top of the ninth inning of my pregnancy and I'm ready to have this baby out.

"Helllllloooo," I call out. I knock on their back door as a courtesy, but I enter before getting a response.

"In here," LeChelle calls out from the kitchen. "Come on in, girlfriend."

This is how it has been. I've become their bottomless-pit, heart-monitor-carrying neighbor who freely comes and goes. Their house is always inviting. I'm all too happy to be sucked in by their warmth and welcoming, but I keep my guard up. I'm suspicious and fully mentally armored because I'm leery of their feel-good Christian-family behavior. No one can be that happy all the time. I don't need any *Big Love* kumbaya sessions.

Somehow, some way, in this house, we always get around to Jesus, Jesus, Jesus. They talk about Jesus like he's a familiar cousin always up to something. I've got nothing against Jesus. I'm just not buying what they're selling. I'm good with it all—*for them*—as long as they keep feeding me and they understand I'm not coming to their church, if for no other reason than to protect them.

If I went to their house of praise and worship, lightning would hit it. The skies would fill with large, muddy flying swine and flocks of angry momma swans would attack the congregation. Outside, swarms of locusts would devour the crops in the fields. There'd be nothing edible left and everyone would die. Thus, no church for me.

As I sway through the Jacksons' living room, I can't help but notice over and over that everything in this house is big. Enormous. I feel like Jack when he climbed the beanstalk and entered the giant's castle. And by the way, I'm not small. Not anymore.

The tan leather sofas are deeper and longer than normal sofas. The matching chairs are wider than any chair I have ever owned, the flat-screen is larger and brighter than the one Burton has, and the vases and flowers are taller, fuller, and more elegant than anything I have ever seen—with the exception of the Creative Artists Agency lobby in Century City. It's a big house for big people, which is perfect for the now-175-pound version of me.

Like a basset hound, I follow my nose. I'm hot on a scent as I round the grand piano. Somehow I manage not to knock over the family photos that are carefully arranged on top. Generations of Jacksons are crowded together under glass, framed by polished wood and gleaming silver, their smiles and grins and purity all caught on film.

There are three Jackson girls, ranging in age from twelve to seventeen, and twin boys who just turned seven. Five kids and two grown-ups joined together under one roof. Tim Jr. and Kyle are sitting on the couch, their backs propped all the way back so that their bare feet don't even reach the edge of the cushions. The twins are wearing 3-D glasses and playing the Madden NFL video. Their heads tilt left, then right in perfect unison to follow every move of the game. I pat Kyle on the head. Oblivious to me and totally engaged in their game, they elbow each other and groan out loud.

I say a silent prayer to the Shopping Goddess and thank her for making sure the kid in my belly is a girl. Little boys are so cumbersome and strange to me.

The kitchen has a Tuscan feel to it. It's elegant but rustic and relaxed. The counters are long and wide and built for prepping a lot of food at the same time. The espresso-colored granite countertops give way to dark wooden cabinets and rough-looking stucco walls with glossy tile borders. Giant wood beams stretch overhead. Hanging flowerpots and wrought-iron pendant lighting fixtures hang from them. The kitchen's deep sinks, hidden refrigerators, Wolf stoves, and brick pizza oven built into the wall leave nothing to be desired. Tim and LeChelle knew what they were doing when they designed and built their castle.

Michaela, the eldest daughter, who is tall like her mother, is regally posed, sitting at a grand table set back in an alcove. Her casual school-basketball clothes contrast with the high, arched windows that frame her perch on every side. "Just take this, and divide it here," she patiently explains to her youngest sister, Debbie, who is sitting at one of the twelve chairs at the table. Debbie is either going to take after her daddy—she's big-boned and more solidly built than her mom or Michaela—or just hasn't had the time to sprout up and lean out yet.

"It doesn't make any sense. It's stupid!" Debbie gripes. "I'm gonna be a singer anyway, and I'll hire someone to do my taxes and stuff like that," she says with a double snap of her fingers for emphasis.

I can't help but laugh out loud.

"Hi, Miss Alice," Ava, the middle sister, greets me. She has caramel skin like her mother. She smiles at me while helping

LeChelle beat eggs in a bowl. Ava's wearing a high, pink, pointed party hat on her head.

She is my favorite. Perhaps it is because Ava has always been in the middle, even before the "oops boys" came along and stole the title of *babies,* and put Debbie in the middle too. I believe middle children are more eager to please because it's easy for them to feel invisible—something I can relate to. Or it might be that I like Ava best because she wants to be a writer. It's a dream I once had as a fifth grader, long before pictures sold magazines and when my mom was still alive and read *Reader's Digest* to me. Ava is the unbroken, bright-eyed version of me I see in my flashbacks.

"I didn't know it was your birthday," I say as I climb onto the cushioned barstool next to her, feeling cruddy for not bringing anything.

"I'm just happy you're here," Ava says, grinning while trying to cover her braces, which are full of green rubber bands.

Had I known it was her birthday, I'd have brought her a gift certificate to the local mani-pedi place. I hate being empty-handed.

When I first was invited over by the Jacksons, I'd bring along something for Mom and Dad—perhaps a good bottle of Pinot Noir—and an apple pie for everyone to share. It wasn't until the second or third visit that I realized they don't drink alcohol and they make things from scratch, so booze and my Publix grocery store bakery pie offering were nothing more than nice gestures.

"My babies are getting soooo big!" LeChelle hugs Ava with a squeeze that would make me uncomfortable, but Ava seems to relish the tight embrace. "All y'all got something to say?" LeChelle's tone changes to stern as she addresses her other children.

Michaela and Debbie look at their mother. LeChelle's eyes

are so wide that they look like they're about to jump out of their sockets.

"Hi, Miss Alice," the girls say in unison.

I turn in my chair to properly respond. "Hello, ladies," I say.

Shaking her head in disgust, LeChelle says, "Those girls are losing their manners in public school." She mixes hot sauce with the eggs in a bowl until the mixture is bright orange. "Okay, now take the dark meat and dip it in this," she instructs Ava, who soaks a piece of chicken in the slimy orange concoction and then puts it in the seasoning.

"What's in that?" I ask, pointing at the floured pan.

LeChelle looks up at me with concern. "Can you eat this? I'm so sorry, I didn't even think . . ." Her voice trails off as she shuffles dishes and darts between the cabinet and fridge, clearly mentally planning a special dish for me.

I interrupt her thought. "*Stop!*" I slightly roll my eyes at my own condition. "I've given up everything good in my life for the last eight months. I'm eating fried chicken tonight."

"Okay, as long as you're sure." She winks at me and returns to her frying pan.

"I just want to know what's in it in case I ever have to, God forbid, cook."

With a zing in her voice, LeChelle shares some of her secrets with me as she coats the thigh and tosses it in a cast-iron skillet that is popping hot with peanut oil: "A little salt and a little peppa. Some flour and Big Momma's secret spices."

Ava repeats the dipping process with two more pieces of chicken while LeChelle moves on to finishing her biscuits.

Just then I see Tim sneaking into the kitchen from the back staircase. He's now fresh from the shower. He silently creeps behind Ava and LeChelle as he holds his finger to his lips. He carefully maneuvers behind both his girls before wrapping his arms around them like a big grizzly. As he scoops them up off their feet in what is arguably the biggest hug ever, LeChelle and Ava both let out a frightened scream.

"How my girls doin'?" he asks matter-of-factly as he releases them.

Ava punches her dad in the arm. "That's not funny, Daddy."

"Sure it is." He nods at me.

I shake my head in response and smile.

Tim pushes LeChelle's long, straightened hair off the back of her neck with his hand and plants his full lips there. "Nothing like the smell of Chanel No. 5 mixed with fried chicken. Ummm-hmmm!" He does a little bend in his step like a broken dance move. "Makes a man realize how blllesssssed he is." I love the way he sings the word *blessed*. In my mind, I freeze this moment in time so I can take it all in.

The Jacksons are exceedingly extravagant and perfectly homey at the same time. I sit in their house and I want so much to be one of them.

But I am not. I never have been, and I'm not now. But it would be nice to be normal for once. To be peaceful in my own skin, in my own family, at home in my own home. To understand what the word *family* means. Is it wrong to want to be one of them? Even if just during my pregnancy sabbatical?

LeChelle pours buttermilk into a mixing bowl containing flour, baking soda, salt, and butter, and heats what appears to be lard in a frying pan.

Awesome! Real lard!

She puts the dough on a floured board and rolls it out with a wooden rolling pin.

"Come on over here," she says, handing me a biscuit cutter. Putting her hand on my hand, LeChelle shows me how easily the cutter goes through the dough and how to twist it gently to make the cut. Together we lift up my biscuit and place it on a cookie sheet. It's funny; her hand is so much darker and softer than mine.

It is the first time that I've really noticed that we are very different colors.

Growing up in a strip-mall town set against a desert backdrop, I never experienced racism the way it's written about in the history books. I had a lot of Latino friends simply because we were seventy miles from the Mexican border. We had different cultures but were all stuck in our prefab-constructed life: Native American kids, black kids, Mexican kids, and poor white kids.

Tim was right: LeChelle does smell like Chanel No. 5 and fried chicken, and the mixture is delicious. She's about three inches taller than me, so for the first time in a long time I'm okay feeling vulnerable and open to taking direction from another woman. We are just women, after all. This is something that was lost on me for the past fifteen years in Hollyweird.

"Look at you, baby girl. Makin' biscuits." Tim hands me a big glass of sweet tea.

"I wouldn't go that far," I snicker, trying to not show Tim and LeChelle how much it means to me to be included in their family, even if it is just for fried chicken and biscuits.

Twenty minutes later, their heads are bowed, hands clasped. We sit around a table filled with food. All eyes are closed except for Tim Jr.'s and mine. We are peeking.

"Lord, today we just thank You again for this family. For our health and providing for us for another day," Tim prays.

Just then, Tim Jr. leans to his left, head-butting his unsuspecting brother. "Ow!" Kyle yelps.

Tim, without opening his eyes, bellows, "Booooy, you better quit." Without missing a beat he continues, "We thank You that fourteen years ago today You blessed us with Ava, another perfect and special baby girl. We ask You that You keep her safe, keep all of our children safe. We are blessed to live a life that pleases You. We thank You for this food and for the hands that made it and we ask that You let it nourish our bodies. And Lord, we thank You for our friends Alice and Burton and their baby girl on the way."

This makes me smile.

"We pray in Jesus' name"—Tim pauses—"and all the people said?"

The entire table, including me, answers, "Amen."

Grace is over, so of course pandemonium breaks out. People start talking and passing plates around.

"All right, who's gonna go first?" Tim looks around the table as the food is being scooped up. He makes eye contact with me and explains, "On your birthday you get to pick your favorite meal and favorite cake."

"So I should thank Ava for the chicken?"

"Yes, ma'am," Ava answers.

"And we use this minute or two to speak life into the person whose birthday it is," LeChelle says as she passes the gravy to me.

What an interesting concept: speaking life into someone.

Tim doesn't wait. "Okay, then I'll go." He looks at me. "You just need to have something encouraging to say about Ava. You have time to think while we're all goin'."

Ava adds, "It's a one-line affirmation. It's a Jackson tradition. You'll get it too on your birthday."

I could have used that, say . . . oh, I don't know, the last thirty-eight years of my life. Maybe then I wouldn't be so jaded inside.

"Ava, my baby girl," says Tim, "you got a light in you that can't be denied. That light is gonna lead you to great, great joy and adventures."

"I like it, Daddy." She blows him a kiss.

Next round the table is Tim Jr., who smirks and says, "You're gonna look reeeaaaalllll good when you get those braces off."

Kyle takes his turn, talking while mashed potatoes spray out: "Ava, I'm glad you're my sister 'cause you help me with my reading."

Next up is Michaela, but the timing is off. She helplessly points to her mouth, full of garlic greens, so they move on to Debbie.

"I appreciate that you share your favorite clothes with me and that you braid my hair and that you love me. You're an awesome sister."

The table lets out a collective "Awwww."

"Ava, I love that you're more confident in who you are every day," says Michaela. As her big sister, she's clearly privy to more of the birthday girl's backstory than I am. "You've recognized that you're smart and fantastic and full of God's joy."

Another collective "Awwww."

How does she do that? I mean, talk about God without a hint of embarrassment?

"Oh! And that you've grown out of the Jan Brady phase," she adds, and talking like Jan from *The Brady Bunch*, cries out, "Marsha, Marsha, Marsha!"

Everybody laughs.

"You're up." Tim looks at me.

"Ahh, no. Moms get to go before party crashers."

"Momma goes last, after y'all are done eatin' and passin' them plates," LeChelle says, raising her brow.

"Kinda like the opening credits in a movie. The most important person is last." I laugh nervously as they all look at me like a cucumber just sprouted out of my forehead. "Oh, okay. Well, Ava, I haven't known you that long, but I will say that I like you a lot."

"Thank you," she acknowledges.

"And I think you have a great talent in your writing," I continue. "The short stories you've shown me are really creative and have good characters, so I think you'll go far with that . . ."

"Gift." Tim finishes my sentence.

"Yes, gift, talent . . . go far . . . Okay, I'm done." Seriously, I am really good at giving speeches, but this touchy-feely, family-dynamic stuff is all new to me and very unnerving.

"Thank you, Miss Alice." Ava shyly shrugs her shoulders at me.

I just wink at her, wondering what all that love feels like when it's poured into you.

Dinner has come to a close, and Tim gets up to clear some of the plates.

"Y'all hold up one second." LeChelle gets up from the table and goes into the kitchen. She disappears inside before coming back with the candles blazing on top of a homemade, three-layer angel food cake. It's topped with mounds of fresh strawberries, and gooey white icing is drizzling off the sides. Yum.

Everyone sings "Happy Birthday." When we finish the song, with her eyes clenched shut, Ava takes a deep breath, holds it, and wishes as if it were her last wish before finally blowing the candles out.

LeChelle pulls the candles off the cake and says, "Happy birthday, my baby girl. You know it's fitting that you'd pick an angel food cake every year, 'cause you're like my little angel."

Her tone changes to serious and I understand now what they mean by "speaking life."

"I want you to know that you can do anything in this life because the Lord made you special. Special! And He equipped you with many, many strengths. You got a good heart and a clever mind and strong beauty that comes from in here," she says, first pointing at her heart and then up at the heavens, "and up there. There isn't anything in this world that you're not going to be able to do. You understand me?"

Ava nods with tears in her eyes.

"Nothing you can't do!"

Okay, where in the heck was that speech when I was four-teen? Where is that speech now? Doesn't everyone need that speech?

Ava gets up from her chair to hug her momma. They both cry. I'm going to cry. I look around. The whole freaking table is crying.

"That's why she goes last," Tim says softly.

After I grub up the cake, my bloating sets in and the questions begin. I'm now in the Jackson family's Jesus hot seat. This is the one time since I've been pregnant that I really, really need a glass of wine, and a big one at that. A fishbowl-sized glass filled to the brim would do. A tolerator. I'd just slowly guzzle away the uneasiness of intimacy and drown the truth in full-bodied red. All the ugliness and uncertainty would flow down, down, down and be gone.

"How about you come tomorrow?" Ava asks.

Oh, great. Tomorrow is Sunday. This dinner, a birthday party for my favorite of their five kids, and her innocently inviting me to go to church. Nice. A new tactic. Using the kid. Tricky yet obvious. I'm no fool for their Bible brainwashing.

"Since you didn't get me anything and all. How 'bout you come with us, for me? It will be my birthday present."

"Ava, your daddy knows I'm not big on organized religion. No offense."

"Then you should like it 'cause we're about the most unorganized bunch I've ever met," Tim pipes in.

The table is silent. I look around at them all looking back at me. We've had this discussion before, and although I love what they have, the whole holy-roller thing isn't really for me. I glare at Tim.

"I swear, I said nothin'!" Tim puts his hands up in the air, feigning innocence. I almost believe him.

"I bet."

"He doesn't lie," LeChelle says. "That's just the Lord using that precious girl to reach your heart."

"Come on, lil' momma!" Tim Jr. adds, making me smile. He must've heard that in church.

"Let me ask you this." Tim looks me in the eye and stops gathering the dishes. "How 'bout you come and tell me what you think. Straight-up honest. If we look crazy, tell me. I could use some outside viewpoints and all. You lose nothin' by comin'."

I lose an hour of my life I can never get back, I silently grumble.

"I promise you won't be asked to do anything freaky. Just come and check it out. Who knows, maybe there's a way you don't know about."

They sit looking at me. It's not a look of pressure. It's not a look of pity. It's a long, quiet look of . . . Hmmm, I guess that must be what hope looks like. Yes, I think it is. They are looking at me optimistically.

Maybe it's my blood pressure, or maybe it's the chicken rounding third base next to the collard greens in my lower intestine. Maybe my baby is ready to be horizontal. I don't know, but I feel tired. Real tired. How many times can I say no? How many times can I reject their faith?

"There might be something there to experience. See if it's real. If it connects. See it for yourself." Tim carries the plates to the sink.

"Commmmmme," pleads Ava. She's the last nail in my coffin.

"Fine, preacher people! I'll come, but I'm not going early."

The table claps. "Yay!"

"Oh, don't get too excited. I'm sitting in the back just in case the heavens open up and hellfire and brimstone shoot down on all of you as punishment for bringing me to your holy place."

LeChelle laughs. "Girrrrrrl, you crazy."

You have no idea. You have no real idea how crazy I am.

I'll try one service with this family at their freaky church. Honestly, it can't be worse than the rabbit hole, can it? And, at the very least, if I go once, maybe Tim will stop inviting me every friggin' day. Maybe he'll just leave me be on my familiar guilt-free path of nothingness and moral oblivion. It's tarnished, and that's just the way I like it.

3

The United Nations Musical

Getting dressed is always interesting when you're fatter than you'd like to be. I feel good in absolutely nothing but my giant grandma cotton panties, Burton's extra-large worn-out Johnny Cash T-shirt, his wide-legged work scrubs, and my Ugg slippers. And feeling good is all about comfort, not looks.

Showering at this point is tricky, as it requires waddling in total nakedness in front of the bathroom mirror into our frameless, stone-encased waterfall area. As alluring as that may sound, the whole catching-a-glimpse-of-my-extra-pounds-of-flesh-following-behind-me-like-a-shadow is horrific.

After going through numerous elastic-waisted skirts in my closet, I settle on a navy, stretchy, cotton mid-calf-length number from A Pea in the Pod. I top it off with a silky cream-and-navy short-sleeved striped blouse. I'm the freakin' Skipper from *Gilligan's Island* with a bobbed do.

"Casual yet respectable," I mumble while eyeballing the enormity of my bottom cheeks in a full-length mirror. I make a muscle like Popeye and shake my arms. My reflection, I note, has an inch of floppy flesh now dangling with absolutely no tension, even when flexing.

I kick my ruffled, cream leather Jimmy Choo flat sandal over to the edge of my bed and climb onto it. Then I curl up onto my side and stare at the wall. I'm sweating in places that don't have sweat glands. From the heat of the shower, the blow dryer, and the excess weight, I'm an overheating Pontiac on a long stretch of desert highway with no coolant in the radiator. As a result, the baby is having a tantrum on the right side of my ribcage. I can feel my heart racing just slightly above the approved safety limit. I lie there thinking that these are all perfectly good, solid reasons to stay in bed.

Just then I hear a buzz. My phone.

Are you coming?

It's a text from Tim.

I preached a good one at the 9:00 service. Just making sure you're getting ready and know how to get here.

I lie there, feeling the *thump, thump, thump* of the vein in my neck pulsating. Breathe in. Breathe out. Wax on. Wax off. I try to channel Mr. Miyagi in *The Karate Kid*. *I'm okay*, I think, feeling everything but okay, and trying to calm down and not have an anxiety attack, stroke, or coronary. "I'm not dying. I'm not dying."

I take a deep breath and release it. Leave it to a real life-or-death health issue to kick in all of my hypochondriac theories of impending personal doom. Like I wasn't insane enough already.

I decide to rally. I sit up and strategize as to how I am going to get my shoes on today. There's no chance I'm gonna be able to see what I am doing on account of my enormous belly. I must go for the exterior shot. With considerable oomph, I bend my right leg to the right side, pull my foot up so that it flanks me, and hold my breath as I fasten the absolute last hole available on the ankle strap. I am just recovering from successfully repeating this gymnastic feat on my left shoe when the phone rings.

I grab my purse, head toward the garage, and bark into the phone, "I'm on my way already!" No *Hello,* no *Good morning,* nothing.

"On your way where?" To my surprise, it's Burton.

"Church," I say nonchalantly.

"Reeallllly? Is everything okay?" Even after simply passing me like a ship in the early-morning fog over the past five months, he knows church is not really my gig. That's putting it kindly.

"I'm going to solidify my invitation to a Sunday night meal."

"I'm glad you're going," he says with coziness in his voice.

Burton was raised going to church every Sunday. He's got that God thing already organically entrenched in him. Yet he's smart enough not to push it on me every Sunday these last few months when he's not at football practice and leaves to meet the Banister bunch for bending on knees and brunch at the club. *"No, thank you,"* I say. No amount of food or pretty white linen tablecloth presentations would make me reach out to religion with them. This I know, as their religion isn't working for them. They are awful, judgmental, and hypocritical. With them at church, at any moment I could become their sacrificial goat on the baloney-selling altar.

I can hear the Tennessee Titans minicamp music blaring in the background at Baptist Sports Park, practice facility and home of the Titans. "Don't get too excited or tell your family or anything. It's a one-off. And I'm late, so I gotta run."

"Okay, I'll call you when practice is over. Love—" he begins but I hang up, not wanting to hear the rest.

No *love you, love you back* sign-off. Perrrrrrfect.

I mean, do we really even *love*-love each other? Some days I think we might, some days I'm not so sure. I did agree to marry him after about five months of our cohabiting. His family thinks it is more about insurance benefits, baby legitimacy, and other tangled pieces of life than it is about love. Love? What is it, really? I haven't experienced anything remotely like love since the age of fourteen. Not real love, anyway.

We're not in that mushy love, at least I'm not. It is more a newfound tolerance and healthy respect on my part and true caring, concern, and conscious consideration on his part. We have been thrown into a life under the same roof and committed ourselves to one another for a lifetime, or at least for the time being, to raise a child. I mean, I've had other kinds of passion, hot sex, and erotic out-of-body experiences. I have mooned over the kind of love they write about in romantic movies like *The Bridges of Madison County* and *Love Story*. And this is nothing like any of that. I have no solid life plan at this point, other than birthing this being inside of me and jamming out of Dodge City. If you had asked me one year ago where I'd be today, I would have said at the Emmy Awards in a fantastic gown with a glass of Cristal Champagne in one hand and a hidden camera in the other. Seriously, if—and I mean *if*—there is a God, it has a pretty decent sense of humor. I'm preggo and married to a dude named Burton.

Ahhh, Burton. We've become increasingly aware of each other's idiosyncratic behaviors. Like the way he takes a bite of his food and chews it a hundred times before swallowing. Or the way I floss my teeth and leave the floss on the bathroom sink. And the way he snores like a donkey. Okay, the way *I* snore like a pregnant donkey. There's the flatulence, there's the body hair, and there's the mascara stains on the pillowcases. We've become aware of it all without becoming too emotionally intertwined. He is much more patient than I am. Much more tolerant. Perhaps he plans to just take care of me nicely until our offspring has sprung and then he's going to hand me over with a satchel of money to some third cousin who lives in Dickson with instructions to hide my body in a hunting ditch somewhere. (Wow, I've got to stop watching *Law & Order*.)

Honestly, I think Burton loves what he knows, which is that I'm having his baby. He keeps learning little bits here and there, but mostly he appreciates that I do like sports and can tolerate almost any situation he puts me in, with the exception of churches and long dinners with his family, without booze or prescription medication. The point being, I do care about him and he does care about me, despite my rough edges and my serrated scars. We have had a few moments. Private, meaningful moments. He's an honest, honorable man, and those are hard qualities to come by nowadays. I'm learning to appreciate more than the fact that he has a nice tush. His Southern drawl simply makes me warm inside.

As I drive north down Hillsboro Road past acre after acre of rolling pastures speckled with cows chewing on green grass behind white fences, my mind flips to Burton on the football sideline at the Titans' practice. I can only imagine the Titans cheerleaders rehearsing their high kicks and panting at him like hungry, hot, tight-bodied temptresses. What is it that makes a grown woman want to do a shim-shim with her pom-poms like that?

Annoying. Why do I care anyway? Such contradiction in my own heart. Like a tennis match of my emotions. Some days I feel Burton is totally mine, and some days I'm ready to pound the pavement of freedom. I am falling for him or perhaps I have fallen, but I will not partake in all of the sensitive drivel that comes along with actually loving a man that turns women ridiculously silly.

I turn onto Granny White Pike off Old Hickory and pull my Navigator into the jam-packed parking lot. A large white church is set back on the property. I'm surprised I am in the right place. It doesn't look at all churchy. There's no steeple or anything like that.

An off-duty police officer frantically waves his arms, trying to show me that I've entered the exit flow of traffic from the service before this one. *It's private property,* I am tempted to mouth at him as I quickly snag a coveted open spot toward the entrance.

I probably should have noticed this was a sign. I was entering through the exit after all. I get out of the truck and slip on a piece of paper on the asphalt. My shoe digs into my ankle as I grab my door handle for support. I suppose I should wear more suitable shoes, but I will not relinquish the one lavish thing that still fits my feet.

More waddling up to the side door of the church. "Quack, quack, quack," I ridicule myself.

"Welcome to Bethel!" A smiling, balding gentleman with a name tag that says GARY greets me at the door. He places a service pamphlet in my left hand and eagerly shakes my right. Noticing my belly expanding out of my skirt, he exclaims: "What a blessing!" Gary drops my right hand like a hot potato in favor of touching my ever-expanding stomach. *Space, people! Get out of my personal space!*

It creeps me out. I want to smack him and scream, *Don't touch my baby belly!* Why do people always touch my belly? *How about if I rub your big belly, Gary? Huh? How about that?*

Mother of pearl! I am so cranky.

I escape the middle-aged man's overly friendly petting and look around at the inside of the church. There are already more than a thousand people assembled. Row after row of filled pews form a semicircle that surrounds a stage equipped with a band, choir, and singers. The musical collective is creating an unfamiliar yet catchy tune.

The gathered are singing and swaying, creating a mass of sound and fury from black, white, and tan believers. Red, white, and blue. Rich and poor. Americans and Africans. Chinese and Filipino. Mexican and Ethiopian. The celebration of color is increased by the fact that people are dressed in their corresponding national garb.

This bizarre tapestry of God's parishioners all woven together looks more like a United Nations parade than any Sunday service I've ever seen. Not that I saw many at St. Matthew's growing up.

Another greeter-type person tries to direct me down the aisle to the front. *Not so fast, buddy*, I think as I wave him off and duck into the very last row. He just smiles and helps me get seated.

I marvel at the stage. Three long panels hang vertically from the ceiling with gold and black lettering: DEVOTION. DISCIPLESHIP. DIVERSITY. The latter would explain the hodgepodge of visual and audio entertainment gathered: a potbellied Middle Eastern guitarist, three white dudes rocking a horn section, a gray-haired grandma on the fiddle, and Johnny Rocket on the drums. The mismatched musicians are backing up twenty-five purple-and-gold-clad, rainbow-skin-toned choir members. A very large fifty-year-old black man and a very pretty thirtysomething white gal stand in front, belting out heart-pounding notes about Jesus the Redeemer.

I thought they were singing that Jesus was—wait for it—the *Reindeer* until I read the screen behind them with the lyrics on it.

I'm going to hell. In the express elevator.

At this moment, all I can think is, *Who do I need to call at FOX to get this girl on* American Idol?

Taking a long look around at the hand-waving, tear-spouting, jumping and dancing Jesus followers, I wonder, *What in the hell have I gotten myself into?*

I sit back in my easy-exit pew to watch the "show."

My pulse is racing and the baby is dancing. I suddenly feel a strange sense of connection, at least to that music. What is it about music that can find its way to my heart? I can't help but remember a time long ago, at the beginning of the end, when my faith in God was about to be altered, when all innocent goodness ceased to exist in my realm of possibility, and my life started to head toward catastrophic self-destruction.

Spring 1980: My mother is working with me on my seventh-grade spelling homework. Being a schoolteacher, she usually keeps her long blond hair in a ponytail to look neat, but at home with me it is loose and dances on her shoulders. This is the way I like it. Every move she makes sends the scent of Breck shampoo my way. She's so cool in her yellow bell-bottom pantsuit and big gold hoop earrings.

You'd think she'd get enough of teaching kids at Whitmore Elementary and Middle School and wouldn't want to come home and do it with me. She's an eighth-grade history teacher. Her classroom is across the playground from mine. Every day, we drive home together in her black-and-white Dodge Challenger and talk about our day.

We live in a modest, older, three-bedroom, red-and-white brick-and-stucco ranch house. Oleander bushes have taken over our carport. A fountain trickles water into a makeshift four-foot pond for snails, worms, and birds. Potted flowers bloom at the base of the bay window. Gravel and four big palm trees make a ring around our small front yard. Our lawn is brown, the grass dead from the Arizona heat.

Next to the six-foot concrete retaining wall that protects the sides and back of our house is our prized yellow-and-white Terry Travel Trailer. It is currently grounded on the side of the driveway in an improvised parking space, killing more grass and upping the trash factor of our lawn.

Every July, we hitch up the trailer to Daddy's Oldsmobile and head to Show Low in the White Mountains, determined to escape the 115-degree heat of Tucson. It's my favorite time of the year; we play crazy eights and rummy in folding chairs and I camp in sleeping bags between Mom and Dad amid the smell of pine needles and burned wood from an open fire pit. Mom taught me to bait a hook last summer, and I caught bluegills for the first time at Becker Lake.

It's the middle of the school year now, so we are home and in the family room. Daddy is rocking in his brown leather La-Z-Boy recliner. It is torn and fire-charred on the right armrest, a constant reminder that sleeping with a lit cigarette between your lips can "nearly burn down the house!" as my mom used to say in a raised voice.

Dad has his Dallas Cowboys T-shirt on with his work suit pants. He's half-comfortable after a long day at the office. I swear he's still mad the Cowboys lost the Super Bowl to the Steelers. He's a big football fan and is always telling me that the Cowboys are America's team.

A pot roast with baby carrots and potatoes is in the Dutch oven slow cooker. The smell is so heavy in the air that I can see a thin layer penetrating the plume of Daddy's Marlboro smoke by our low popcorn ceiling.

Daddy's got some type of gin drink in his hand. He mixes it in a measuring cup and stirs it with ice. It's gross. I know this because I pulled it out of the refrigerator and drank it, thinking it was 7UP. I nearly threw up all over our yellow-and-white linoleum kitchen floor.

He's rocking in his chair, gulping his drink, and watching TV. A gray-haired man named Walter Cronkite is giving us the news of the day. Mr. Cronkite is showing black-and-white pictures and looking like he's got a lot to say and not enough time to say it.

Mom and I are seated at our octagonal Formica dining table doing my spelling homework. I watch as Mom turns her attention away from me and to Mr. Cronkite on the TV. Her head is shaking and her eyes are sad. It makes me feel like the blood is draining right out of my legs and into the orange shag carpet.

"What's going on, Mom?"

Realizing she has upset me, she pulls me out of my chair and onto her lap and tries to explain. "Those men there with white blindfolds on are Americans," she says. "We're Americans. And those people with the guns, they've been keeping those people with the blindfolds on, as hostages, for a long time. Prisoners. The men with the guns, they're from Iran, which is another country, far, far away."

As she speaks she strokes my hair gently. She is trying to make it all sound normal, but the way her blue eyes continue to pierce the images on the TV gives her away. She's concerned and scared.

"Did those prisoners steal something? Is that why they are prisoners?"

"No, honey. They weren't bad. They were just in the wrong place at the wrong time." As she lets out a deep sigh, I sink further into her body.

"Kinda like Granny and Granddad." I look up at her.

It is my dad's turn to look stern. He is staring at me and his eyes are dart throwers. It's as if I said a curse word or something. I'm suddenly aware that I've done something I shouldn't have done. Then his eyes soften at Mom.

She shakes her head at him. Without a word, they both go back to watching those hostages.

My mom hugs me tight and kisses my cheek. "Yes, baby. Like Granny and Granddad."

My mom's mom and dad were on a plane from Chicago that crashed when they were coming to see us at the beginning of last summer. Now they're in heaven.

"Well, that's not fair. That's just not fair they're keeping them there away from their families."

"No, it isn't, honey."

The news is coming to an end as Mr. Cronkite looks into our family room in his yellow tie and silver mustache and says, "That's the way it is, Tuesday, April 1st, 1980, the 149th day of captivity for the hostages in Iran. This is Walter Cronkite, CBS News. Good night."

"Mark my words, between botched US attempts and heart-breaking disappointments trying to free them over the past five months, if it goes on much longer it's going to cost Carter the election." My mother spits out her opinions with a passionate verve and conviction for history and politics and our country that makes me proud.

Then she spins me around on her lap and shuts my spelling book, smiling, and totally changes the mood. "That's why we gotta live life, honey. We have to live every precious minute we get. Now help me make those cookies!" I climb onto her for a piggy-back ride into the kitchen, where she turns on the portable radio next to the coffeemaker.

The Bee Gees are singing "Too Much Heaven," and Mom and I start dancing around the kitchen like a couple at a junior high school dance. My hands are on her slim hips, and her arms are around my neck. We just dance and giggle until Daddy comes in the kitchen and takes Mom in his arms. He dips her and then kisses her for such a long time that it makes my cheeks warm. We keep on dancing and singing in the kitchen as the radio plays.

She has no idea while dancing in the kitchen that day that she will be dead soon. No idea at all.

It was the last time I remember feeling safe. Normal.

The music on the church stage at Bethel has slowed and the young woman is still singing. I am hit with the realization that for the first time in twenty-five years, I'm sober enough to recall a good memory of my mother. There are plenty of angry, painful ones to draw from. But this was a different emotion. Having such a pleasant memory awakened and clear gives me pause. The music has shaken me out of my emotional slumber and warmed the waters in my pot.

A pot that eventually became filled with secrets, lies, and shame.

4

How Many Calories Are in That Biscuit?

I was raised Catholic. The two things I remember most vividly about church were filtered through the mind of a naive twelve-year-old. The first was the fact that our priest could turn a biscuit into Jesus and a pitcher of Kool-Aid into His blood. These supposed miracles are beyond gross for a kid.

The second thing was that church was not fun. For me, it was quiet, scary, damning, and hard to understand. Jesus was hung, beaten, and killed. This horror story was told to us every Sunday. Isn't the point of religion that He arose from the dead?

I always wondered why they didn't focus on the risen, happy, miraculous version of Jesus. Jesus skipping on water like a smooth, flat rock expertly flung from the fingertips of a little boy. Jesus who defied the naysayers and Roman and Jewish odds-makers to slip out of the death tomb and float like a lost balloon to the happy land in the sky called Balloonia. A place my mother promised me that all the helium balloons went after they had slipped from my grip.

As I sit at Bethel today, in a mainstream glee-club–inspired reproduction of an old-school tent revival, I am being reintroduced to the concept of a Jesus-infused Keebler biscuit. I am being asked to drink the blood and eat the body of Christ.

Little plastic shot glasses are being passed from person to person and I think: *Doesn't anyone in this place remember Jim Jones's Peoples Temple and how he mass-murdered more than nine hundred of his followers in Jonestown, Guyana, with laced Kool-Aid?*

I do. And that thought gives me pause, as I don't want some altar boy slipping me a roofie.

Never mind the fact that I look like I ate someone. My gynecologist, Dr. Nicole Schlossberg, an attractive, fortyish, purple-crew-cut-sporting pit bull of a Jewish baby doctor, has become a medical Marxist to me, making sure I don't die on her watch. The Vanderbilt graduate and Los Angeles transplant has quickly become the only person I trust at Burton's hospital. Both she and Burton have been hounding me about absolutely everything I do and eat. "No salt. More water." I can hear her San Fernando Valley accent in my head.

Apparently there's a mandate at Baptist Hospital that I not croak. Dr. Nicole is amusing to me because she scares the heck out of all the nurses. She's an ob-gyn on a mission to raise the bar of excellence at the hospital. I find it ironic that a woman who spends her days elbow-deep in other women's private parts bringing new life into the world has chosen a peaceful existence with her husband and no children of her own—just two Rottweilers as her babies. She has to know something I don't know. I keep giving her a run for her money on the Alice good health Tilt-a-Whirl.

Whether she can rein me in or whether she's going to have me committed to the maternity ward on bed rest remains to be seen. Oh, sure, she threatens, but I've managed to escape her commitment papers so far. Fingers crossed.

Here's a consideration I can sink my teeth into for Dr. Nicole and myself: *Jesus, how many calories are in that biscuit? Because I really don't want to eat it and end up facedown in your* Masterpiece Theater *God-production.*

January 2005: My thoughts on Catholicism are laid bare on my Nashville move-in day last winter. That's when Tim really starts talking to me about what I believe in. The weather is turning from cool to warm and the bees are swarming the bushes on our front porch. I have agreed to move to Tennessee and live with Burton to get away from the stress of work, which is forbidden for the baby, and be closer to a real doctor who has the common goal of keeping me alive. If nothing else, I am to stay alive as Burton's baby pod. My plan is to live with him and see how it goes. This is the beginning of the seeing.

I have lost my temper with the two knuckleheads outsourced from the Sprintz furniture store. I love Sprintz, as it has absolutely every little knickknack and I need to add pieces of me—like my new dining-room table—to Burton's house. But the delivery guys make me want to throw rocks at them. Big, sharp rocks.

"Can you two get it together, or do I have to call Bruce?" I screech sarcastically as they scrape the doorframe for the fourth time. Bruce is the guy on the Sprintz furniture TV commercials.

"Y'all need some help over there?" Tim walks up my driveway uninvited. I'm not exactly speaking in hushed tones here.

With back-support belts cinching their guts and chewing tobacco thrusting their lips out caveman-style, the two guys are clearly unable to carry my new dining-room table into the house. A third man is needed. Tim the neighbor is our third man.

With moving trucks arriving from various furniture stores and bringing my must-haves from my house in Los Angeles, my layover sentence in Nashville has begun.

Yes, I am doing exactly what you think I am doing: I am redecorating Burton's house in Laurel Brooke and making it a space of my own. His sixty-year-old cleaning lady, Tee-Tee, is milling around frowning while I load things into the PODS container stationed in the driveway. It will be packed up and stored far, far away in a warehouse somewhere in East Nashville. As long as I have to live here, I figure, I might as well have it the way I want it. Don't get me wrong; it is pleasant enough the way it is if I were a character from *Designing Women*. It is Queen Anne, pastel-and-floral *Southern* nice. Not *West Coast* nice. It more resembles his mother's moldy taste than that of a hip bachelor. June-Rae had hired some swanky designer from Belle Meade to turn his place into a Laura Ashley home for a Mr. Belvedere–type. I would have been more at ease with a futon and milk-crate bookshelves.

Tim has known Burton since Tim's football-playing days with the Houston Oilers–turned–Tennessee Titans, so there is a history between them. Burton was one of the first and youngest team doctors here in Nashville. That football familiarity along with what I presume to be a local curiosity about me—masked by Southern hospitality, of course—is what brings all the *y'all*s here to get a good look at me.

My arrival as the suddenly and famously knocked-up new girl on the block has spread like yellow fever from neighbor to neighbor. One after another, they come over to deliver their cheerful, nosy welcomes. It feels more like the Spanish Inquisition than a warm Southern greeting.

The women are perfectly dressed with their trendy clothes

and tight bodies. I totally get it: they all look like a version of me from about a year ago. But with a lot a more Botox. Tons more. Don't get me wrong, there are some nice ones. Like the lady neighbor across the street, Mellissa. She is from Arkansas. Her little boy looks like a young Brad Pitt. She works downtown doing . . . oh, I don't remember what. We met at the mailbox. She looks like a perfectly normal forty-year-old and what I like most about her is that she, like me, is a transplant and therefore not obtrusive or transparently curious.

But then there are the others. They usually appear in smirky, judging pairs. When they flash their toothy white smiles, they are a scarier sight than a great white while you're on a boogie board in open water. Their visits are more about them than me. They giggle and talk among themselves, finishing each other's sentences, and I just stand there wide-eyed, wondering what weird Tennessee Williams play I am acting out this week. They occasionally break away from their banter with a random and inappropriate question like, "So, when was your wedding?" while they peer at my pregnant belly. They are asking the question but they are already in possession of the answer.

"Oh, we're not married," I repeat, over and over, to Jane, Belinda, Erika, Sue-Anne, Robin, and Blewett.

I'm not naive. I know their point is simply to let me know that *they know*. They tilt their heads and bat their lashes as I stand sweating and sober, dying for a cocktail and daydreaming about knocking their heads together like something out of *The Three Stooges*. I just can't figure out what their motive is other than getting a chance to judge me.

Tim has helped the guys unload the dining-room table and they are back in the furniture truck saying their good-byes.

"Ummm, Tim?" I say as he heads out the door. "Would you mind . . ."

He turns and looks at me as I point inside the house. "You got more?" He asks with a voice that really sounds like, *Sure . . . no problem.*

"Yes, sir, she has more." Tee-Tee rolls her eyes. "It's very"—she looks at Tim—"interesting." She walks away.

She's a spy sent to gain information for Burton's family. She does not know this, but today will be her final visit.

Minutes later Tim has a plump bronze Buddha in his arms and I'm trying to figure out where it looks best. "There. Over there." I point to the giant wooden chest I picked up in Bali. Tim places my lotus-position statue next to my dear old lonely friend, the hookah pipe. Our Eastern-themed meditation room is virtually complete.

Tim stands back from the Buddha's final resting place and takes a good look around at the remnants of my mind-bending quest for inner logic. These are all my items from Los Angeles, and I relish the opportunity to showcase my spiritual treasure island. After all, he is a preacher man.

Tim stands scratching his head as he scans the room. He lifts a brow and correctly identifies the elephant in the room. Other than me, of course. "Girl, where you been in your spiritual journey?" he says.

I hear a "Huh!" come out of Tee-Tee's mouth from around the corner.

At this stage of the God-game I think he and I are on par spiritually, when actually I don't have a clue. "Oh, come over here, sir, and let me tell you." I motion for him to get comfy. He's the first friendly guest I've had. Well, he's the only real guest I've actually invited into the house.

Tim sits on the canopied daybed-cum-bench. The piece was built on the island of Java for a fifteenth-century prince. It's a true collector's item. I wonder if Tim's weight might actually crack it. I cringe at the sound of the wood creaking. "Dear Jesus, let this thing hold me," he says.

"I'll second that."

"My enlightenment?" I throw out nonchalantly. I am challenging him to bring it on and give me all he's got. I feel perfectly at peace surrounded by the trinkets, beads, and deities that represent my many attempted pathways to self-realization.

He scoots back against the maroon-and-silver velvet pillows and says, "I mean, you got all this different"—he pauses—"stuff."

In addition to the Buddha, I have two metal hands with the tips of the thumbs and forefingers touching in Chin Mudra. There's also a wooden cross, a sacred OM syllable encased in a metal plate, a weathered antique Bible, and a mini replica of a Hindu temple. Until now, it has never occurred to me that, to the untrained eye, the souvenirs from my journey may appear to be a mishmash of spiritual remnants.

I watch him scratch his head again. Ha! I have really impressed him!

"It just makes me wonder whatcha really believe in," he says with genuine, questioning interest.

I'm not sure how to respond. I gaze at the rosary beads that are dangling from a lamp. I think, *What kind of crazy question is that?* The spiritual arrogance and ease I enjoyed five seconds earlier has rapidly descended into the depths of discomfort and is fast-tracking toward the south side of agitated. I have gone from being excited to explain my travels to him to being asked to bare my soul to him. I am neither prepared, capable, nor willing to do this. It's really none of his business what I believe. I mean, isn't what we believe a personal question?

Wait . . . didn't I start this?

I have a few ideas of what I believe in. But honestly, over the years I have come to believe only in myself. "Do you want some iced tea?" I ask, trying to change the subject.

"Sure," he says. He leans forward to stand up but discovers he's stuck in the meditation bed.

I walk away and smile. I have just given myself a moment to come up with an answer. And him a moment to ungracefully pry himself out of my Zen pillow collection.

"I'll help you get some of this stuff out of these boxes," he calls after me.

I am swimming in his question and thrown back in time. I stand pouring tea over ice and I feel lost. Lost in a time long, long ago.

1981: My happy life has been knocked off its normal course by death. My mother has died. The details are foggy. But the fact remains that early in my fourteenth year, I experienced something supernatural. The Occurrence, as I like to call it, has happened.

The Occurrence has changed me forever. The Occurrence has caused my father to vacillate between thinking that I am losing my mind from the trauma and that I am the most committed little liar around. Either way, he has grown to resent being stuck with me. He either doesn't want me or doesn't know how to deal with me. He does what any old-school, all-unknowing, unable-to-communicate parent does: he sends me to see a priest.

We had started going back to church after Mom discovered that she had a ticking time bomb inside of her. The cancer was going to take her away from this world and into another, and I wanted to know what that world was gonna be like.

There is nothing like an old man in a collar to wring any real sense of spiritual belonging—no matter how small—right out of you. For the record, I don't have anything against Catholics. There is something beautiful about their ancient cathedrals and the methodic rituals of their Mass. I have a lot of friends who love Catholicism and are helped tremendously by their Hail Marys and all that kneeling, but let's be very clear: I am not one of them.

Not surprisingly, our gray-haired priest does not see the beauty in a fourteen-year-old's Godly epiphany. My personal miracle. The Occurrence. He, too, is split between two conclusions: I need either more mind-altering medication or less. At the very least, he is certain I can benefit from Catholic summer camp. Cha-ching!

I remember his exact spirituality-squashing words: "Don't ask God for a sign." I am crushed.

But wait a minute. I have already been given my sign! The priest is wrong. And I want to share my hope and revelation. I want to be validated that something has moved me, healed me, touched me! But instead of being celebrated for uncovering, and being encouraged to continue my exploration of, the mysteries of faith, I am shamed for believing.

I am humiliated, confused, and ultimately angry.

Why pray at all if God doesn't really want to answer us? Why not ask for a miracle or a sign? Besides, I haven't asked for a sign so much as I have been given one! In what universe does that make me disobedient? Or a sinner?

If I am going to be a bad girl, I am going to do it right.

By late in my fourteenth year, the curtain rose on my very own personal tragicomedic play. Faith: exit stage left. Bong and hookah pipe: enter stage right. I start smoking weed in the seventh grade.

Flash forward to today, where my trusty pipe and the other symbols of faith have fallen into the rabbit hole with me. These trinkets have lost their luster and now are simply broken mirrors reflecting my past back at me.

Tee-Tee stands in the kitchen holding out one glass of iced tea in front of her. She's holding another back. I'm sure she's eager to eavesdrop on how I dodge the religion bullet.

"Thank you." I take the tea she's offering me as she follows me back to where Tim is sitting.

I think that I did give up on religion, but somewhere inside I haven't given up the search for happiness. So now, in the meditation room in my quasi-new house, the question is asked again.

"What do yoooouuuuu believe in?" I singsong the question back at him. "I mean, I know you believe in Jesus and all. Goes hand in praying hand with the whole preacher-as-a-full-time-job thing. I guess I want to know why."

He takes the iced tea from Tee-Tee. "Thank you, kind lady."

Tee-Tee is anything but kind.

Her face softens, "Of course, Pastor Tim." Then her gaze moves to me, her eyes narrow, and she turns on her heels and leaves only to continue to mill around.

I just shrug at Tim as if to say, *What the heck was that?*

He smiles at me. "I know what you're doing," he says.

Do you? Do you really know that my life strategy has been built on denial and counteraccusations? I gobble up agents and publicists and Hollywood studio executives for fun. This whole preacher thing doesn't scare me. I truly doubt you know my life strategy, preacher man.

"Really?" I cock my head to the right. "What am I doing?"

"You ain't answering my question," he says triumphantly.

"I'm not answering your question yet," I spit back.

The only sound in the room is the rustling and crinkling of

newspaper as we unfold and unwrap various items, unpacking the boxes I had shipped from LA, and Tee-Tee clearing her throat from the kitchen. The air hangs between us, but I refuse to give him the satisfaction of my vulnerability and introspection. Before long, after the awkwardness has turned to thoughtfulness, he starts to talk.

"I wasn't always a believer, you know," he says, pursing his wide lips. He takes me back to his childhood, a time he re-creates for me like a perfect craftsman. He tells his story flashing from the past to the present better than Ridley Scott.

"It was 1960 and my momma—who they called Big Momma—and her sister, Sue Nell, who worked as a midwife, were at the country hospital. Big Momma was about to give birth to me."

I can't help but smile. He just has a funny way of telling things.

He takes a long swig of his tea. "I should have known then I was meant to do something special with my life since Jesus helped me get into this world. Big Momma was screaming"—he pauses before launching into his best lady-screaming impression—"ohhh Jesus! Dear Lord, he'p me, Jesus!"

I burst out laughing and almost pee my pants.

"And out I came. All ten pounds of me. Big, round, and bald."

"Kinda like now." I can't help myself.

"That ain't nice." He takes another drink. "Anyway, a few years later Big Momma said we had another Jesus intervention. I was playing on our dirty kitchen floor with a buncha pots and pans and a skinny black man with a big afro and a tattoo on one hand and a beer in the other came in our kitchen. My birth father. He shoved my Big Momma hard against the counter. It wasn't the first time I'd seen him hurt her, but I started to cry. I was just a preschooler, now. I ain't no crybaby."

"You remember that?"

"Like it was yesterday," he said, picking up my antique Bible off my table and cocking it back like a baseball bat. "But then Big Momma, she picked up her Bible off the counter and she completely leveled him upside his head, dropping him like a fly." And he swings to the track. "I remember her saying, 'Lord, have mercy' as he just crumbled to the ground."

I give him a look that says *I don't believe it. Come on, man!*

"For real," he assures me. "I had barely known him before the day when she laid him out on the floor. I was just five years old. He never came back, so I grew up with no father, but that was okay, because a lot of kids in my neighborhood didn't know theirs either. Big Momma said if we lived our lives by the Word, it'd never let us down."

"So you grew up believing in Jesus?"

He tightens his lips together in a little smile, but then he throws me off: "Not really. See, we lived in a one-bedroom country—*real* country—slum house with broken windows and clotheslines hanging from house to house and graffiti painted on the walls. We even had a pool. Granted, it was a big ole garbage can filled to the rim. Me and my boys used to soak in them cans while Big Momma sprayed us with the hose."

I can imagine their heads bobbing up and down. "When did you start playing football?"

"We were always playing something. At about eleven years old I was one big 'cuz. 'Bout 160 pounds and I could run like I was chasing the devil who got a hold of my pork sandwich."

It is riveting the way this man can tell a yarn. It's as if the G-rated, Alabama-double-sized Eddie Murphy is talking about his childhood.

"But it wasn't till high school." He stops unpacking for a second and bends down like he's on the football field at the scrimmage line. "I was a defensive tackle. I could read the quarterback's eyes. I could see his fear. It was just something I was born with. A gift."

He looks at me and then starts to demonstrate various moves by dodging the unpacked boxes in the room. "He'd say '*hike*' and I'd push by the tackle, toss the running back to the ground, spin left, and *wham*! I'd punish the ole boy quarterback." He sits back down. "I believed the game and that football, not Jesus, were gonna save us. That was around 1982."

"That's easy to believe." I nod.

"Do you know who Bobby Bowden is?" His head cocks.

"The Florida State coach. Of course I do."

"Well, he showed up in our house, and I can remember him shaking hands with Big Momma and Aunt Sue Nell and giving them official Florida State sweatshirts."

I ease my pregnant body down onto the floor so I can sit cross-legged. I'm mesmerized by the preacher preaching his story in my house. But it doesn't seem like preaching at all. More like a one-man show that is the most entertaining experience I've had in weeks.

"Sure we went to church, but I'd been livin' like a heathen. Booze, ladies, skippin' class."

"Didn't we all?" I raise my tea glass to toast him.

"I'd never been out of Pahokee. I was lost in college. I was lonely and angry. I had a lot of questions about who I was and where I was going. I even tried a psychiatrist at one point. I was playing hard and hurtin' people on the field. Punishin' those boys across the line with my pain from the past. I was partying hard, trying to ease bruises and tears in my muscles and spirit. There was pressure in the classroom, pressure on the field. I couldn't take it. Then by chance I heard some campus minister preach."

"And the rest is history," I sigh as I begin to heave myself up, disappointed that I fell for it. "What a nice ending to a nice story."

"Heck no! I found that minister offensive! I didn't think I was a sinner. He come in all preachin' I was a sinner. Heck no. Whadda he know 'bout me?" His face scrunches together. He almost looks angry. "I was an academic and athletic All-American. My record spoke for itself. I made it out of the wooded hood. He didn't know me." His voice raises an octave. "He sure didn't know where I been or where I was goin'." Shaking his head, he said, "I felt something in my heart when he talked about forgiveness." He shrugs. "But I blew it off."

"Why?"

"Oh, 'cause it's easier to keep on running. So I just kept on running. I remember being at a frat party and I saw them guys that had been with that campus minister. Now they were gettin' all jiggy with the ladies and drinking shots and I thought, *I'm the only one in this place. Alone in a crowd. They ain't for real.*" His voice fades almost to a whisper. "Like I was in a vacuum. Like my heart had a hole in it. Like I was broke and ain't nothing going to fix that kinda broken."

I feel as if he's found one of my childhood journals and he's reading it to me. I force the knot in my throat back down to where it came from. I fake a nice look and pretend I don't understand the vacuum feeling, or running from the past, or the hole in my heart or my brokenness.

"Then I got drafted! Woo-hoo. The N-F-L! Talk about the big time. A big distraction! Me and Big Momma and Aunt Sue Nell jumping up and down in our living room. I knew life would never be the same. I bought Momma and Auntie a new Cadillac—heck, I bought one for myself, too. Big ole twenty-three-inch rims. And a house for them, and a bigger house for me."

"I can only imagine." I nod.

"Girl, I had it all."

I try to picture him back then in a feather pimp-daddy hat, fur coat, and shopping bags filled, like Julia Roberts in *Pretty Woman* strutting down Rodeo Drive in Beverly Hills. Something about it just doesn't look right.

"The ladies couldn't get outta they clothes and into my Jacuzzi fast enough. I was livin' large. Headed to the Super Bowl and the Pro Bowl and then . . . and then . . . somethin' happened." His voice trails off.

"And then what? What happened?" I shout.

"Then you tell me somethin'," he said, his brown eyes lower.

"Huh?" I squint at him. "You've got me hanging at the end of the second act of your story!"

"You tell me about this," he says, holding up the antique Bible.

"That's not fair!"

"Quid pro quo, Clarice." He imitates Anthony Hopkins in *The Silence of the Lambs*. He crosses his arms like he's not budging. "Quid pro quo."

"Rude." I feebly act as if I can take it or leave it, but the truth is, I am hanging on his every word. He has me really sucked in.

He motions that he's not giving in.

"Fine!" I yank the rosary beads off the lamp and twirl them around my finger and begin a nippy rant: "Primary years spent in a confessional as a Catholic. Uniforms. Priests. Hellfire and damnation, but nothing a couple Our Fathers and Hail Marys from the dude in the closet couldn't save me from."

Next, I snatch up the metal-encased OM and proclaim: "The sacred syllable for Hinduism given to me by my hot Indian professor in college who was married, but who had no problem explaining the world's oldest religion to me in the backseat of his 1988 green Volvo."

I set it down, thinking Tim will be shocked, but he's not. So, I rub the Buddha's head and continue my one-woman show: "The natural progression from my college days of Hinduism was to the New York nightlife and the dharmic philosophy of Buddhism. I tried my hand at Buddhist enlightenment only to realize Buddhism was not a solution for me. Their philosophies hinge on suffering. Through suffering the Buddhist produces peace. For me, suffering produced panic and more suffering."

I then yank the inhalers of the hookah and continue: "Keep in mind that when I was in doubt, the hookah and its friends in psychedelic wrappers were also in the picture. Then Confuuuucius"—I ceremoniously draw the word out for effect—"told me that meritocracy was the way to get rewarded for my hard work. So off to LA I went to study."

I pick up the big ceramic circle with a black teardrop and a white teardrop that come together to make a perfect sphere. "The yin and yang of Taoism, because honestly don't we all have a little good and a little bad inside of us? The main problem I had with Taoism is that their principles of love, moderation, and humility, while lovely, went against my inner and professional principles of lust, greed, and getting to the top of the heap."

"I gotcha," Tim says. I'm kinda surprised he was able to follow my twisted walk down spiritual remembrance lane.

"Oh, I forgot one thing. There was also lunch with an agent at the Scientology compound in Hollywood. But that ended for me when Tom Cruise jumped on Oprah's sofa. Who does that?"

"Brotha went cuckoo. Cu-ckoo!" He laughs.

"I liked the idea of having a sister wife as a Mormon," I continue just for fun. "I could use someone to help me with the dishes and laundry, but life on a compound, hmmm, not so much. So that leaves the Jews. I really still like Judaism and the Torah. A lot of great generational history and tradition. But as insane as it sounds, there's too much evidence for me that Jesus did walk this earth and did turn the water to wine. Did I mention I like the wine part?"

He's just shaking his head, smiling at me like I'm crazy, but in an understanding way.

"But you still haven't answered what you believe in."

Dang. Leave it to Tim to bring the wagons full circle.

"Didn't I?" I take his empty tea glass and ask, "You want another?"

"Nahh, I'm good," he says, staring blankly and waiting for my answer. He just wants me to cut the crap.

"Finish your story." I raise my brow. "I gave you something."

"Yeah. You gave me 'something,'" he says, making the "something" sound like it's a big fat pile of nothing. "Where was I?" He knows perfectly well where he left the story.

"You were chilling with your NFL boys on *Cribs*."

"So I was rolling but I was more lost than ever. Oh, I went to church and did the whole Christian Athlete Fellowship group. But I was a faker till one day I went to help some inner-city kids. The team had set up some meet-and-greet with a couple players and there was a young preacher there, maybe twenty years old, no older than me, and he was giving the gospel to them kids."

"And it touched you."

"Nope. But I was intrigued by the way he was holdin' that Bible. I thought it kinda made sense what he was saying, but I thought I could make it happen on my own if I'd just work hard. I could fix all my stuff with my own ability. I'd made everything else happen up to this point."

You and me both, my inside voice says.

"Then that pastor asked if any one of us wanted the blessings he was talkin' about. I did but I got scared. Those guys on the team, doing the visit with me, they all knew me. So I just sank further down into my seat. I was too embarrassed to admit I needed help. That I needed Jesus."

"No one likes being called out in a crowd," I say to try to make him feel better.

"But then I got up! I don't know why. I just did. And he prayed for me. I thought there'd be some thunderbolt or some miracle, but there wasn't nothing after that day. I didn't have anyone to help me. Anyone to teach me. Coach me up. But the preacher gave me this prayer. Just one little prayer, and I memorized it, and I'd say it over and over. I still waffled in and out of sin, but I kept praying that prayer."

He gets up. "You got any snacks over here? Or you wanna come to our house to eat? My wife, LeChelle, is a really good cook. You gotta meet her."

"Seriously?" I head to the pantry, grab some pretzels, and hurry back after noticing Tee-Tee snoring in the floral Queen Anne chair.

He takes a few in his mouth, really savoring each salty bite. As he chews, he's watching me waiting on the end of the story. He makes me want to bash that bag over his head.

Smiling, Tim finally draws the story to a close. "We were playing the Colts, and it was raining cold pieces of ice."

It's hard to imagine this gentle giant snarling and spitting behind his face mask in the mud. He tells the story like Vince Lombardi reliving the glory years. He describes it so I can see it.

"I beat the offensive tackle off the line, but the running back chip-blocked me like a freight train under the chin. Blew me up in the air with the most violent hit I'd ever felt." He flips up his head and his neck snaps back. He rolls onto the floor, playing dead. "That moment changed it all. Next thing I knew I was in a neck brace in the hospital and couldn't move nothin'."

"Paralyzed?"

"Like a dog run over in the road. I just kept praying that prayer. Over and over. Big Momma said I prayed it in my sleep like I was talking to God Himself. It was the only prayer I knew. It's funny," he reflects. "Sometimes people only look up when they're flat on their backs. I realized in that room I'd been livin' my dream, driving on my road, following the wrong plan. I'd forgotten what Momma had taught me. Only God had the power to heal and rescue my life . . . to fill up the hole."

"And He did, right?"

Tim sits up, takes my Bible back off the table, and holds it like a precious gift.

"Yup. He must have heard me 'cause I got better. And then some men from church came and helped me rehab, and I got healthy and played three more years. I got baptized and the power of the Holy Spirit did something to change my heart. I still struggled—but God changed me. He brought the right people in my life. People to equip me to deal with the pressure. People to teach me how to read my Bible. People who showed me it just starts with a simple prayer. A desire for somethin' better. A surrender to saying 'I got this,' 'cause I didn't . . . It's a process."

"That's a nice story."

"It's the only one I got."

He left that day giving Tee-Tee a hug and without pushing me again about what I believed. That day five months ago marked the beginning of another chapter in my spiritual journey, just when I thought I had closed the book for good.

Sitting today in Tim's church, where he is the preacher, I am still pondering that conversation in the middle of the crowd.

Truth is, I don't know specifically what I believe in and I

think he understood that. But it's not that I don't believe. I believe in something out there. I'm just not ready to jump into this Kool-Aid crew of organized religion. Been there, done that. A few times.

Tim left me with a lot that day, but mainly it was the beginning of an honest friendship. No pretense, no judging. No condemned-soul talk. An invitation. Two people connected by a sea of historical pain and past bravado—yet his was healed.

He also threw me what I believe he thought was a life jacket: that prayer he's been praying over twenty years. The prayer that got him praying. It was a worn photocopy folded four times to fit in a wallet.

I dig in my purse while the altar boy is still passing the trays of sacrament. I pull out my wallet, open it up, and slowly read the text.

A Prayer for Hope

I will pray for hope, and I will pray as a broken man—
To the Creator of the trees and streams and of all
great things, give me hope.
As I go out today into the world, I walk with my head
down and a heavy heart.
Put Your hand on me, guide me as I wander the paths
of my life that can lead to happiness and success.
This day of all days, I call on You for hope.
I don't need money or jewels or even a day's wages;
instead lead me that I can find Your hope that soars
beyond my cages.
If the tiger can hunt and the eagle can soar, so can I
find the purpose of my life. Send me on my way, the way
only You know.

Mark my words with honest favor.

Let me stumble and fall so I may remain humble. Do not hide my way from failure or pitfalls, but stay with me to show me how to get up with You.

Give me a job that is only for me. Plant the seeds of success and watch them grow.

Bring me challenges and fears and peace in my spirit.

Let me be courageous and able to laugh at my weaknesses and misgivings.

Help me to reach for my dreams and live my days as a gift of no more.

Let me ride the waves heading toward the shore.

Give me the time to finish my goals and help me love the people who need loving the most.

Break my spirit of addiction or of lust or of greed and let me feel the grace that is my only need.

Expose me to danger, to bigotry and those who take, so I can witness a stranger's walk and love them versus hate.

Bring the love of a family and the touch of a friend, let me be surrounded by their kindness until the very end.

Love me, oh God, and guide my every step. Help me. Show me the way that is best.

Today I pray for hope and not for an easy day. I pray that You are with me until my last breathing day.

And when my days are past and there is nothing left to say, I hope that Your face will be with me and I will no longer be afraid.

There was something about that prayer that kept me reading it. I read it that night before bed and again in the morning. For a while I kept it in my makeup drawer and would read it out loud as I got ready for my day. I'm not sure why.

Maybe it was the fact that it was honest and beautiful and hopeful and not overly preachy and religious, or maybe it was the fact that it gave Tim hope when everything appeared hopeless. I flirted with the possibility that his type of hope could be something I might have one day if I read it over and over as he had.

Finally I put it in my wallet, secretly desiring that it cut through all the layers of my dysfunction. Perhaps I kept it because of the simple fact that Tim cared enough about me to give it to me. Somewhere I want to believe it can work to change my mind, my heart, but mostly I think it's going to take a lot more than a prayer to heal my wounds.

But I still keep it.

5

Say a Little Prayer for Me

The people-watching at Bethel is pretty good. Nearly every available inch of the pews is now full. I am getting a good look at the gathering from my bleacher seat.

A shot glass full of grape juice has been placed in a little holder in front of me. It sits next to my untouched "Communication Card." Like I'm really going to give the Bethel people my address. Next thing you know I'll have two missionaries on my doorstep trying to drag me back, send me off, or better yet, promise to keep me in their prayers. No, thanks.

The whole shot glass experience is a little reminiscent of my baby shower in Nashville.

* * *

Late January of this year: I sit on our couch, blindfolded. Burton plays Enya's *Amarantine* CD for me as he prepares my surprise. This feels bizarre, as I barely have gotten settled. I can hear his shoes on the hardwood floor as he makes his way toward me. "Sit still," he says with a laugh as he places something on my head.

"What?" I exclaim. My hand makes the discovery of a tiara.

"Listen, pregnant lady. Move it again and you're in trouble," he instructs.

I hear paper rustling. I want so much to peek. I hate being in the dark. It makes me feel vulnerable—an emotion I loathe.

"Okay. You can look now," he says, pulling the soft black handkerchief from my eyes.

Our house is decorated with pink and white streamers thanks to the Jackson girls. LeChelle, Tim, the kids, and Burton all start singing "For She's a Jolly Good Fellow." A pile of presents sits on the table in front of me along with a cake with candles set aflame.

I don't want a bunch of people I barely know throwing me a party. I don't want people I *know* throwing me a party.

I freeze. I want to run . . . or cry . . . or hide. Their faces are happy and they are looking at me, but it's as if they are not singing to me. The normalcy of it all is causing an out-of-body experience for me. I'm living someone else's life for a moment. It feels sore and tranquil all at the same time.

"It's a baby shower. Get it?" Burton says, looking around at all the weird cherub wrapping paper.

I hate baby showers! I think. *Diaper games and presents and cupcakes. Women sitting around talking about milestones for their toddlers. I'm not sure I even like babies. Ridiculous.* Nor did I tell Burton, my baby daddy, or any member of the Jackson family I wanted a baby shower.

I'm seriously a green monster inside wanting to spit fire breath at everyone.

They have sneaked around me, under my very nose, and plotted to celebrate my life and the life of my baby. Why? Granted, these are good people who want to be here for me. But it's so unfamiliar and uncomfortable; I've never felt more undeserving or less desirous of attention in my life.

But just at that moment, from out of our bedroom I hear a familiar voice yell, "Surprise!" It is Amos. My Amos. A glimpse of life from my home planet. Someone who knows all the broken parts of me.

I burst out crying.

"Hormones," he says with a flourish to the room, as they all seem worried about me. He sits down on the couch and wraps his long arms around me and hugs me. "Happy shower, lucky lady," he says, and it was as if he had handed me a gold coin. My treasured Amos. "Never thought I'd be at a baby shower for you, doll." He ribs me. "You're so fancy." He touches my tiara. "What's next, my suburban princess, Avon? Tupperware? Pyramid schemes?"

I want to kill him for making fun of me. But it is so good to have him there to meet the Jackson family and see what Burton and I are doing in our paper-doll house. I need his perspective to dissect if I am slowly being brainwashed by fried food and a Southern niceness potion. It is good to hear about our business and all of the new treasures in our scandal vault. It is good, and I want to be a part of it. The life I built in California is rolling along without me. Here I thought it revolved around me, and now I'm just an afterthought. Sure, I'm sneaking an occasional conference call, but Amos keeps me at bay, for my own well-being.

As I watch him flit and sparkle and entertain in all his Amos glory, I am surprised that I feel slightly disconnected from my old planet. Not from him, but from that life. I listen intently and with excitement, but as a reader of our webpages and not as the creator or insider. I've told him that I will be back, that this move is temporary. But he has moved on without me.

Life in LA keeps going, and it's been only four weeks. Daily Garbage keeps transmitting and Trashville keeps succeeding without me. It doesn't make me sad, it just makes me feel . . . in between. A purgatory state of being. But I will be back! I will be back!

My friend still loves me, and I him, but he doesn't need me the way I thought he did.

We eat cake and open presents, and then Burton and I drive Amos to the airport. He has come for exactly four hours. He has to be in New York for Tiffani-Amber Thiessen's birthday bash. It's rotten having to split your baby shower with a famous person's birthday.

That night in bed Burton asks me, "It was weird, wasn't it?"

"What?" I look at him staring at the ceiling and think, *What could be weirder than lying here with you after you impregnated me while I was in a wasted stupor? Life as I knew it doesn't exist!*

"Amos. The shower. The whole thing. I know you're not big on surprise parties."

"Or holidays in general," I say, trying not to sound completely ungrateful. "I like to point the lens at other people, not myself. It's just how I am." *Be careful, that's a little too much insider information to share.* But I keep going so he can at least not make the same mistake again. God forbid he actually tries to love me. I might try to eat him alive. (Wow, my hormones are morphing me back into the big green monster!)

"But you deserve it, you know?" He turns and looks at me with compassion in his warm brown eyes. "You deserve to be happy."

I've told him so little about my past. He lives presently and honestly. He has never asked about my dark secrets. I'm grateful: the less I tell him, the less I have to be dishonest.

"You know, Alice, your life is like a car." He smiles at me.

"A Mercedes," I say hopefully, trying to hide my discomfort.

"And you got me sitting next to you for the ride." He ignores my sass. "We're looking out that big front window together and it is filled with all kinds of good, exciting stuff—if you'll let it be."

"Very profound." Again with the humor.

"There's a reason the rearview mirror is so small."

"Why's that?"

"'Cause what's in the past is already gone by." His sweet Southern charm oozes out and onto the welcome mat of my memory house. And, with the slightest pressure, the door cracks open, fresh air fills the room, and I let him in for just one peek.

"My mother," I start, and just as abruptly stop. Burton's soft gaze encourages me to continue. "Before she died, she taught me a quote. I memorized it. She had a funny way of teaching me fairy tales with happy endings, but this quote was by a philosopher named Hugo Grotius." The memory makes me smile. "She used to tell me I could tell my prince from the frogs by his character. His integrity. His morality."

Burton is still watching me intently. He props himself on his elbow, his brows raised.

"Grotius said, 'A man cannot govern a nation if he cannot govern a city; he cannot govern a city if he cannot govern a family; he cannot govern a family unless he can govern himself.'" I pause, taking a deep breath, then let it out with relief. "She would have liked you."

"I did have sex with you on the first night." He grins. "I don't know how well I was governing myself."

"Everyone makes mistakes." I wink. "My mom was more interested in character."

He leans into me and kisses me, then says with all seriousness, "Alice, you were never, and are certainly not now, a mistake."

Our lips press together with more than the usual passion, which makes my feet tingle. Sometimes I wish I could be more open, but I can't. I'm just not wired that way. I don't want to share my past, my issues, my secrets—the truth. I wish my truth wasn't what it is. So I plan to keep it safely tucked in my own personal vault of scandal and dirt and shame.

Leaning back down onto his elbow, he says, "Thank you."

I nuzzle into the nook of his arm and shoulder, close my eyes, and just try to be present. Before I know it, I have fallen asleep.

I look down at my throbbing feet tucked under the Bethel pew in front of me. They are swollen like big white sausages bound by Jimmy Choo leather. The blue veins on the top are poking out of my skin. It's not a pretty picture.

A middle-aged, suited man with short red hair, rosy cheeks, and freckles makes his way onto the stage. As the ushers help the remaining stragglers find a seat, I anxiously scan the back wall of the church. Where is Tim? Where is my neighbor friend? I clench my fists and grit my teeth. Did Tim get called away on some God emergency? Did this Opie Taylor, a second-string stand-in, get called up to the big show from triple-A Jesus ball camp? It's a bait-and-switch after months of luring me here. I'm starting to regret my decision to accept Tim's invitation as Red makes his way to the stage.

First the Kool-Aid and now Opie. I feel an urge to whistle the theme from *The Andy Griffith Show*. Oh, if only I had a fishing pole to complete the image of me joyfully skipping toward the exit sign. I am about to make my move when a young girl with glowing, milk-chocolate-kissed skin and long, soft chestnut curls slips in alongside me in the pew. The seven-year-old-ish girl, accompanied by her mother, looks like a junior version of Halle Berry. She is striking, and I am caught off guard by her young beauty. I stare at her as I scoot over without a word of protest.

So much for my big escape.

"Goooood morning! How great is our worship team?" The fill-in pastor bellows his greeting over the church's sophisticated sound system.

What's a worship team? Is that the singers? It must be the singers. So the singing is *worshipping*? I would have thought worshipping was a bunch of folks on their knees bending forward and then flying back up, or virgins getting tossed into volcanoes.

In response, the parishioners hoot and holler. He continues, "Who's happy to be here this morning?"

The congregation responds with more clapping.

"Who's happy to be filled with the Holy Spirit?"

He's filled with something, that's for sure. Tanqueray? Don Julio?

These people are loud. They are happy and they are noisy—two things I am not accustomed to experiencing while sitting in a pew. I can still hear my dad telling me, "Sit still! Be quiet."

"Who knows their life has been changed by the love of Jesus?" he asks.

There's more hooting and hollering.

"Give Him a hand. I'm Pastor Bruce, good morning. I'm glad

you've had a chance to partake in Communion this Sunday, and I'm happy to see you on this wonderful Mother's Day."

The music slows, and now it's just the solemn melody of the keyboards. I suddenly feel as if I have landed the starring role in a very, very sad movie.

My heart sinks: it is Mother's Day.

How did I not know that? Then again, why would I know it after all these years of being motherless?

"Let us pray."

Everyone bows his or her head but I sit, first staring blankly ahead, frozen, before melting when I look at the little girl next to me. Her eyes are full of innocence, warmth, and confidence. She meets my gaze as she takes my hand in hers before looking back at Pastor Bruce. He continues with the morning prayer.

"Lord Jesus, we're so happy to be here with You today. This morning we pray for all the women of the world, Lord, and for their families. We pray for our mothers."

She catches me staring at her and smiles. I give her nothing but lostness, which makes her squeeze my hand tighter.

The prayer, combined with the warmth of the young girl's hand, comforts me. I just concentrate on her hand in mine until a soothing, safe feeling begins to envelop me like the warm water of a gentle bath. Looking down at our hands wrapped together, I am taken back to a time when life was not confusing, scary, or isolating.

Summer 1980: I can see my mother tossing her head back, laughing at me as I try to relax in the tub. She's sitting cross-legged on the floor in her sundress next to the bath with a glass of wine. I put my elbows on the side of the tub and rest my head in my hands and close my eyes. She traces letters on my face with her soft pointer finger. It makes me smile. Her tracing letters on my face was a game we played when I wore diapers. Her finger gliding over my skin now makes me feel happy inside remembering how creative she has always been and how she taught me to use my imagination even as a toddler.

"*I.*" I open one eye to look at her, letting her treat me like a small child.

"Yes, you peeker! The letter is *I*." She bonks my head. Next, writing with big swooping cursive letters, she tickles my eyelids.

"Love," I guess with a snicker. "That's so easy. 'I love you.' You've always written the same things."

She pours some water over my head from a big plastic cup. I sink under the water's surface. I look up at her from under the water and can see through the blurring surface that she's looking back at me.

We've been talking in the bath since I can remember. There was a time when we both fit in this tub. Not anymore. Now one of us is forced out while the other gets the soak. Either way, it is one of our times together. It's a special time when I don't have to share her with other kids from school, her friends, or my father.

"But I do. And you need to know it. I love you. I love you. I love you," she says, handing me a towel. "Now, off to bed."

This is the very last night before I know she is really sick. I remember it now, vividly.

Pastor Opie's voice snaps me out of the recollection of my mother. I try to shake it off. The resurrection of these long-buried flashes is making me feel uneasy.

"We pray for the single fathers who are raising children alone, and we pray for unborn children in the womb. We ask that You let

Your love be on them, Your peace be with them, and that their hearts know You."

I close my eyes tight and shudder, trying to shake off my mother, but my memories are washing over me. It's a tsunami of emotion and I am unable to swim against it. It swallows me whole.

I am transported back to when Corey Hart's single "Sunglasses at Night" blared out of the stereo of my mom's 1976 black-and-white Challenger.

Early fall 1980: As we pull into our driveway, my mom jams the center gearshift into park. "Let's go, we got things to learn." She reaches back and heaves the brown paper bag of medicine and drugstore paraphernalia out of the backseat with determination.

Her headscarf gets caught on the seat belt as she gets out of the car. The scarf slides away to reveal a mostly bald head with patches of blond fuzz. There are still a few long golden strands, but she loses a few more every day. Gone are her Breck-infused golden locks that blew in the wind at Woodstock. Gone are her eyebrows. Gone are most of her lashes.

I know her students snicker at her baldness, but I see only her beauty. Her eyes now seem bigger and bluer; they practically leap out of her pale-yellow skin. Her face is thinner and more sunken than ever, but her spirit for teaching and loving is still big and bold.

She is determined to live. She will beat the odds and survive the various stages of her treatments. I heard her say, *"What the heck do the doctors know?"* one night as I stood hiding in the hallway. My dad wept like a child at our dining-room table. It made me feel small and afraid. I sank to my knees just watching from the darkness of the hallway as he buried his head in her belly and she stood stroking his hair. Funny, she's always the brave one.

Yesterday's lesson was about how to handle a woman's time of the month. My period has not yet started, but she is preparing me for a life without her.

"Okay! Let's figure this thing out." She smiles as she pulls some lipstick, lip liner, mascara, and foundation from her brown paper bag. Today's lesson is on how to properly apply mascara and lipstick. I learn by mimicking whatever she does. We stand side by side, just inches apart, leaning toward the mirror. She carefully traces her lips with red liner; I do the same with pink. "The trick is to *barely* touch the liner just slightly around your lips," she advises as she leans back to admire her handiwork.

As I follow her every instruction, I notice her eyes light up. "You don't want to look cheap. It should look natural but enhanced." She leans down and kisses my face. "Your God-given beauty." She squeezes me tight. "*Oh!* You're so pretty. I did such a terrific job making you."

We both laugh. "What about Daddy?" I ask, bumping my hip into hers.

"Oh, I suppose he had a little something to do with it too." She bumps me back.

But she's right. I do look like the thirteen-year-old version of her.

"What's more important than being pretty?" she asks with seriousness in her voice. She has asked me this question since I was five.

"Being nice," I answer, rolling my eyes. I heard her the first thousand times she told me.

"You mock me," she says slyly, "but girls get meaner as they get older. You're just at the tip of the teenage mean-queen iceberg. You gotta keep your soul pure and protected. Always kill 'em with kindness. Even when they are total jerks. Don't let someone else's ugliness make you ugly." She wipes a little of the liner off my face. "Remember who you are. You're smart. Like your mother." She giggles.

"Remember . . ." her voice trails off into a cough. The coughing starts dry and small at first. But something about it makes me stop lining my lip. Then it increases and causes her petite frame to heave up and down, her back arching like a cat. I watch her in the mirror as she tries to reassure me with her face that she's all right, but I know she's not.

Her coughing grows so deep that she braces herself against the countertop and in an instant I think she's going to throw up. She covers her mouth and blood spills into her hands and spatters onto her white, ruffled blouse from school.

Then I go from trainee to trained.

As I have been taught to do, I wet a towel and quickly bring it to her. I wrap my arm around her waist as she leans on my shoulder. I'm suddenly aware of how bony she has become.

I help her down the hallway to her bedroom and place her on her bed. All of a sudden she looks very tired. Very fragile. Very sad.

"Baby, I'm fine." She dismisses my concern with a casual wave of her hand. She is trying to shield me from the inevitable.

I begin to unbutton her blouse. "Let me get this to soak or it will stain." It takes all I have to concentrate on the task at hand and not start crying like a scared kid.

She sits up a little as I slip her blouse off. The little white camisole she is wearing underneath is also now spattered and soaked through with blood and mucus. I pull it over her head. "No big deal," I reassure her. "Bleach will get it out. Bleach . . . right?"

She smiles and nods.

You'd think I'd be alarmed at the deep-purple caterpillar scars that crawl across her chest where her breasts used to be, but honestly her missing nipples are what seem most strange. *Even boys have nipples,* I think. I get her favorite nightgown out of the top drawer of her dresser and help her pull it on.

"You're too young." She faintly smiles at me.

"Too young for what?"

"Just too young."

I'm too young to know what words like *breast cancer, ductal carcinoma, lymph nodes,* and *stage four* mean. I'm too young to know that *metastatic* means the sickness has moved to other parts of your body. But I know what she means, so clearly I'm not too young.

I'm thirteen and I know how to give myself a breast exam although my breasts are little more than swollen acorns. More than anything I know what it means to try to *keep someone comfortable.* It means there's nothing else to do.

"Miracles do happen," she tells me that night when I lie next to her, listening to her breathe, soft little sighs going in and out. "Miracles happen every day." We wrap our arms tight, face-to-face, chest-to-chest, as if we could melt into one another. Our unbreakable embrace.

My body is shaking all over and I realize that I'm back in church. I'm safely in the pew still holding that little girl's hand.

Pastor Opie finishes, "We ask, if it be Your will, that You touch each person here who only by Your hands will have their needs met."

My needs met? Seriously?

I'm very aware that I'm sitting in this house made for God-people, not Alice-people. Here's a need I want met: I want the ghosts of my past to stop being so present here. What is it about this place that I am haunted by these painful memories? I pushed them down, buried them so long ago. Why are they suddenly buoyant here? What does it all mean?

The baby kicks and I feel woozy with my mother's weight once again on me. I feel her sickness, which is dark and frightening. Damn it! Even when she was sick, I somehow managed never to feel it. Why now?

Long ago I shoveled my denial and faux strength into piles, building a fortress, a shield to protect me from any of her pain. I was strong. But today I feel something else. For the first time, I remember a specific feeling. It's what I felt the day she was coughing in the bathroom.

Afraid. Thirteen-year-old afraid. A tear escapes my eye at the thought. I wipe it away wishing I could, again, wipe the fear away.

I was afraid then. Even worse, I'm still afraid now.

I want so much to get out of this place, but the warmth of this child's hand in mine and the curiosity of *Why these memories now?* keeps me leashed to my pew. I wish I knew where Tim was. I wish I knew where the entire Jackson family was. I'm craving their comfort and warmth. I close my eyes again and think about them. I think about being safely hidden in their family, away from the snares of my own.

Earlier this year, as the winter season finally gives way to spring: I find myself hiking the trails at Percy Warner Park with Tim and LeChelle. I tuck myself behind Tim on the way down the mountain like Jimmie Johnson drafting on Jeff Gordon's bumper at Talladega. I want to be able to grab hold of his waist pack and have him steady me if I stumble, especially on the last steep slope before the carved-stone, pre–Civil War era staircase where we started.

When the winter days are warm, the park has become one of my favorite escapes in Nashville. With its hiking, biking, and horseback-riding trails, you can easily get lost in the solitude. I watched a snake three days ago as it tried to eat a frog—whole. As disgusting as it sounds, it was fascinating. I finally had to get a stick and bat the snake away. I felt sorry for that big, slow toad trapped and wrapped up in that striped green slithering menace.

There's something about getting lost in the trees of the park, on the paths of silence, something here that makes me feel found. The park is heavily wooded so the trails stay nice and shady and cool. It is a peaceful place.

On this particular Saturday, LeChelle is following me as I drift behind Tim. We are all wearing shorts and sweatshirts to keep us cool and warm at the same time. My sneakers get caught on a protruding tree root. I can't see anything on the ground in front of me because of the enormity of my lower half, and I still have three months of pregnancy to go, but at this moment I am certain I am about to meet my end on this dusty, narrow path face-first.

Without missing a beat, LeChelle grabs my arm and catches me before I hit the rocky ground.

It is a perfect metaphor for our relationship: me trying half-heartedly to follow the hidden lessons Tim gives, almost falling on my bonbons, and LeChelle always there to scoop me up before I soul-plant—heart-first.

At the mouth of the trails we hit the rock stairs, which open onto a wide grassy field, just as a big golden retriever, beside its owner, a short-shorts-wearing, ponytailed jogger with absolutely perfectly toned legs, bounds by me, taking with her any sense of accomplishment I had felt.

"You okay?" Tim asks with real concern.

"We went like a hundred yards," I joke. "I think I'll make it."

"One point three miles. A good afternoon vein pusher."

"If you're ninety." I shake my head in disgust at my condition.

LeChelle makes her way to the grassy clearing where on any

given afternoon you'll see families picnicking on blankets, couples smooching on benches, kids playing badminton, or a lone dude tossing his Frisbee to an insane Jack Russell terrier that leaps six feet in the air to catch it. It's picturesque.

To my surprise, I miss Burton—well, a little.

It would be nice to not always be the third wheel on Tim and LeChelle's faith tricycle. It would be nice to actually be a couple at more than the occasional dinner or Saturday lunch. Burton is always working. But perhaps that is what has made this transition, as weird as it seems, slightly bearable. I'm a thirty-eight-year-old woman who has lived on my own terms for as long as I can remember. To avalanche into being together all the time, having someone in my space, or being in his space all the time, and having to make small talk with a nine-to-fiver might have thrown me off the cliff. As bizarre as it seems, easing into our pretend family has been relatively smooth, if you don't count the unplanned pregnancy.

This week he is on the road teaching another clinic. I sure hope he has learned his lesson about hooking up with ladies on the road, as I don't need anyone else moving in, at least until I'm gone. That just leaves me here, sober, sweaty, and mooching off the Jacksons' companionship.

LeChelle sits down in the soft, green grass, and I slide down next to her, panting like a hot basset hound.

Tim kisses the top of her head. "You want some water, baby?" He hands her the bottle as I drink from my CamelBak. He sits to my right.

"We look like an Oreo cookie," I say nonchalantly, looking at our legs all outstretched.

"You're more pink than white." LeChelle cracks herself up.

She's right. My fleshy thighs and calves are blotchy from the heat.

"Have you guys always done this?" I ask.

"Done what?" Tim questions.

"Taken in strays."

"Baby girl, you ain't no stray. You're our neighbor. You got a home."

LeChelle chokes on her water. "He's been taking people in for twenty-five years."

He gets his serious but funny face on like he's about to tell a tale. "Oh yeah, she's right. I do like to bring people home, don't I, baby?"

"Yes, baby, you do."

"It started when I was playin'—"

LeChelle interrupts with a laugh. "Oh, you just wait till you hear this," she says with a little umm-hmm attitude. "He brings home some fan of the Steelers that came into town to watch an open practice during preseason."

"You mean to your house?"

"Yes!" LeChelle's eyes get wide. "To our house! I was pregnant with Ava and had my other baby girl in diapers, and here's Tim invitin' some man we don't know into our house."

"He had nowhere to *stay*," says Tim.

"He wasn't homeless," LeChelle counters.

"Hilton. Best Western," I add under my breath.

"Riiiiiight?" LeChelle nods.

Tim takes advantage of our side conversation to continue the story. "I was all fired up about Jesus. That was my second year back since the neck accident. I wanted to tell everybody about Jesus. He had healed me!"

"This brotha coulda been Jeffrey Dahmer and he still woulda invited him," explains LeChelle.

"So what happened?"

"He was okay. I mean, we had a nice dinner, and he spent

the night. I talked to him about the Lord and gave him my testimony."

"What's a testimony?" I ask.

"My story of how I came to know the Lord."

"Oh, the Big Momma story," I answer, kind of pleased knowing I've also been given the testimony.

"Girl, well, Tim leaves for practice after this man spends the night at our house. First night was fine. I mean, I locked me, Tim, and the babies in our room the night before, but he seemed okay. White guy, nice enough. And, well, he comes downstairs for breakfast and it's just him and me, and the babies are still sleepin'. Tim's at practice."

"I don't know what I was thinkin', leavin' him there," Tim recollects.

"And so I take out my Bible and I start talking to him about Jesus." LeChelle pretends she's thumbing through her Bible. "And I'm talking about Jesus and the brotha keeps nodding like he understands. But somethin' ain't right."

Tim jumps in, "I was just being a good Christian."

"Not smart," I mutter.

"And the guy says, 'I know.'" LeChelle deadpans. "I say, 'You know what?' And the guy says, 'I know Jesus.' And I say, 'That's good.' Then he says"—LeChelle turns and looks at me straight-faced—"brother said, 'I know, for I am Him.'" Her voice tightens. "And I say, 'Whatcha mean, you are Him?' And then he says: 'I am Jesus.'"

"Shut up!" I laugh.

Tim shakes his head, embarrassed, "It's true."

LeChelle continues, "I'm like, 'Yes, Jesus lives in all of us.' Tryin' to help him out. Tryin' to make it all okay. I mean, we do have the Holy Spirit in us. But then he went on and said it: 'No, I'm Jesus. I am the Messiah.'"

"He's crazy?" My brows go up.

"Oh, yeah," Tim says.

LeChelle keeps going. "So I slowly get up and I go into the other room and I call Tim at the field and say, 'Get home! Your new friend thinks he's Jesus. *Jesus!*'"

"She did," he confirms.

"Then I went back downstairs and said, 'You got to go!'" She recounts how she lost her temper.

"And he went." Tim shrugs.

"Twenty-five years." She places her arm around me. "Twenty-five years with the strays."

I put my head on her shoulder and don't feel so crazy. This is why I like them. This is why I think their God loves them. They are good and funny and unconditionally caring. But I am not. I have no idea what unconditional love is anymore. I get why God loves them, but I don't think God could ever love me that way. He knows all of the secrets that lie in the shadowy places of my heart. He knows the truth about me.

6

The Dunk Tank

They are raising the curtain high above the stage at Bethel. What could possibly be next? I gently settle my aching hips into the wooden pew and try to find a position that relieves the pressure on my swollen lower back. I have finally released the precious little girl's hand. But I like that she's there, she and her mom on this Mother's Day.

I make a mental note to remember to bring popcorn and a lumbar pillow next week: a snack for the show and a cushion for my pain. I find a position that I can tolerate for the next five minutes before looking up again. When I do, I gasp.

No! They couldn't have possibly.

But they did. They have constructed a ten-by-four-foot-wide, glass-encased dunk tank on what might have been a balcony at one time high above the stage. My pupils dart from left to right. I don't see it. I'm confused. Where's the red bull's-eye target? And at what point are they going to hand everyone in the crowd a softball to toss? It's a dunk tank!

And bravo! My neighbor, Pastor Tim, who has been AWOL, is also high above the stage. He sure knows how to make an entrance. He is wearing a long white smock and is submerged to his waist in the tank. The glass magnifies his dark feet and they look enormous even from the back row. He is using a wireless microphone. It's tucked behind his ear but I am certain it will slip out, fall into the water, and electrocute him. I hold my breath.

"Good morning, all God's people!" he speaks in a voice deep, raspy, and with a hint of ethnic street flavor.

He makes me smile impulsively.

"This morning we are excited and honored to watch this man, Jason Dodson, be born again," he says.

As if birth the first time around isn't hard enough.

He pauses to acknowledge the parishioner, standing in jeans and a T-shirt next to him high above the stage. On dry land. For now.

"Acts 2:38 says, 'Repent, and be baptized every one of you in the name of Jesus Christ for the forgiveness of your sins; and you shall receive the gift of the Holy Spirit.' With this baptism and faith, all sins of the past are forgiven."

Wait—what? Is my pregnant state affecting my hearing now, too? They get a do-over? How is that possible? A dunk-tank do-over? And if they get a do-over, can *anyone*? What about murderers? Rapists? Child Molesters? Politicians? Agents? Paparazzi?

Tabloid editors?

"And love, joy, peace, patience, kindness, goodness, faithfulness, gentleness, and self-control"—Tim smiles—"will be theirs with the Holy Spirit as their guide."

It's that easy? I'm doubtful.

I watch the man walk down the stairs into the water. He says something to Tim. I lean forward and strain, but I can't make it out. My ears must be swollen, too.

Oh! I hate secrets!

But then I hear Tim say to his fellow swimmer, Mr. Dodson, "Is Jesus Christ the Lord and Savior of your life?"

He replies, "Yes, He is."

"Have you committed to following Him the rest of your life, no turning back?"

"Yes. I have."

Tim finishes, "Upon the confession of your faith, I now baptize you in the name of the Father, and of the Son, and of the Holy Spirit, in Jesus' name."

I watch as the man falls back into the safety of Tim's strong arms and the former defensive lineman submerges him in the water.

To my surprise, the water remains crystal clear. Where's all his internal dirt? I'm wondering when all the spiritual blockages are going to come streaming out of his body, mucking up the water. I guess I expected it to be like an energy-balancing system where you soak your feet in a tub of water with this weird machine and your biochemical energy pathways with blockages are released into the water. This gross black, blue, yellow, and green goop comes out of the pores in your feet. It's nasty.

Let me set the record straight: there isn't enough water in the Cumberland River to wash me clean.

Seeing all that clear liquid takes me back to our apartment complex in Tucson. We were in the lower unit of a three-story building, the last in a line of six with a fantastic view of the Dumpsters.

January 1982: The first time I notice how much my father drinks and realize that he has become an alcoholic.

He is a self-medicator. So I come by it naturally. I've been self-medicating for decades.

It is a Friday morning. Our television replays grainy footage of the assassination of the president of Egypt, Anwar Sadat. He was killed three months ago. The same footage over and over for months of their president riding in the back of an open-topped Cadillac wearing his fancy military uniform dripping with medals, and then him sitting in bleachers at a military parade as his troops pass by him.

It is astounding to see the naivete of this president when a uniformed soldier jumps out of his truck from the parade of vehicles and President Sadat salutes him, only to be pelted by grenades and bullets. It makes me sad that no one does anything until it is too late.

My mother would have been appalled. He was a man who once ruled Egypt with an iron fist, but then he had released the hatred from his heart. My mother always believed people could change for the better, and President Sadat ultimately accepted a peace treaty in the Middle East and won the Nobel Peace Prize—only to be gunned down by fundamentalists. I feel a kinship with the children of the dead man.

My mom loved history, that it showed the desire of men and women to make a difference. She had taught me about leaders like John F. Kennedy and his brother Robert, and their untimely deaths. She communicated her admiration for women who bravely paved new paths for other women to follow. I remember well her telling me the stories of Florence Nightingale, Margaret Chase Smith, and Harriet Tubman. I vicariously felt her horror and regret when she told me about the assassination of a man who she said preached nothing but peace, equality, and justice: Dr. Martin Luther King Jr. was her hero.

That October day, it is another murder of another peace activist, but more than that, it is a reminder that my mom's private lessons are over. It is the realization that I have lost my mother's passionate speeches on character and peace and how history repeats itself and how we should not sit on the sidelines while others are doing what is right and making their mark. We should be the mark makers. The risk takers. Stand up to oppression. Hold lawmakers accountable. Love the unlovable. Change laws, views, and opinions, and be a patriot. Be *that* American.

Some good that did the peacemakers of history, I think.

We moved into this shoddy one-bedroom apartment almost a year after we buried my mother. I don't remember much from age fourteen to fifteen, except that I revolted. I had command of the tiny bedroom and my father slept on the pullout sofa. What began as a sweet acknowledgment of my girlie teenage need for privacy swiftly turned permanent in more ways than one. Dad stayed on the pullout from the start of my freshman year through the end of my senior year of high school. Day and night. He was either sleeping or was passed out. It was hard to tell the difference.

We were two variables. The constant that had once connected us was out of the equation. Now we had no connection at all.

I often want to talk about the Occurrence after her death, but I become muffled by my fear that he will somehow, in some way, convince me that it never happened. That he will send me away again to a priest or Catholic summer camp, or make me talk to professionals who will try to convince me I have some type of traumatic stress disorder.

I walk out of our apartment, bitter with the death of both of them. He is as dead as she is to me. I heave the Hefty garbage bag I am carrying over my shoulder and it rips at the ties. Perfect! Just great.

Four empty one-gallon Smirnoff Vodka bottles crash onto the cement and roll next to the Dumpster. I take the trash out twice a week to protect us both from the reality of Dad's addiction. I am irritated that the bag hasn't done its job. I knew what was inside; I don't need to be slapped in the face with it.

Call it mourning. Call it teen angst. Call it rebellion, but whatever it is, I am pretty much in a constant state of pissed-off-ness. My grief turns to fury. My belief in something bigger and beyond this life has been bagged like those vodka bottles and thrown into the symbolic trash bin in my heart.

AC/DC's "Rock and Roll Ain't Noise Pollution" cranks off my turntable in my bedroom. My hair is dyed black and I am wearing goth-style makeup. I am the inspiration for Winona Ryder's character in *Beetlejuice*. I have morphed from my former sweet, earnest, believing, and open self into a methodical, silent bundle of rage. For two years, I anchor my loneliness to an equally rebellious group of friends. They provide an answer to my immense loneliness. We have a faux friendship fueled by LSD and 'shrooms and nickel bags of Mary Jane.

I wear this new, all-encompassing ache poorly. It didn't exist when my mother could still pepper my face with her Oil of Olay–infused kisses. There would be no more indulgences of her smell or the sound of her laughter. I have to shake off all the memories of her beauty and her strength. Shake off the possibility of a happy ending. There are no happy endings. People get gunned down, run over, poisoned, and dragged behind life's stain-laden train—and that's just how it is. You're either the bug or the windshield. So just grow up, and stop daydreaming about what was, because all there is, is now. It is what it is. This self-defeating principle is my mantra.

My dad's boss at the insurance agency gave him time off after Dad accidentally wrapped his Buick around a palm tree. He's never gone back to work. He has morphed, too. The demands of being a stay-at-home drunk soothe his pain, I suppose.

He died with her that day.

Around the age of fifteen, I realize that God doesn't care. He's way too busy for me. Why had I ever been so arrogant to think that my prayer to spare my mother's life, over and over—my one simple prayer for her existence—would be answered? I realize God has left me rudderless on a ship with a drunken captain. I walk a shaky plank of insecurity every day. Living with my dad and without her brings a newfound darkness upon my life. It follows me everywhere, a wild combination of madness and sadness. I thrust it upon anyone who tries to get close.

The grinding of my teeth snaps me back to real time in church. Tim is still teaching his guppies the spiritual breaststroke in the pool of enchanted fresh starts. His eyes are squarely focused on his last soul in need of cleansing.

LeChelle is in the front pew of the church. As the first lady in this house of worship, she's totally in the VIP section for the God people. Her head tilted upward, she is engrossed with pleasure watching her other half put on a heck of a Sunday Waterworld show.

I'm hoping she's got something good planned for brunch, as lately she's been making me do more walking and talking than sitting and grubbing.

Watching her gaze upon Tim up in that soul-washing bathtub, I get a sense of her love for him. A love I knew only once. An unconditional love I felt for my mom.

Shake it off, I command myself. *You gotta shake it off.*

LeChelle has the same love my mom did, a love my mom gave to me and to my father. A love she felt for the strays, too. A love I'm reminded of today in this place even as I try my hardest to forget. My mind keeps drifting back to her.

My mother knew what would become of my father after her

death. In her last weeks, I believe she was more worried about him than me.

A cold beginning of 1981: "You're like me," she says in her breathy voice as we lie in bed. The Arizona sun is trying to peek through the pulled curtains in her bedroom. "You're a fighter, a survivor."

But she doesn't survive.

He, my father, is weak and she knows it. How can I blame him for falling completely apart without her? She didn't have to say it. Even then, a part of me knew that all the good in life originated with her. She was our connection, our light and our glue.

In her final weeks she finishes all she can teach me. How to make him coffee, do the laundry, and make their bed just how he likes it. She's taught me how to balance my own checkbook and told me to deposit all of my paychecks from my job bagging groceries at Safeway directly into my own account, to keep my money separate from his and be responsible for it.

I heave her seventy-five-pound body into the tub to help her bathe, and she says, "I love you."

I rebut, "I love you more."

And she whispers, "Not possible." She pauses for a moment before speaking again. "I'll miss you the most," she says, holding back tears. "I am sad, but not for the reasons you think. I'm not afraid. I'm going home to see my mom and dad, to be with God. But I am sad because I'm going to miss seeing you grow. I'm going to miss you every minute until we are together again."

Her words dredge a gorge of deep sorrow in my body.

"I promise to watch over you from heaven," she says, smiling. "I'll send the angels to kiss you good-night in your dreams and look out for you during the day. I'll have them report back to me, so you better be a good girl," she warns.

But later, in the darkness of her bed, I feel her real sadness when she sobs. It makes my teenage eyes well up. She hears me sniffle and then she rolls over to face me. I cling to her and she to me so tightly that I think one of us will break.

I am the one, not him, who changes her nightgown and bed-pan. I am the one, not him, who soothes her to sleep by putting ice cubes on her lips after I have coated them with Vaseline. I am the one, not him, who calls the hospice doctor for more pain medication. I am the one, not him, who sprinkles her face with tears and kisses when she is slipping from this world. I am the one who is here when she takes her last breath.

In her death, my mother and I become one. I lay there birthing her into the next realm. There is no fight left in her. She just slips out of my life and into another dimension that people call heaven.

I don't move for three hours. I just lie there, hugging her limp body. Hugging and pulling her closer, knowing she will never, ever pull me back.

It is only me and her. I feel so special to be the one with her.

I finally let go when my arms go numb. When I go numb.

Later, I stay until all of the dirt covers her coffin. My dad has gone to sit in the limousine after all of her friends from school, and my classmates with their pity-filled faces, have gone. I sit here frozen in a blue plastic chair holding an 8×10 framed picture of her on the beach at Coronado Island as two men load her white and pink carnation–draped coffin into the ground at East Lawn Cemetery. Now it is just me, and me alone.

I close my eyes and trace I-L-O-V-E-U on her face in the picture and smile.

She had handled every detail of her death, including getting rid of all of her clothes and writing her own obituary. She knew my dad couldn't do it and she knew I would if I had to. She tried to shelter me even in the end.

But she ran out of time for the stuff I need to know now. It wasn't fair then and it isn't fair today. You never know how much you need and miss them until their absence becomes your free-falling, heartbreaking never-ending abyss.

I was only a baby! I want to scream. *I was only a baby.*

Now I long for the water in Tim's tank of tricks to magically wash all of that pain away. I wish it were capable of healing the still open and tender wounds of a brokenhearted fourteen-year-old who grew into a livid adult.

How I wish it were that easy to just submerge in the safety of secure arms and lie in the stillness of deep, healing water. Maybe then the joy and happiness and peace would return. If only it were that easy for people like me.

As far as I know, people like me don't get do-overs. People like me push past the pain. They run into thick layers of mental pain management. Medicated, self-destructive, sometimes euphoric, blissful pain management. We run into the empty, never-satisfying arms of others and we most certainly do not end up in the arms of Jesus.

Maybe that's what Tim's tank is all about: God-medicated people.

I hope it works . . . for them.

7

Money, Money, Money

Part I

The dunk tank is draining and Pastor Bruce, aka Pastor Opie, is back onstage with a Bible open in hand. He exhales audibly and says, "The Bible teaches us to give."

Oh, here we go. I knew there had to be a door charge. They just wait until you're sitting and can't get up.

"Why give? Why not save? America has it rough right now. In fact, the world has it tough right now. Tsunamis, floods, droughts, earthquakes," he continues. "You might have it tough. Foreclosures? Up. Unemployment? Up. Recession. Repression. It's all up. Everything says it is time to save, not to give."

"Amen to that," I grumble.

In an obvious contradiction to the sermon, at one end of every pew, burgundy velvet bags are being dangled in front of everyone's purse strings. It wouldn't be a church if the coffers weren't out, now, would it?

Fall 1984, senior year: I am back at St. Matthew's. I smell stale vodka every time my dad exhales. It bleeds out his pores and mixes with the hour-old cigarette smoke. The scent of him makes me loathe the hypocrite that he is—sitting here pretending to be holy. I'm still mad that he made me wear a stupid flower-covered dress when his shirt is not ironed and I'm pretty sure he pulled it from the hamper.

There's not much I can do other than wallow in my disgust. We're locked together in a hard oak pew in the third-to-last row. I prop my unlaced Dr. Martens boots on the velvet kneeler with more than a hint of unruly satisfaction.

My dad is watching as the gold-tone collection platter is being passed my way. He digs his elbow into my ribs, an indication that I should get my dollar ready.

The gray-haired priest, the same dude who shipped me off to Catholic summer camp after he was told about the Occurrence, is now saying if we love God then we must love His people. And we must show our love for His people by giving to those who are oppressed and poor. The children and the widows. Wait . . .

"Dad, you're a widow, right? Am I a widow?" I whisper urgently in his ear.

"Shhh." He squeezes my leg.

The priest is well-intentioned. "We don't buy our way into heaven by doing good deeds," he says. "It is by God's grace alone. When we believe in Jesus Christ, when we love Him and follow His teachings to use our money not just for ourselves but for others, then we are good stewards."

"What's a steward? Like on a plane?" I mutter under my breath.

My dad's chest heaves up. He's frustrated that I'm not playing along. "Be quiet," he says under his breath with his lips still together like a ventriloquist's.

I am hearing the wrong things. The priest did say *steward*. I have questions—what's wrong with that, bud? I go to public school, but I still have questions. What's he expect? Have another shot of vodka, Pops.

"You must accept that your money is not yours alone and you must give with an open heart," says the priest.

Huh? I've been saving every dime I've made working at Safeway for over three years. I've got to escape and find happiness, and money is my means! These were my dying mother's instructions to me.

Well, not verbatim, but I got the gist.

"Second Corinthians 9:7 says, 'Each one must give as he has decided in his heart, not reluctantly or under compulsion, for God loves a cheerful giver.'"

I don't feel seventeen; I feel forty. I'm not cheerful and I'm not a giver. I cannot wait to be done with all of this force-fed religion. I cannot wait to be done with high school. I want so much to get out of Tucson. I want to leave the brown, barren, thorny existence that has become my life. I want out of our dirt-stained apartment and away from the Formica TV trays that serve as nightstands/footrests/dining-room tables. I want away from the sickening one-two aromatic punch of frozen-dinner Salisbury steak and spilled vodka and orange juice.

My mother was right about keeping my money separate from my father's. He has spent every penny he made working as a handyman in our apartment complex to pay off her medical bills. He has collected a little from his accident, but it went exclusively into filling our freezer with potpies, ice-cream sandwiches, and booze.

I want to get away from him. I want to leave him like my mother had before me. He has given up on life, and he is trying to take me down with him.

I look around the Catholic congregation for my boyfriend, Scott. I see him across the aisles toward the left front. He's with his fancy mother and father and two sisters. They are the perfect, unbroken family with a country-club membership.

Let them give. Me and my dad are all out of cash. And faith, but who's counting?

Scott's soft, dark, Jim Morrison hair curls just above his Polo shirt collar. He makes my legs tingle. I'm filled with sinful desire, and no religious teaching can suppress my teen hormones. Every night I sneak out of my bedroom window to see him, the love of my life. He fills up my darkness, if just temporarily.

Despite my dad's nearly always being passed out, when I sneak out to find my fulfillment with Scott, I take the added precaution of rolling the primer-spotted, dented Buick out of its parking space before turning the engine on. My parking place outside Scott's parents' house is equally premeditated. I have a short hike in the desert dodging prickly pear cacti and keeping an eye out for coyotes on my way to the six-thousand-square-foot house in Tucson Country Club.

"Stairway to Heaven" on the *Led Zeppelin IV* album has become our theme song. The greatest thing Scott has done for me has been to turn me on to good music like Petty, Joplin, and The Doors—as well as open my mind to magic mushrooms, purple-haired weed, and the paper-tablet LSD that dissolves on my tongue. All in all, I'm a pretty typical teenager.

The screen on the window of his room is simple enough to pop off. Jimmy Page's guitar solo from the record floats around the room. I stand in the darkness of his bedroom and silently take off all of my clothes and crawl into bed with him. Lying there sweaty after we teenagers engage in a somewhat gawky carnal experience, I can feel something again. I feel connected to the carbon world and sewed back together, if only by Silly String.

I'm pretty sure Jimmy Page and Robert Plant wrote *IV* for these exact moments.

I imagine that Scott and I are grown. That we are in our own house. That I am a rich, happy, and loved country-club wife and Scott is my strong, protective, faithful husband. In those tender hours before dawn, I lie awake next to him. The soundtrack alternates between quail calls and Scott's gentle snore. Unbeknownst to him, I picture exactly how I am going to reinvent myself once I am free from the hell that is my present reality with my father.

Unfortunately, Scott will probably be collateral damage. Shot and killed by Alice's emotional friendly fire. So sorry.

I've become bold enough to walk down the long hallway in the cover of darkness past his parents' master bedroom wearing nothing but my underwear and a Pink Floyd T-shirt.

"Don't do it," Scott whispers loudly, and watches as I walk out into the hallway.

Despite the alert perfection on display in the family pictures along the hallway, I know they are passed out in a benzodiazepine bliss. I examine the photographs on my way to raid their fridge. I am like a half-dressed grinch here to steal chocolate milk and Ding Dongs.

I come back with my hands full of munchies and crawl under the covers. "You're crazy," he says and then kisses me like it was a good thing.

It isn't until I get fully dressed, jump back out the window, and embark on my teenage walk of shame that the guilt and humiliation hit me. Driving back home, I feel dirty . . . sneaky . . . cheap. Not like a respected country-club wife at all.

I can see the truth of my future as a straight-A student who will waste her life striving to be the manager at Safeway. Scott will go off to some Ivy League school and I'll still be sitting on the Buick's ripped and weathered seats. I'll be knocked up at nineteen. I don't want this to be my destiny. Where is the angel that my mom was supposed to send to help me?

I have managed to do this night after night, this teenage angst/ love–fueled dance with the devil, without getting caught, and I'll be graduating at the top of my class.

I listen to "You Got Lucky" by Tom Petty & the Heartbreakers and take at least three bong hits every morning before algebra. Mr. Stetson, my first-period teacher, who looks like Ed Asner on *The Mary Tyler Moore Show*, has no idea I wake-and-bake. He thinks I'm just a brainy, introverted, goth girl whose mom died and who now has a case of the nervous giggles. All of the teachers who knew my mother feel this about me. Grown-ups are blind to what they don't want to imagine can be their own children.

The early-morning sun is already scorching. I can feel its heat bounce off the top of my desk as me and Scott's song replays in my head: "And she's buy-uy-ing a stay-air-way . . . to hea-uh-ven."

In my protective, hazy bubble, I anonymously and invisibly cruise the hallway, methodically avoiding the perky cheerleaders and serious student-council members bobbing up and down, getting ready for a pep rally in the auditorium. I was as invisible in high school as I am now in church. I hide in my bubble, hoping no one will pop it and try to engage me.

This year, two weeks after Valentine's Day: Burton and I are standing in the lobby of Escape Day Spa in Nashville. Tami, the owner, who has a young Stevie Nicks wardrobe–vibe thing going, greets us in the lobby. It is open and spacious with whitewashed woods and hints of Eastern traditions. The salon upstairs is airy with glazed-cement floors and paper lamps illuminating the small stones piled decoratively in the corners and along the walls. There are ten or twelve hair stations where various ladies are getting blown out, highlighted, or shampooed.

"Burton tells me you're from LA," Tami says nonchalantly.

I nod, snobbishly wondering exactly how much Burton has told her about me.

"Me, too," she says, surprising me. "Well, I grew up here, and then went to LA to do photography and met my husband. We did a lot of music stuff. Album covers, that kind of thing. We lived in Malibu."

"Really?"

"Yep. Till I got pregnant with my daughter, Daly. I gained like fifty pregnancy pounds and we moved back here so I could be around my family. Then we opened a spa. I work my butt off, but it's totally worth it."

"There wasn't anything like this here in Nashville." Burton waves his arm around, as if he's showing off the place.

"Like you come here," she banters back at him. "Your sister comes here. But you don't. Too busy for us, huh?" She ribs him a little.

"I'm here now."

"Yes, you are. Let's get you downstairs." She smiles and turns to me. "You want some cucumber water? A glass of wine or something?" She eyeballs my pregnant belly. "One glass will help you both relax."

Oh, how I love her. I don't know exactly why I love her, but I do.

We take the elevator down one floor. It opens onto about ten thousand square feet of pure heaven. The sound of gurgling water and meditation flutes makes me both lose control and connect to myself again.

As I cozy into a giant robe and lie down in the meditation room on an oversize brushed-suede-and-chenille sofa, my eyes gloss over the ceiling twinkle-lights. There are exotic touches everywhere, from the tall bamboo sticks to the praying hands and Buddha in the corner. I see a small wooden carving on a table that reads, RELAX, REFLECT, REVITALIZE, REJUVENATE.

Burton comes out in his robe, tugging it closed, a bit inelegantly. It forces a laugh out of me as he lies down on the sofa next to me.

"Not much of a spa guy?" I already know the answer. "Can't wait to have a hairy man rubbing your naked body."

"Oh, I got a woman," he shoots back.

"I bet you did."

"Tami told me you'd like it here. Being that you're a spa connoisseur." He smiles.

"More like a spa snob."

At that moment Nicole Kidman and Keith Urban walk silently by us in the dimly lit meditation room, past the cascading wall of water, and lie down on the sofas across from us.

Why don't I have a camera? This is perfect stuff for Trashville. Nashville Trashville . . . My brain starts getting creative.

"Stop. Just stop, now," Burton says in a stern whisper. "I can see your wheels turning and I can feel your pulse racing."

I pout for a second before relaxing. I know he's right.

Two massage therapists come into the room. "Alice? Burton?"

Burton gets up and offers a hand to help ease me off the chaise. "Darling," he says with a British accent.

"Oh, yes, darling." I sound like a drunk Elizabeth Hurley.

We go into the couples' massage room. It is more perfect than I could have dreamed. It has dark woods with more Eastern decor and symbols of peace and harmony. There are two levels divided by a giant soak tub with purple lights glowing at the bottom. The room is warm and the aromatherapy suds are cooling my senses.

"No tubbing for you," Burton says. "Well, maybe just your feet."

Like I want to be seen in the buff at all at this point in my pregnancy, let alone be submerged with my boyfriend.

After our ninety-minute heavenly massages, I learn that Burton has arranged for us to have a private lunch in one of their VIP small dining rooms. I am sure this is where Nicole and Keith must lunch. Amid the lit candles and champagne glasses filled with sparkling water, I can't help but feel grateful for the effort Burton has put into making me feel good for this Hallmark holiday.

I lean back in my chair, take a deep breath, and put my hands in my pockets, just relaxing and wondering how I got here. The key to my locker is dangling out of my robe pocket. As I pull it out, Burton's face changes from relaxed to slightly nervous. Something's up. I look down at the locker key and see a yellow diamond ring has been tied to it with white satin ribbon.

I'm confused. This isn't my key chain. Burton's lips start to move as the pieces of the puzzle start to come together. *Oh no. No. No!* I want to scream but I say quietly: "Don't do this. Please don't do this."

"Alice, don't panic. Please," he says.

They're not exactly the romantic words I thought were coming, even though I'm not sure I'm ready to hear any.

"I want you to have this."

"Why?"

"It's a little obvious, don't you think?"

"But—"

"Look, I don't care what other people think. But I see your

face every time we meet someone new and they know you're pregnant, and then their eyes move to your left hand."

My chest drops a little. How did he ever notice my defenselessness?

"I see your look. I know you try to hide it. That you try to put on this tough image like you don't care, but I can see you do. I see it when no one else does."

"It's not that," I begin. "It's just, none of this is how I had my life planned out."

"Sometimes our plan and God's plan are pretty different."

"Now you sound like our neighbor."

"But it's true. Alice, the more I get to know you, the more I'm falling for you."

"You don't know anything about me. It's been, like, six months—and four of them we didn't really talk."

"I know you're smart. I know you're a good businesswoman. I know you're brave: you moved here!"

"I had to move here or die." I eyeball him. "That isn't really being brave."

"Okay, I'll give you that. But I know that deep down, where you think I can't see, you have a nice"—he pauses—"yes, a nice side to you."

"Oh, that's good. 'A nice side.'" I mock him. "You so don't know."

"I know you like mint-chocolate-chip ice cream all mushed up with milk in it. I know you put three spoonfuls of brown sugar in your decaf. I know you like to read the whole paper in the morning before you talk to anyone. I know you brush your teeth from left to right and top to bottom the same amount every time. I know a lot more than you give me credit for, and I want to know even more."

"That's it? You just want to know more with this?" I hold the ring up.

"Yes, that's it. Well, that, and if we get married, you stand to gain a small fortune and really good insurance benefits."

"Very romantic." I smile.

"What?" He laughs. "You like the insurance part?"

"I was sold at 'small fortune.'"

And at that he gets up and comes around the table and kisses me. One of his long, wet, strong kisses that makes my feet tingle.

I slip the ring on my finger and much to my surprise, it fits. A perfect fit even with my swollen digits.

"Look, no promises," I say between kisses.

8

Money, Money, Money
Part II

Back in Bethel, as the service goes on, something catches my eye. It's the flicker of light caught by a pen as it moves across paper. The elderly black man to my left, with a gray-speckled Afro, is doing the writing. He is dressed in a tattered blue suit and is in desperate need of new shoes. In my peripheral vision I see he is writing a check for two dollars. No, wait. There are too many zeros. Two hundred dollars?

I slap my hand over my open mouth. It's all I can do not to say *holy moly* out loud. Grandpa has lost his mind. He is getting milked out of his Social Security money by a smooth-talking character from *The Andy Griffith Show*.

I sigh under my breath and whisper to no one, "This is nuts." Still shaking my head, I look back up at Pastor Opie. I feel as if he is staring at me. His eyes are boring holes in me. I stare back at him, as he's really starting to get on my nerves. *Poor Gramps. Gramps needs his money, con man!*

"This is the time to help your brothers," he says, pacing back and forth. "Let's just face what some of you are thinking. Money is a hard thing to talk about in church."

Seriously, I think. *You're draining poor Pawpaw here. The dude needs shoes.*

"Tithing your money isn't about me, or Pastor Tim, Pastor Broocks, or Pastor James having a new car."

I gulp. He is reading my mind. I'm thinking all those pastors are high-fiving their way to the local car dealership to get a new gold Caddy.

Opie continues, "In 1 Timothy 5:3 it says, 'Advance the kingdom of heaven on projects outside the church, such as feeding the needy and providing assistance to struggling families or communities.'"

April of this year: I'm outside of my house admiring the white blooms on Burton's cherry trees while getting the latest *People* magazine out of the mailbox when LeChelle comes barreling down her driveway in her black Escalade with tinted windows. She revs up next to me, making me jump up on the curb. The shaded passenger window rolls down. She looks annoyed. "Girl, whatcha doin' right now?"

I squint at her suspiciously. "Why?"

"'Cause I need your help, that's why. Get in the car."

"I got . . ." My voice trails off as I helplessly point to the house as if I have things to do.

"What? What do *you* got to do?" She cocks her head at me. "Not like you're supposed to be working."

"I have stuff I'm doing," I lie. My blood pressure is through the roof and I'm tired all the time, making it so hard to do anything that I have stopped trying.

"Get in the car," commands LeChelle as she leans over to open the passenger door for me.

We have a ten-second stare-off before I huff and puff and get in the car. She scares me when she wants to get something done.

I have just barely clicked my seat belt into place when LeChelle presses the pedal to the floor. I glance over in time to see the speedometer passing 50 mph. Hillsboro Road is a 45-mph zone. When she speeds through the yellow turning arrow onto I-440, I double-check my seat belt.

"Where are we going, Earnhardt?"

"Girl, I got all this stuff from the church." She points in the back of her Escalade. I notice now it is filled to the roof with boxes. "EJ was supposed to help me, but her baby got sick. I can't take this all by myself."

"Where exactly are we are going?" I ask.

"We're going to the Nashville Rescue Mission."

"Am I supposed to know what that is?"

"It's a homeless shelter," LeChelle says as she whips off the freeway onto Rosa L. Parks Boulevard and makes her first left into the parking lot. A few women stand around smoking cigarettes and making small talk. I suddenly feel awkward. I want to lock the door but have no idea what I'm afraid of.

"What do you need me for?" I wonder if I should cover LeChelle's purse. It's sitting out for all to see on the floor in the backseat as we get out.

She walks around the back of the truck and the electric button eases up the hatch. "Get a box," she commands.

I sometimes give money to people on the side of the road; I'm not a completely selfish piece of work. I also donated to the Save Darfur fund. Granted it was because George Clooney personally asked me to promote it on Trashville, and I would do anything for Clooney. But I gave a thousand dollars, and about five hundred in advertiser space. I'm not terrible. I give—kinda.

I've just never, well, been up close and personal with where those dollars supposedly go. Does that make me vapid and egotistical? Or is it self-preservation? My dad often teetered on the edge of desperation, and I spent my life getting away from the possibility of needing help from places like this.

A sign hangs above the door with a cross. Purple letters spell out NASHVILLE RESCUE MISSION FOR WOMEN. THE HOPE CENTER.

As we go through the metal detector, an older white woman named Miss Mary Cruthers, who could not be more country or more grateful, meets us at the door. Everyone calls her Miss Mary. She takes the box out of my arms and sets it down. She hugs LeChelle like she's the Queen of Sheba, breaking all the rules about personal space in my book. LeChelle doesn't seem to mind, though.

"Miss Mary, this is Miss Alice."

"Well, nice to meet you, Miss Alice." She looks down at my belly. "You ready for that baby, sugar?"

"I'm working on it."

Women from the shelter follow Miss Mary's lead and start unpacking LeChelle's truck. Again, I can't help but worry about her Chanel bag and wallet and her laptop sitting unprotected and up for grabs in the backseat.

"We're just so thankful," Miss Mary says. "Let me show you around."

Ugh, I really don't want to go lurking around here. It's not my business. I don't need to know. "Umm, okay."

With her hand on my shoulder, Miss Mary leads me through a set of glass doors and around a small chapel area. "We do services here every night and have a lot of great guest speakers," she explains before heading down the cement corridor and climbing upstairs to the second level. As the door opens, the smell of Clorox hits me and then I hear the pitter-patter of little feet as they race by me, followed by laughter.

"There are homeless children in Nashville?" I think I am saying this in my inside voice but it comes out of my mouth for all to hear.

"Hundreds," LeChelle says, "and hundreds. These are the lucky ones." Mary points at the game room where tweens are mixing with two-, three-, and four-year-olds. Some are clearly siblings and some are just connected by this place of refuge.

I'm overwhelmed by how totally unaware I have been of so many things. We move on to a large area that has rows of bunk beds. "We never turn anyone away," Miss Mary says. "We find a place." Each small bed has a shower bucket, a lone suitcase, and personal belongings light enough to carry. This room is where the bleach smell is originating. The white linens on the beds are all the same. On some beds I see a crocheted blanket. A small doll is propped on a pillow. My heart sinks upon seeing the little shoes in a row. Little hairbrushes. *Little* lives here.

I rub my belly, feeling my unborn daughter tucked in the safety of my womb.

A woman with a short brown pixie haircut and a clean black-and-white polka-dot blouse and blue jeans walks by. She's got her four-year-old in tow. "Hello," I say.

"Pat, this is Alice." Miss Mary introduces us. She looks like . . . me. She could be me. She doesn't look dirty or crazy. She just looks, well . . . displaced. She blinks her heavy lashes. "Nice to meet you."

"And this is Mya." LeChelle picks up Pat's daughter and hugs her. "You doin' good, baby girl?" Mya shyly nods in response. Then the ladies carrying the boxes from the truck come by. "We gotta run," LeChelle says. "You got everything?"

Miss Mary looks at a woman in a Nashville Rescue Mission T-shirt who is carrying a box. The woman says, "Yes, ma'am."

Then Miss Mary puts her arms around me the best she can with my protruding belly and hugs me tight. "You come back now and I'll give you a proper tour. I'll be praying for you and that baby." She looks deep into my eyes and then back to LeChelle. "Thank you. Thank you so much. Both of you. God bless you."

I feel sick, as I have done nothing to deserve this outpouring of heartfelt gratitude. I was just abducted by my crazy Christian neighbor.

Back in the Escalade, I am surprised to see LeChelle's purse, wallet, and laptop exactly where she left them. We drive home in silence.

I keep thinking about that woman, Pat. Why is she there? Why is her daughter there? Where is her family? That could easily have been me. What separates me from those walls? Nothing.

We hit the guard gate at Laurel Brooke. "What was in the boxes?" I ask LeChelle.

"Easter baskets. About sixty of 'em. The church puts 'em together."

"Easter baskets," I repeat with the sudden realization that there is no Easter egg hunt or Halloween or Christmas morning under the tree in a shelter. Even in our dungeon apartment, my drunken dad and I still managed to have a Charlie Brown tree.

"You did this on purpose to me, didn't you?" I ask, opening the door and getting out.

"I did not make EJ's baby sick, but I did feel led to bring you when I saw you from the road. I'm just listenin' to the Lord. Listenin' and obeyin' the Lord," she repeats for effect.

I shut the door a little hard, pretending to be a little put-out, but I'm not.

LeChelle rolls down her window. "It's not me," she hollers as she floors it up her driveway. "It's a *God* thang."

Back on the stage, Pastor Opie is still encouraging giving. "Give to help provide shelter," he says.

Or Easter baskets, I want to say.

"Give to a teenager who needs a new jacket or backpack. A mother who needs shampoo. A dad who needs a bus pass. A kid who dreams of going to college. Sow a seed of hope into a broken soul."

Wait a minute, I think. *Where were these Jesus people when I needed to go to college? Where were LeChelle and her filled-to-the-brim-with-goodies truck?*

"Only you can decide how much to give. The amount is in your heart." Pastor Opie's voice sounds in the speakers. "Don't do it because you have to, or because you feel pressure to. Do it because you feel it in your heart."

June 1985: My father is sober at my high-school graduation. It is a rare thing, to have him sober and functional during the day. He comes to the noon Sabino High School service in a clean shirt and freshly ironed pants. He is shaved and smells of Aqua Velva. Later he sits next to me at Denny's, where we celebrate my milestone with a lunch of blueberry pancakes.

He blows smoke from his cigarette and studies me intently. We sit there just looking at each other. "You look like your mother," he finally says, "with your hair curled like that."

Through his seeing me, I see him for the first time in a long time. I see worry lines that are too deep for a man just forty-eight years old. I see his suffering. I see his weakness. I see him so still. So small. He doesn't look like the man he was when he, my mother, and I danced in the kitchen. He is changed. We are both changed.

"I want you to know that I'm sorry," he begins. His voice cracks. It makes my heart pound. It makes a lump in my throat grow painful. Who is he? Who has he become? He used to wear a suit, and we played cards at the dinner table. Who have I become? We have, in four-and-a-half years, ignored, buried, and rebelled against everything she tried to leave us with.

Just then, the waitress comes with the check. As he reaches across the table for it, he changes course and places his hand on mine, touching me kindly for the first time since she died. "I love you, Alice," he says. "More than you'll ever know."

As he drops me off in the Safeway parking lot—I work the night shift—ABBA belts out their hit "Money, Money, Money" on the radio.

Later that afternoon, my dad goes up to Mount Lemmon and drives that old Buick off a cliff. The police rule it an accident, but I know better.

He left a life-insurance policy on the table in the kitchen and a note.

I've gone to be with your mother. You have earned the right to go to college. This small policy should help pay your tuition. Burn this letter immediately so they will never know.

I light a joint and take a long inhale. I want to be numb to all of it. With the cherry of the joint, I burn that letter. It is a convenient way to keep our secret. It is an extremely ineffective way of dealing with my pain. Sure there is a piece of me that wants to cry and kick and scream. To pound my fists on the table sobbing and bellowing *Why Daddy, why?* like a tragic television Movie of the Week. But I know the answer and honestly, what is the point? There are no more tears left in me and frankly, I'm surprised he hung on as long as he did. He had already been gone for the last four years and this was just his final curtain call.

So long, Pop. Thanks for the memories, rolls around in my brain.

It may seem cold or callous but how exactly am I supposed to process this? Is a teenage kid going to seek out a shrink so she can kick back on a couch and discover the *healing process?* There is no one left to hold my hand and guide me through it. This is now my solo performance and I will not let the crowd down. I am, as always, in complete survival mode.

"What a quitter!" I say, watching that paper burn.

I decide then that I will be happy only with a new life. Only then will the void created by my mother's death and blasted open by my father's untimely and unsavory demise be filled. I will rewrite the past. I will create a new future. I will find comfort in a life filled with success and money and without a care in the world.

It is the beginning of truly being alone.

Pastor Opie finishes on the steps of the stage, saying, "When we give, regardless of our lot in life, or our uncertainty, you can know this for sure: God will give back to you with His grace, mercy, and blessings that you cannot measure."

A female singer comes to the stage: "Blessed are those who give."

2

Burning the Past

A petite, pregnant Latina singer who, unlike me, is thin but appears to have swallowed a basketball in her pretty floral maternity skirt and orange, silky blouse, comes to center stage as the musicians start playing. I'm half-jealous and half in awe: for being in the sisterhood of the knocked-up, she's awfully tiny.

The Sunday-suited ushers are making their way toward the back rows. They are collecting checks and MasterCard numbers from most of the easy-to-fleece audience members. I watch in wonder as every last morsel of hard-earned cash is sucked into their offering bags. I focus my attention again on the beautiful and radiant pregnant lady on stage. As the music plays, she begins to softly sing:

The room grew still
As she made her way to Jesus

She stumbled through the tears that made her blind
She felt such pain
Some spoke in anger
Heard folks whisper
There's no place here for her kind

My baby kicks hard as if telling me from the inside to get ready for the money dudes and to contribute to their overflowing satchels full of green and silver.

I am torn between my previous disgust at the pocket-pillaging and my new wonder at the generosity of God-givers and their trust that the church will do the right thing with their paycheck. Why is it that even after knowing the Jacksons, after being a witness to their good deeds and seeing them put the God-money to work, I'm still a skeptic? Why am I so jaded?

Still on she came
Through the shame that flushed her face
Until at last, she knelt before His feet
And though she spoke no words
Every tear she shed was heard
As she poured her love for the Master
From her box of alabaster

I pull out my checkbook and start writing. I cross out my cursive *Twen*—and change it to *Fifty*. I fill out the contact form so at least my tax guy will have one charitable deduction to make for me this year. I set the envelope in the velvet burgundy-lined basket and inhale deeply. I pass it to my left and the weirdest thing happens: instead of feeling suckered, I feel good.

At this point, the choir joins the soloist's song:

And I've come to pour
My praise on Him—like oil
From Mary's alabaster box
Don't be angry if I wash His feet with my tears
And dry them with my hair
You weren't there—the night He found me
You did not feel what I felt
When He wrapped His loving arms around me
And you don't know the cost
Of the oil in my alabaster box

I am not above admitting that the Jesus folks can carry a tune. In response, my baby is dancing on my bladder, causing alternating sensations of back spasms and having to pee really badly.

The pretty, pregnant singer's voice stands out from the choir's singing. I try to pinpoint what it is about her voice—is it her purity? her boldness?—that is connecting me to this church-a-palooza, but nailing it down is difficult. She sings with her eyes closed, raising her right hand above her head to belt out:

I can't forget
The way life used to be
I was a prisoner
To the sins that had me bound
I spent my days
Poured my life—without measure
Into a little treasure box
I thought I had found

What a song concept: some poor, broken, slutty, dirty woman makes her way to Jesus with all her possessions in a box ready to give them to Him just because He loved her. That must be some great kind of love. Isn't it ironic that the religious people were ready to kick her out? I'm glad the people at Bethel aren't on to me, plus I'm not quite ready to hand over my money, my faith, my hope, or my life to their God.

Until the day—when Jesus came to me
And healed my soul
With the wonders of His love
So now I'm giving back to Him
All the praise He's worthy of
I've been forgiven
And that's why
I love Him so much

January 1985: We have been poor in a barren wasteland of the desert. I fantasize about putting a hundred and fifty miles between me and the poverty and living a reinvented life.

Five months before my dad takes a header off the side of Mount Lemmon, I turn eighteen. He marks the occasion by drinking vodka that has been dyed green and passing out while my red-velvet birthday cake burns in the oven.

I come home at seven thirty after working the late-afternoon shift at the grocery store to find our apartment filled with smoke. The fire alarm is blaring. The green and white streamers he has hung from the doorframe are barely visible through the haze.

You'd think coming home to such a scene would shock and panic me, but it doesn't. These episodes of lunacy are the norm. Each day I wake up and brace myself for the crazy-quake I know is coming. I never know exactly where, when, or how it will happen, but I am always prepared to battle the invisible demons of broken dreams and promises, and duck and dodge the raging alcoholic.

My dad is draped goofily on his recliner. I kick the footrest to throw him to the floor, where the air is cleaner. He gasps for oxygen. The recliner ejection causes the TV tray to fall over, his glass to break, and half-melted green ice cubes to spill onto the carpet. With a broom, I whack the alarm off the ceiling to shut it up. I crawl to the kitchen and turn off the stove, and, using my Safeway apron as an oven mitt, pull out the culprit. I open the kitchen door before running back to the open front door and throwing the smoking cake into the parking lot. Fresh air pours into the apartment. I sit down on the orange shag carpet next to my dad and wait for the room to clear.

"Sorry about the cake," he mutters, putting his head on my lap.

I touch his hair, petting him the way my mother used to pet me to help me relax after nightmares. "It's okay, Dad. I don't really eat cake anymore anyway."

These are the tender moments that usually follow the drunken openhanded slap to the face or the sucker-punch shove against the wall. Precious moments like these accompany his sober realization of what he has done and what he has become.

We'd have our moment and then I'd wipe up the blood on the carpet, pick the shards of broken glass out of his arm, and clean him up, and we'd eat dinner as if nothing had happened. We'd have amity for one night. I'd feel clean and renewed and the knots of anticipation would loosen and deflate, until morning, when the tension and fighting would start anew.

My Safeway name tag had fallen off my apron as I was flailing around at the alarm. As I pick it up, the pin pricks my finger, drawing the tiniest bit of blood. I suck it.

"Oh, yourrrrr'ee bleeding," my dad slurs as he gets to his

knees and uses the La-Z-Boy to steady himself. "Let me get you a Band-Aid." As he stumbles into the bathroom, I wonder how my mother didn't see the wickedness in him when she married him. But I understand.

I also love him. Loving a man so defeated is full of compromise. We had made exceptions for the shattered shell he was, and the fact that he was ill equipped to master the job he'd been given, because he showed us a glimpse now and then of the good man we hoped he could always be.

My eighteenth birthday marked the last time I would feel trapped by the poverty of loneliness and disappointment in the Ferguson family.

April this year: I am squatting over the toilet peeing into a cup. I look at my trusty dark-brown gallon bottle with a funnel purposely stuck in the top. It's almost full.

"Burrrrrton, I may need another bottle," I call out from the master bathroom with my underwear around my ankles.

He comes in just in time to see me pouring my own urine into the funnel.

"Whoa! Whoa! It's about to overflow!" he says, wide-eyed.

"I know. I need another jug," I say, holding the cup and funnel.

"Where is it?" he asks, frantically looking under the counters.

"Where is what?" I sound exasperated.

"The extra jug." He looks at me, confused.

"I don't have one. I need one!"

"What? You don't have one?"

"No!" Now I'm starting to get frustrated with the fact that not only have I been pouring my own urine in a bottle for an entire day, but now my cup runneth over.

Burton goes into doctor mode. "Okay. I can handle it. I just need to boil some water."

"I'm not having the baby," I call after him as he jogs out of the bathroom. I sit on the floor, wearing Burton's scrubs, straddling my trusty pee bottle and holding the pee in the cup, careful not to spill one precious drop.

Burton returns with an old Miracle Whip jar.

"Seriously?" I shake my head. "What is happening to me?"

"I sterilized it. Move the funnel over."

"Seriously." I pick it up with my fingertips. "Okay. Fine." I move the funnel out of the brown jug and into the mayo jar. "Gross."

"Good, right?" He smiles.

"Nothing about collecting my own pee for an entire twenty-four hours is good. Particularly watching it go into a sandwich dressing jar. I'll never spread Miracle Whip the same way again." I finish pouring my almost-clear liquid into the jar.

Burton comes around behind me and places his forearms under my armpits, then lifts me up. "It's the best way to really test your proteins. Dr. Schlossberg just wants to make sure you're okay."

I squint my eyes at him. "You put her up to this, didn't you?"

He shakes his head no. But his face screams yes. He's such a bad liar.

"Oh, no! You did?"

"Maybe I did. But only 'cause your levels weren't consistent last week."

"That's fine!" I say with a huff, turning my back on him and facing the mirror.

"I did it . . . 'cause . . . I love you."

I look at him in the reflection.

"You love me?" This all seems very confusing. "You pick now, over a bottle of pee, not red wine, to tell me you love me?"

"Maybe I do. So what?" he says.

I pick up my jars and hold them out to him. "Then you can take these to Dr. Nicole, your partner in crime."

His whole face scrunches.

"You're a doctor." I thrust the bottles forward.

"But that's pee. I hate pee. The nurses do the pee stuff."

"But you loooooooovvvvve *my* pee." I shove the jug at his chest.

He reluctantly takes my jars and turns.

"That's true love, baby!" I call after him as he leaves for work. "Real love!" I yell for emphasis before catching my reflection in the mirror.

"Real love," I repeat softly.

August 1985: It has been two months since I buried my dad next to my mom at East Lawn Cemetery, and there are still Scotch-taped corners of the birthday streamers stuck to the smoke-stained wall. I look around our apartment, thinking that it is time to move on.

But there is so much evidence of my history. I need to get rid of it, torch it. Finish the job my birthday cake didn't get done.

I dismantle our existence piece by piece. His clothes, shoes, pictures, toothbrushes, and pillowcases—every remembrance of a life with the failed Ferguson family and every tangible trinket God abandoned when He took my mother—I pile it all onto rugs and bedsheets and curtains to drag across the hot asphalt parking lot and heave it into the Dumpster. Items like appliances and the sour milk–stained flooring that carry no emotion for me I leave for the next loser occupant of apartment 307. I am done with it all.

I save only the two things that could identify who I am. The first is a file containing legal documents like my birth certificate, my parents' death certificates, my Social Security card, transcripts from high school, and my acceptance letter to Arizona State University. The second file contains a picture frame with two photos: one of my mother and father on St. Matthew's steps on their wedding day, and another of the three of us with Santa at the mall when I was six.

The choir continues to belt out praise. Despite my best intentions, I feel the melody begin to loosen my furrowed brow and clenched fists. I don't remember clenching them. I feel a stirring inside of me.

> *I can't forget*
> *The way life used to be*
> *I was a prisoner*
> *To the sins that had me bound*
> *I spent my days*
> *Poured my life—without measure*
> *Into a little treasure box*
> *I thought I had found*

The pregnant singer is really feeling it now. The lyrics pour out of her and caress the people in the room. A warm, clear-blue tide has broken over us. I'm starting to feel it too when a woman in front of me suddenly throws her arms in the air and jumps to her feet.

Really? I mean . . . seriously? How rude. I can't see anymore! I'm ready to yell, *Down in front!* as lots of other people join the lady in front of me by standing up, too.

I am outnumbered. But I am also pregnant. I am not getting back up. I wiggle around impatiently in my spot on the pew. I learn that if I lean forward and lurch to the left, I can see the singer again.

Tears are streaming down her face. What the—? Are they tears of happiness? Tears of pain? Tears of gratitude? What is going on with these people? What is going on in this place?

> *Until the day—when Jesus came to me*
> *And healed my soul*
> *With the wonders of His love*
> *So now I'm giving back to Him*
> *All the praise He's worthy of*
> *I've been forgiven*
> *And that's why*
> *I love Him so much*

Just then, something strikes me about my dad: in all his screwed-up, failed weakness, he paid a price for me. Was that it?

My father had done the best he could. He snaked the clogged toilets of strangers so he wouldn't leave me in debt. We never went hungry. He slept on a pullout sofa with a lumpy mattress an inch thick to allow me the privacy of my own bedroom. He did these things because he loved me.

He had left me before I could leave him. That was one mistake I wouldn't make again.

Was his suicide a cop-out? Absolutely. But at this moment, awash in a foreign feeling and surrounded by faith-freaks, I feel sad for him. I feel like I could forgive him. I take a deep breath as the realization forms fully: as totally pitiable and regrettable and pathetic as his suicide was, it was his way of setting me free. He drizzled his own life into a paper guarantee for me. He had no sense of his own value.

He set me free.
The singer's voice starts to rise.

And I've come to pour
My praise on Him like oil
From Mary's alabaster box
Don't be angry if I wash His feet with my tears
And dry them with my hair

Her voice sings out triumphantly, making a cause for every lyric.

You weren't there—the night He found me
You did not feel what I felt
When He wrapped His loving arms around me
And you don't know the cost
Of the oil in my alabaster box

In his sick and twisted way, he did it for me, and I've been running from that responsibility ever since. He put all his dreams for a future in one envelope and left it for me. It wasn't his fault. And, I finally realize, maybe it wasn't mine either.

Late August 1985: I've gone shopping at the Gap with some of the money I collected from the insurance agency. Three bags of new clothes lie on the empty floor where my bed used to be.

I rinse the Clairol blond out of my hair and admire my new honey-kissed color. It looks like my mother's hair. I stand back and gaze at myself in the mirror. For a second, through my foggy reflection, I see her smiling back at me. I'm startled but unmoved. I want more. I wipe the fog away in order to see her more clearly, but she has vanished. I want to climb through the mirror to be with her and my dad on the other side.

It wasn't like the Occurrence, but I did see her there.

Still staring at myself in the mirror, I am dizzy. The room spins around me. I grab a pair of sharp scissors. I want to be with her. He has gone with her, why can't I? It would be so easy to end it all here and now.

I take a hit off my joint and exhale. I blow the smoke at myself in the mirror, creating the illusion that I'm disappearing. The pot is helping my dad's antidepressant pills kick in. It's either the pot or the fact that I washed the pills down with grape juice and vodka: I feel nothing. Although nothing does feel like something. To quote the Pink Floyd song playing on my boom box, it feels *comfortably numb.*

"You're strong." I hear her voice in my head. I shake my head in reply. *I am not strong, Mom.*

The light from the blade reflects off my face. I stare once again at the blond version of me. I pull my hair to the side, admiring my throbbing vein, and then I place the pointed scissors next to my throat. How simple it would be to just slice into my flesh.

I take a good long minute to admire my long hair before slashing and cutting. I chop off four inches. I have created an ear-length bob with straight bangs just over my eyebrows. I have no choice: I cannot go with my parents and I cannot stay here. I have to start over.

The apartment purge is complete. A mountain of memories spills out from the mouth of the Dumpster. I hurl two gallons of gasoline on the mess. Once everything is good and soaked, I light a match and toss it on top.

Whoosh. Sparks dance across my parents' comforter. Flames tickle my dad's shirts. Pictures and paintings and fake flowers and plastic burn, and any attachment that these items have to me or the last eighteen years melts away.

I have traded my black leather Dr. Martens boots for Sperry sneakers and white ankle socks trimmed with lace. I am wearing a khaki tennis skirt with a madras blouse to complement my new bob. My full lips are lacquered with a light-pink sheen.

As I back away slowly from the heat of the inferno, I invent a wonderfully tragic story about my past and my family. Oh, how the girls on sorority row will marvel about how my two loving parents had died on their way to Sunday brunch at the club. I accessorize my new look with a tragic background story and a fairy tale of a popular girl who cheered for the varsity football team, was student-body treasurer, and had vowed to remain a virgin until marriage.

Like a phoenix, I am born again from one hellish bonfire.

A police car pulls up as the fire dwindles and the officer asks me what I saw.

Practicing my new plastic grin, I feign concern and innocence and say, "Some crazy girl with black hair and dark-purple lips just burned all this stuff up."

Never thinking an innocent preppy girl like me would be such a juvenile delinquent, he asks, "Where'd she go?"

"She's gone." I shake my head. "She's just gone." As soon as he leaves, I run. I book my new-and-improved self a ticket on an Arizona Highways Shuttle and leave Tucson for Phoenix for a fresh start. I never tell Scott or anyone where I am going. I make a clean getaway from the past to my future.

I get off the shuttle with my suitcase full of new clothes, old drugs, and fresh beginnings at Arizona State University.

Free. Free at last.

Oh, happy day, here I come.

10

The Show

Part I

I'm in real need of a back rub. You'd think that cramps would cease to exist when you haven't had a period in thirty-six weeks. But no, here I am, painfully bloated and practically doubled over in pain. I feel like I'm at a Bon Jovi concert and the opening acts were awesome, but I'm tired of waiting. I want Jon in his tight jeans and feathered hair on the stage. Now. I'm ready for the main attraction. The event. The show.

And without further ado, my main man, my neighbor, my brother from another African mother, Pastor Tim, appears in the aisle and takes his place in the center ring of this puzzling circus.

My man has a serious sense of style. Perhaps it is the former NFL player in him who knows how to put together a runway-ready look. He is styling in a custom-made Italian suit with a luxurious polished sheen. The tan fabric makes his chocolate skin glow. His crisp white shirt and striking light-blue-and-silver tie pop against the three-button jacket.

He is standing behind the Plexiglas pulpit. He sets down his Bible and picks up wire-rimmed, octagon-shaped glasses. His bald head glistens, creating a weird halo effect. His earpiece is still perfectly tucked in his ear, the microphone arcing toward his mouth. A warm smile spreads across his face. I swear I not only see but hear a sparkle bounce off his gleaming-white teeth as he begins addressing the congregation.

The *giving* portion of our entertainment this morning is over, and the jovial singing-and-clapping flock is petering out.

"Thank you," Tim says casually, knowing full well we have all been waiting anxiously to hear him. "This is a special day and I'm just privileged that I could call my mom, who is seventy-two years old. A lot of you have heard me talk about my momma. She was a school-bus driver for twenty-six years. She worked two other part-time jobs and raised six kids on her own with a brown leather belt to keep us in line. Some of you might have had spankin's, but Big Momma gave whoopin's."

Tim pauses before changing his tone. "But there was more to Big Momma than carrying a big strap. She was a Godly woman, a praying woman. My momma would pray for anything and everything. Big Momma would pray for money to pay the electric bill. She would pray for help for gettin' all her babies off the streets and into the church. She would pray for protection from the gangs who were on every country corner trying to sell drugs to all us kids. Oh, my momma pray-hay-ed. She wore us *out* with her prayers."

I like the way Tim sings the word *prayed* and punctuates the word *out* with his inflection. The audience laughs. "She was a praying momma who prayed over, under, and around her babies. There was power in her prayers. So on this Mother's Day, I thank Jesus for my praying momma."

He looks down, opens his Bible, then looks back up at the crowd and says, "Happy Mother's Day. I'm Pastor Tim Jackson, and if you haven't been told already, welcome to Bethel. We're glad to see you this morning."

While he scans the room, his eyes connect with me ducking in the back. It's just for a nanosecond, but it is enough to make me feel happy inside. I feel a part of something, a part of the group. As much as I hate to admit it, I feel optimistic here.

"This is a day where we honor mothers but also women in general, as last time I checked, a mother would be the one thing we all have in common. We all got mommas."

A knowing ripple of laughter rolls from pew to pew. My own personal Cedric the Entertainer doing the Bible.

"We put together this little video clip that I'm going to show now." He steps sideways as the room goes dark. A screen scrolls down, covering the dunk tank. The video begins with a sweet little six-year-old boy with a blond crew cut and two missing front teeth who says, "I wanna thank my mommy because she lets me eat a lot of candy."

I smile as the screen fades and then a teenage black girl with long, straightened hair and wearing a pretty purple shirt states, "I want to thank my mom for always caring for and loving me. Even when I wasn't too lovable."

I hear a woman in the crowd call out: "True dat."

Next a man who has a large purple burn on the left side of his white face shares, "I want to thank my mom for teaching me how to be a man and a father when my own father wasn't around."

Just then, there is a pinch right above my bladder. I close my eyes and wince to deal with the pain of the cramp and I hear, "I want to thank my mom for never giving up on me." I open my eyes to an Asian woman who looks like a biker with her tattoos and shaved head. Her eyes are filled with pride and love.

This continues until an eight-year-old pigtailed girl giggles and asks, "Is it on?" She covers her mouth shyly. "Okay, here I go . . . I love you, Mommy, because, because . . . you teach me about Jesus and how much He loves me. You teach me that this birthmark"—she pulls her shirt off one shoulder—"is a reminder that God made me special. He made us all special."

Then she looks innocently into the camera, unpins a thoughtful grenade, and lobs it at me directly: "Why are *you* thankful to your mom?"

After my mom died, I tried hard to forget her. I pushed all my memories of her deep down inside me and locked them away. I didn't throw them away, though; I couldn't. I close my eyes trying to remember what it was about my mother that I am thankful for. The good things. I remember things that are special.

My years one through seventeen are encrypted on my heart hard drive. Thanks to Pastor Tim and a shy little girl on a video screen, I'm reconsidering my attempts at self-preservation. I have recovered the password and jumped back into my past. A file titled *The Occurrence* opens in my frontal lobe. A file that was locked away so very long ago.

January 1981: I am fourteen years old. It is the day I buried my mother. Night has fallen on the Tucson sky and darkness fills the air and my heart. I am naked except for my yellow hipster underwear. I look at my body in the arched mirror atop my mother's makeup table. My reflection looks like a skinny boy instead of a girl and is in stark contrast to the feminine carved roses and ivory detailing on the mirror frame. I run my hand over my breasts; they are barely nubs. Will they ever grow? I pick up my mother's floral antique brush and pull it through my hair, remembering that she hadn't needed it since her seventh chemo treatment.

I finish combing my wet hair and set the brush back down. My strawberry-blond strands are intertwined with her dead strands in the bristles.

My dad had moved into our guest room to let my mother be more comfortable and not have to listen to his snoring. Although toward the last few days, I am not sure she heard more than my whispers and prayers. The hospice workers would come in every other day as I sat next to her watching them drain her tubes, administer medication, and check her vitals. But it was me who changed her clothes and kept her clean. I did not want them touching her privates. I remember them touching her feet and calves those last days and just smiling at me as if to say, *Not long now, sweetie. Not long now.*

I walk into her closet. There are only a few things left. After the doctors stripped her of any remaining hope and filled us with the grim reality that there was nothing else they could do, she donated most of her clothing to charity. I couldn't decide who I hated more: the nasty dream-killing doctor or the sad-eyed Salvation Army lady who came to our house about a month ago to collect the clothing Mom didn't want.

My mom left me the fox stole that was her mother's and her tie-dyed overalls and an old, faded Dr. Martin Luther King Jr. *We Have a Dream* T-shirt. Her green-and-white bell-bottomed pinstriped suit that she was to be buried in was hanging in there, too, beside a few of her cozy nightgowns and housecoats. In the end, she didn't have much energy. When she had company, she modestly covered up her nightgown with one of the housecoats.

I pull a white cotton nightie off the hanger, slip it over my freshly showered body, and crawl into her queen bed. I draw the afghan and light-blue sheet up to my neck and stare at the ceiling. I am looking at nothing really but the ugly popcorn ceiling.

She is gone. Dead. Entombed in a shiny, long, bolted box, buried deep in cool soil. I am alone.

The drapes are open. The Arizona sky is aglow in moonlight. I have not cried, and I am numb. I lie in the shadowy darkness of her bedroom, just barely a teen and already broken into little pieces.

My gaze lowers to the wooden clock perched on her wall. Nine forty-five at night. Before I know it, the words that have been bouncing around in my head—*Mom* and *why*—begin to escape my mouth in muffled little cries.

I can't breathe. I feel suffocated by sadness. I pound my head on the pillow and finally hot tears of acceptance of the end begin to stream down my face. For the first time in the months since her diagnosis, an immense sadness blankets me like a thick, wet fog. I am frozen in my teenage grief and fear and aloneness.

The reality hits me: what has happened isn't some nightmare that I'm going to wake up from. The truth of it all is almost too much to take. I want to die, too. I lie there sobbing. Muffled, bone-crushing pleas of pain are released into the night air.

And then it begins. Like a dog that can sense the arrival of an earthquake seconds, even minutes, before it hits, my heart begins to pound. The hairs on my arms stand up. My body tingles as if all of my extremities have fallen asleep. I am acutely aware that something is about to happen.

Nervousness takes over and then abruptly my blanket of darkness is yanked off. I'm neither happy nor sad nor numb. I feel nothing at all.

At first it feels good. It is a relief. But then I wonder: *How is this possible? Am I going crazy?* I don't feel dead, but I feel apart from this world. How can it be that my heartache has been erased from my soul? I am losing my mind from sorrow. I am totally insane.

An ethereal, teal-colored mist is hovering in the air. Colorful sparks of light dance on the walls. It's as if a prism has been hit with billions of rays of sunlight. It should be blinding, but it's not. I want to cover my eyes but I don't.

The air has changed. I breathe in its coolness. Something is in the room.

Something is here. Is it her? An angel?

The mist begins to take form. My breathing is deep and full and finally peaceful. I can see my mom's hair gently caressing her shoulders. She is first a translucent silhouette. Then the illusion takes semisolid form. My mother is standing in front of me, at the foot of the bed. She is wearing the bright-yellow-and-cream daisy sundress I always loved.

She is not alone.

I sit up and pull my knees to my chest, my feet scooting me back quickly on the bed until my back presses against the headboard. I lean forward and look deeply into her green eyes. She looks as if she's afloat, yet she's real. Perhaps it is an angel in her form. But it looks like her. She is holding someone's or something's hand. I can't see who or what it is, but I am not afraid of it and I know she and I aren't alone. She is smiling. She looks healthy and lovely.

I'm motionless but wanting to feel her. *Mom,* I want to cry out. *Mom!* But nothing escapes my lips. I am frozen in an emotional, spiritual time capsule. I watched them bury her. I know she is dead, but then she is here.

She reaches out to me. I want to feel our hands pressing together. I try to reach out to meet her but I am still.

Whoever or whatever is her companion exudes compassion in waves. It fills the room and in turn fills me with a courage that is not my own. I lift my hand to meet my mom's. I am flooded with bliss. I close my eyes.

I melt as our fingers intertwine. I feel faint at her touch. I want so much for her to snuggle me in the bed and fall asleep with me. I want her to hold me tight just one more time. One more night. Our tight, face-to-face embrace.

Having her near and having these memories feel fresh and present is warm and soothing. As she pulls her hand back, I plead: *No! No! No! Mommy, don't leave me. Take me with you. Mommy, please!* But my cries are silent. Hot, salty tears pour from my eyes. She immediately lifts her palms open toward the sky and drops to her knees.

Her companion raises its hands. Light shoots out from holes in its palms. It looks like a sparkler that a child would hold on the Fourth of July: beautiful, powerful. Controlled yet with an element of surprise.

It takes my breath away.

It must be God. Or Jesus. Right?

Kneeling, my mother reaches out toward me, sprinkling me with composure. At once, I understand. An understanding that I've never been more confident about, coming from a source not of this world. My tears stop. My sadness is wiped away by peace.

She stands and comes nearer to me until she is right next to me. The presence boldly stands behind her as she takes my cheeks in her soft hands. I sit, mesmerized, as she peppers my face and eyelids with kisses, exactly as I had done to her in the moments after she died.

With that, I knew she was still here with me. I knew that, yes, she was gone, her body was in a box covered with worm-filled dirt. But she, the essence of what made her *her*, had been raised up to wherever it is that good mothers go. I knew right then that there was something beyond where we are now.

My head is heavy in her hands. I close my eyes again, trying to absorb every last drop of the euphoric exchange. My heart is pounding in my chest. My lungs heave. The air is electrically charged.

She does not speak, but she clearly tells me: *I love you. I love you. I love you. I'll see you again soon. It is all a perfect plan, my darling.* I am lost in the rapture of it all. There is no drug to duplicate the magnificence of it. There are no words to ever properly describe it. I am dripping with the glory.

With a flash of light as bright as a lightning bolt, my eyes pop open and I see that she is gone. They are gone. I collapse on the bed, mouthing the words *thank you, thank you, thank you* over and over.

I am alone again in the room, but I am no longer empty. She—they—have left something behind. God has left something behind in me. I can feel His hope, His strength, His joy in my heart. He has deposited into the bank of me, the true comfort.

I look back at the clock: 10:45 p.m. Exactly one hour has passed in what seemed like minutes.

I know I wasn't dreaming. I have never been surer of anything than what I experienced that night. I was unquestionably visited by an angel or a spirit of my mom and her friend, who I'm pretty sure was Jesus.

I want to tell my story of the Occurrence to everyone. I want so much to share the hope I have been given with other broken and lost people like me. But I am only fourteen and when I share my revelation with others, there is so much naysaying, so much disbelief. I am told I am crazy. I am made to feel shame and embarrassment. So I tuck the experience into the depths of my mind, far, far away from my day-to-day awareness. But the fact that something supernatural happened to me is undeniable.

That night, around eleven, my father comes in the room to find me sitting up with my feet on the floor, slumped over, my head in my hands, my body heaving up and down. When he turns on the light, I lift my head, flash him a smile, and burst into hysterical laughter. I scare the crap out of him.

"Please stop spraying your mother's perfume," he barks at me before spinning around so quickly that he bangs his shoulder on the doorframe on his way out.

But I haven't sprayed her perfume.

Two days later, the scent of my mother still hanging in the air, I try to tell him what has happened. He responds by sending me to see the priest.

I know that my dad is my witness. I know that in his heart he knows the truth about that night, and that is what gave him the courage to propel his beat-up Buick 285 feet into a jagged ravine.

He knew she was still around, somewhere. Up there in a place we couldn't go. And he wanted more than anything to be wherever she was.

He knew.

But more important than that: I knew and I had forgotten. I had jammed it so far down, so deep within me that it had become unreachable. I had tried to duplicate the euphoria I felt that day. I tried desperately to fill up my open wounds of anger and shame. I used every means possible and nothing could come close—it had all been a wash.

Until now. In this church, on this day, out of the past, with this music and these people, it has been brought to the surface once again.

"I am thankful for that miracle," I find myself saying out loud. I am saying it to the little girl on the video screen, to the pretty, skinny pregnant singer, to Pastor Tim, and to God. I am saying it to whoever will listen. Mostly, I am saying it to myself as, in the safety and wonder of this place, I have finally accepted the truth of that day.

There is something better out there and I have been trying to re-create that feeling for the past twenty-three years.

11

The Show

Part II

"Today is about honoring, celebrating, and loving our mothers," Pastor Tim says as the video screen retracts and the lights in the church come up.

I think back to the moments in my life when I really needed my mother. I needed her so many times after she had died.

Until now, I believed she visited me as an angel and her travel buddy had been Jesus or God or whatever you want to call it. But it was my mom I had needed, so I had focused on her and ignored the rest of it. Had I ignored God? Jesus? The Holy Spirit? Was it just too much to process, so I ignored it?

Why had I buried the whole memory until today?

Honestly, I don't know. I feel as if God had teased me in that room that day with my ghost mom. He had filled me with His love and then said, *Check ya later.* As a result, I totally developed God-abandonment issues.

But after hanging with my preacher man, Tim, and LeChelle, I am coming to understand that perhaps God hadn't abandoned me at all. I was the one who turned my back because everyone I told about my experience had pooh-poohed my miracle. The worst had been the priest my father had sent me to. He was so dismissive that he turned me off to organized religion altogether. Until I met Pastor Tim, that is.

"Turn in your Bibles to John 16:21," he says. "'A woman giving birth to a child has pain because her time has come; but when her baby is born she forgets the anguish because of her joy that a child is born into the world.'"

Oh, please, let it be true, I think as the hip-hop dancer in my belly delivers another swift kick to my ribs.

Pastor Tim looks up and pauses, taking off his glasses. "Lord, we thank You for this Word today and we ask that Your Word would fall onto open hearts and would grow a field of harmony and understanding in Jesus' name."

The crowd says a low *Amen.*

"Being that it's Mother's Day, I want to show the importance that Scripture places on women and mothers," he says, walking to the left of the pulpit, smiling. "First we'll discuss the women in the Bible, and then we're gonna get to all y'all mothers. Often when you think of the Bible, it is the men who get all the credit: Moses, David, Abraham, Noah, and of course Jesus and the disciples. But what about the women?"

He makes a good point. Other than Mary, I'm not too sure of any significant women in the Bible. Which of course makes me feel that the Bible may be a bit skewed. So I like where he's going: power to my biblical lady posse!

"There are incredible women in Scripture. Women who made

a difference—a difference in their families, their friendships, their communities. Women like Sarah, who trusted God to give her a baby when everyone told her she couldn't have one. She was trustin' the ultimate fertility doctor. Rachel, who was confident God would give her a good man, even when it seemed like she'd be waiting forever. Som' y'all single ladies know what that feels like."

A soft murmur of *hallelujahs* ripples through the crowd.

"Naomi and Ruth were what y'all would call BFFs. Deborah was a prophetess and became a great leader in a time of battle. Hannah showed us how to keep our promises to God by giving up her most prized possession: her son. Brave, brave Esther risked her life to stand up for what was right; Mary believed God for the impossible. These are just a few women in the Bible who faced some of the exact issues women are facing today," he says, returning to the pulpit and his notes. He puts his glasses back on. "Jesus utilized women constantly in his parables to show hope, generosity, love, redemption, forgiveness. My point is, the Bible is filled with story after story of great women of *faith*!" Pastor Tim shouts the word for emphasis.

"Faith, faith, faith," I mutter to myself as my baby tap-dances on my spleen. In LA, the malls had expectant-mother parking. Shouldn't this place have expectant-mother cushions at least? I am a woman of so little faith. I remember a time when Pastor Tim and I started delving deeper into the small capsule in my heart where I had stuffed faith.

Something in me still doubts him. I shove questions at him, forever wondering if this God-squad mission is just a facade. I do everything I can to challenge his blind faith. Case in point: one of our many meals this past spring. I daydream as I remember.

* * *

Late March: "The point of blind faith doesn't sound so smart," I say to Tim while pulling out of my driveway. Tim is chillaxing in my passenger seat and Michaela, their oldest, is in the backseat as we all head out to lunch. "It's like going through the world ignoring the facts and just saying"—I switch from my normal voice to a high-pitched, goofy one and mock—"well the Bible says it's true, so I'm just gonna ignore them-there facts about the world being millions of years old."

Michaela looks up from texting and laughs. "Miss Alice, you're pretty funny." And goes right back to texting.

Tim pipes in, "Faith isn't blind. It is being sure of what we hope for and certain of what we do not see. We don't know what *years* or *thousands of years,* or *millions of years* are to God."

As we head out of Laurel Brooke, pass the stop sign at Sneed Road, and turn south on Hillsboro Road, I mull over his answer, trying to digest it.

"Go here!" Tim points to the right as I almost miss a small turn onto Highway 46, Old Hillsboro Road.

"I didn't know this was here. Where are we going?"

"Most people don't," he says, crossing his mammoth legs and looking out of the passenger window at the endless acres of green hills whispering rain-quenched secrets and broken apart by various gated horse farms. He does not answer my question. I guess he'll tell me in his time.

A large bay-colored horse runs free inside the four-foot stone wall that has probably been there since the Civil War.

"Going?" I ask again.

Not that it really matters to me, as the scenery is grand and serene, overflowing with stimuli and beauty. We cross over the deep and slow-dancing Harpeth River. I catch a glimpse of two old men sitting on rocks at the muddy bank. Their fishing poles are in the water, unattended. I have always thought of fishing as a good excuse to be lazy in the water and enjoy the simplicity of the day.

Exploring Tennessee, you get a feeling that in some pockets it is teetering on a bygone era, a time long gone when children could still play safely outside and Coke was something to drink, not snort.

Wow, I've lived in Los Angeles too long.

It's not a backward place like the stereotype developed in my Hollywood-affected, cynical, and highly medicated brain. It is not a place where bucktoothed, morbidly obese cousins get knocked up and hitched. Ironically, I, the city slicker, am the unwed pregnant one.

The Southern charm remains unpolluted by the modern, rude-mannered cruelty of the world. This part of America still has its historic charm and refuses to be changed by transient inhabitants.

I look in my rearview mirror at Michaela. "You good?"

"All good." She smiles, touching her dad's shoulder.

"Well," I say, sighing a little more than necessary. "There better be food at the end of this road."

"Oh, there's food, baby girl."

We come to a stop sign at Highway 96 and I wait for a half-dozen cars to pass before continuing straight on our journey.

"Halfway to nowheresville," he says, smiling, answering my grumbling stomach.

"You'd better not be teasing. Me and the baby, we're hungry. Starving! But enough about me," I say. "What's LeChelle up to today?"

"Girls got cheer practice, boys got soccer."

"No cheer for you?" I look back at Michaela.

"No ma'am. I'm strictly a basketball girl."

"She's going to Virginia on a ball scholarship," Tim says proudly.

"Nice." I look back again. "Well LeChelle's missin' out, but duty calls for her."

"Yes it does." He inhales and exhales deeply. "Love that woman of mine. Twenty-two years. Love her more today than the day we got married."

He exudes tenderness when he talks about his family, and particularly when he talks about LeChelle. It puts me at ease. Our relationship feels very brother-and-sister or, I suppose, if there is such a thing as a spiritual father, Tim would be mine. We have a platonic male-female relationship that would shame Harry from *When Harry Met Sally*. He's a far cry from the smarmy, married, Beverly Hills agent types who were always trying to work some angle with me.

I long for a Tim-and-LeChelle type of love with Burton. I know Burton has grown to love me, and I do care deeply for him, but their type of love requires a vulnerability on my part, and that scares me more than drowning in freezing water with no one to save me.

"So you really believe all that stuff in the Bible, don't you?"

"Yes, I do," he responds without missing a beat.

"Okay, what about Noah? You reeeeaaaally believe he got every type of animal on his ark?" I draw out my *really* to better emphasize my sarcasm.

He just sits there listening and smiling. I'm sure he's heard all of this skepticism before.

"Do you know how many species there are in the world?" I ask, then bellow: "A lot!"

"Noah? That's what you got from the church growing up?"

"Yes. Noah and his big party love-boat full of critters," I reply, mimicking the Southern dialect.

"Girl, you kill me," he says, laughing. But then soberly he adds, "You know they did find the ark on Mount Ararat in Eastern Turkey. It's a fact. Not some good story."

He's good. Real good.

Our split-lane highway approaches a little town and turns into what can only be described as an old-time main street. My eyes squint to make out the writing on a sizable gray antique sign: LEIPER'S FORK. I slow down to the 20-mph speed limit just long enough to read the date *1818* at the bottom of their welcome post.

The sign is set off to the side of the road in front of a red wooden barn. A fence separates several land plots. Hundred-year-old hickory trees rise out of thick grass, and green bushes stand at least ten feet tall. The fields are dotted with cylindrical, seven-foot bales of hay, about one every hundred yards. At the horizon, the green grass and the blue sky meet in a blurry line. It's pretty, but all I can think about when I see the hay is a giant baker rolling out dough to make biscuits. I'm so hungry.

We pass an A-frame log cabin. It's at least two centuries old and, according to the giant American flag draped across it, a historical residence of some kind. Hand-carved wooden and wicker chairs rock gently on the wraparound porch. It looks like the house from *Little House on the Prairie*. We drive past the log house and I see a yellow sign for Puckett's Grocery Store.

"Pull in there," Tim instructs.

Leiper's Fork looks more like a movie set on the back lot at Universal Studios than a real town. Stores line each side of the small street, which stretches about the length of four football fields. A raised wooden walkway right out of a John Wayne western connects the storefronts. At first glance it looks like a ghost town, but then I see that the storefronts are brimming with life. I see antique and art stores as well as the town's real estate agency and post office. To top it off, a vintage Ford police car from around 1940 is parked in front of the police station. It is black and white with one star on the driver's door and a single cherry light on the roof. American flags bookend the storefronts. I shake my head wishing I could call Clint Eastwood, as he'd really like this location to shoot his next flick.

We all head into Puckett's and a few of the farming locals look up from their lunches. The place doubles as the town diner. There's a plaque on the wall.

> Founded by the Puckett family in the 1950s, Puckett's serves as a country store to several communities in Williamson County. From fresh groceries and a good Southern meal, to a tank of gas and a place to catch up with friends, Puckett's is the cornerstone of the Leiper's Fork community.

I look behind the counter and see fresh buttermilk biscuits with sausage gravy and smokehouse bacon. I allow my mouth to water—my new blood pressure medicine is working and my diet is on hold for the day—and I am in food heaven. The chalkboard menu confirms what my nose already knows: they have country-fried steak and ham with creamy gravy, fried green tomatoes, grits, greens, fried okra, fried green beans, and fried pickles. The daily specials, written in loopy cursive, are pork tenderloin and catfish sandwiches. Folks don't come here for salads.

A smiling, lanky, six-foot-three kid wearing a bright-orange University of Tennessee T-shirt is working the counter. He grins at Michaela. She is truly so pretty. Then he looks at Tim and me and asks politely, "Y'all need some help?"

"Yes, I'll have the country-fried steak and some fried okra."

His Tennessee Volunteer college pride transports me away from the biscuits and back to my own college days.

January 1986: I am strutting across the Arizona State University campus wearing my Walkman. The Tears for Fears song "Everybody Wants to Rule the World" is cranked. I'm decked out in a pink Alpha Delta Pi sweatshirt, denim miniskirt, and plaid Sperry sneakers. My big, teased blond bangs—perfectly shaped from my round brush and sprayed into a barrel shape—bounce with every step. I resemble all of the other girls on sorority row—well, at least on the outside. In reality, I am baked from the roach that I finished while walking over the bridge from my sorority floor to campus. The Arizona sun is warming my face as the pot is softening my reality and I feel wonderfully happy.

I make my way into the student union just before my first class at eleven o'clock. Not too early, not too late. I fill a glass with crushed ice and Diet Coke at the soda fountain. I take a long gulp from the straw to moisten my cotton mouth as I pull up a metal chair in an already crowded student television area. I have enough time to watch the Space Shuttle *Challenger* take off. The space shuttle, a warm winter day, a buzz on, and the caffeine kicking in. Who could ask for more?

My Walkman is still playing in my ears as I watch the shuttle climb into the sky. How killer would it be to be seated on top of that rocket thrusting its way into orbit? I pull my Walkman earphones down as I see Tina, one of my new sorority friends, approaching. I take my eyes off of the television for a split second to see her eyes widen in horror at the TV. My eyes flit back to the TV as the *Challenger* explodes into a fireball.

My very first thought is *run*. Blood rushes from my toes to my heart. My hand instinctively covers my mouth as my entire body reacts to the horror. Stunned students look around at each other wondering if what we are watching is really happening. Tina staggers over to me as if searching for consolation, but I am not equipped to manage my own disbelief or pain, let alone hers.

Shock. Carnage. Death. It has followed me. I keep running but I can't escape it. There are no places far enough from pain.

"Oh my . . ." Tina touches my shoulder without finishing the exclamation.

I look at her. I want to scream, *Get away from me!*

"Those poor people," she says softly.

My eyes never leave the television as I stand up. My legs feel like Red Vines licorice. "I'll be right back," I say to her and rush to the bathroom, where I kick open a stall door and hurl all of my Diet Coke into the toilet.

For the next three days, the news coverage of the shuttle disaster is constant. To keep up with the coverage, I am running a pain-free, cocaine-hallucinogenics-and-weed-fueled marathon of sheer denial. I fix my bangs in the mirror of my sorority room bathroom, lean down, snort a big white line off the sink, shake my head, and feel . . . good.

On my way out the door of our sorority heading to a Sigma Nu party, I see a group of my sisters watching the replay for the umpteenth time on our forty-two-inch community television. I want to tell them to look away, run away. I want to remind them the shuttle tragedy is not their tragedy. I want to tell them that it is Saturday night and they should be going out and having fun because one day the bull's-eye will be on their backs and that day is not today. I want to lace each one of their water bottles with a hit of happy LSD or something to alter their minds. But I say nothing.

I stop long enough to catch part of an interview with who I think must be the wife of one of the shuttle's crew members. "I imagine him relaxed and taking control and then—" she says, her face ashen and eyes puffy. She's trying so hard to keep it together, but she can't hold back a new batch of tears.

It's all too much of a pain reminder. *Run away, Alice. Run away.* I hear a voice in my head that isn't my own. How dare she dump her suffering on me? I've been quietly trying to fill the dark cavern of my own pain with drugs and boys for years. Why can't she? I should send her a care package of X and a couple rolled ones. Although I am sure her NASA doctors are writing prescriptions for her as I head out the door.

Annoying. Two years without any real drama. Just an easy, graphic bong street, fairly anonymous, average college existence.

I walk away, choosing not to partake in the aftermath. Tina catches up with me. She thinks I am emotionally shut down thanks to the tragic car accident that my country-club parents had my senior year in high school. I told the story so well during my pledge class interviews that I should have won an Oscar. My sorority sisters know just enough to be at ease with me and yet allow me to keep a safe Heisman distance from them.

The truth of my story and grief is more horrible than any tale I could make up. Why would I tell them? Why should I warn them? At some point in their lives they themselves will be blindside tackled and heart-stained from the fire hose of life.

The hit of Ecstasy I took hits me—finally!—while Tina and I are walking to the Sigma Nu house. I feel a warm wave of temporary safety. I can feel my hair follicles growing from my scalp. Ahhh. The familiar sensation of nothingness and pharmaceutical merriment. Thank God for good drugs.

A bonus is my male medication du jour, Derrick McGrath. Thank God—also—for lonely boys. Once at the party, I beeline for his room. We make out in his top bunk. I allow him to grope me while I look out his window into the pool courtyard. He gently touches my back, causing me to flinch in disgust at my own easiness. Despite Derrick telling me that I am pretty, even after a couple beers and a second tab of Ecstasy I can't shake the familiar dread of the shuttle families left in their onslaught of anguish. I can't sex or drug myself enough not to feel the wallop of the horror hammer. Their cries are chasing my reality.

I hop off the bed to get a better look out his courtyard window. Derrick follows me out onto the three-foot window ledge. The moonlight glistens on the pool's surface. We are three stories up. We both look around at the party going on below. Near the diving board, friends of ours are dancing to "West End Girls" by the Pet Shop Boys. My ears fill with the white noise of laughing and singing and talking and my blood rushing in my head. I put my hands over my ears as I slightly push from the balls of my feet off the ledge and into the air. It's all too quick for Derrick to sense what was coming—let alone even to grab hold of me.

I wasn't aiming for the water but I made it halfway in the pool anyway. I don't remember my head and arm clipping the cement lip of the pool deck before I rolled into the water, but I can see a red liquid mushrooming in delicate columns in the water above me, obscuring the horrified faces looking down at me under the water.

I want to remain submerged under the moonlit chlorine liquid and get washed clean, like the whites in the Whirlpool bleach cycle.

I snap back to the church in real time to see Tim stepping away from the pulpit and walking along the stage before stopping to face the crowd. He is still going on about women. "Since y'all know how important women of faith were to Jesus, today we're going to talk about how to be a faithful mother on Mother's Day. I'm sure all y'all mommas out there are going to get some nice cards and maybe some candy. But I know what you really want is some quiet"—he pauses for effect—"and someone to do the dishes and fold and put away the laundry."

"Amen!" shouts the lady next to me.

"And y'all deserve it," he continues. "Our mothers are the most precious, influential people in our lives. Y'all know what NFL players say into the camera after they make a touchdown?"

As if rehearsed, we all shout in unison: "Hi, Mom!"

He laughs and waves for a camera that isn't there. Then he continues: "But a lot of the time mothers don't get appreciated or they get blamed for being imperfect, or even worse, they get blamed when we, their children, are not perfect." Tim says this with a little hiccup in his step, like someone karate-chopped the backsides of his knees.

He makes me smile as I rub my swollen belly.

"Today, let me let y'all in on a little secret. If you want to be a good, faithful mother—or father, for that matter—teach your children about Jesus. Because at some point, your kids, say around sixteen years old, are going to turn on you."

Again, there is the sound of amusement from the audience.

"All y'all folks with teenagers out there know what I'm talkin' 'bout. They're going to lose their way. They won't think they need your guidance anymore. They will feel pressure to drink, do some dope, have sex, abandon their babies, steal a car, or take their own life. These things will take over and become far more important than y'all, their parents."

He's so right.

"You're gonna get moved out of the driver's seat of relevancy, and the enemy of this world, the prince of pride, ego, self, fear, pain, and insecurity is gonna be behind their wheel." He walks back to the podium. "In Proverbs 22:6 it says, 'Train your child in the way he should go and when he is old he will not turn from it.'" He glances at his notes and looks up, right at me. "So let's be real: if you want to be, or think that you already are, a good momma— and you might be—the only hope that can save your child, love your child, the only hope that can change your child, heal your child, rescue your child, forgive your child, or sometimes slap your child upside the head is faith. Faith in Jesus!"

Is he talking about me? Is he talking to me? Is he talking about me raising my baby? It's all blending together. Watching Tim, I can't help but wonder now what the 1990s would have been like if a higher power had been driving my eighteen-wheeler of escapism, denial, and crazy-making. If faith had been my strength and refuge, would I have needed so many late-night, half-naked bong sessions? I'm sure it wouldn't have been half as much fun if Jesus had been driving my bus.

But looking back now, I paid for it. The cost of my rebellion, my rejection of God, of everyone, even myself, was so high. All of the self-induced body-slam episodes like the one on the side of the Sigma Nu pool might have been avoided. Emergency-room doctors informed me after that warm night in the pool that I had been lucky to survive.

Tim would have me believe it wasn't luck at all. He would have me believe that there was someone watching over me and keeping me safe from myself in those days. That someone cared more about me than I cared for myself.

I can't silence the sad and ashamed voice inside of me. As much as I hate to admit it, it's true. I was scared and ashamed. I am still sad and ashamed.

But piercing my humiliation is a splinter of faith. It irritates my soul constantly, prodding me to believe. Refusing to abandon me despite my destructive habits, it made sure I never completely gave up.

It is this splinter that keeps me in this pew.

12

The Show

Part III

This issue of faith gnaws at me as Tim walks down onto the first step of three toward the audience, his eyes scanning the room. "Let's focus on three quick points of motherhood," he says. "The first is realizing that being a good momma who teaches her babies about having faith in God ain't always easy."

My faith in God or whatever was left of God was tested for the second time after college. I drift back in my mind to that time long ago when the economy was booming and the first George Bush was president of the United States.

Summer 1989: I move to New York right after my last college exam. Instead of seeing all the proud mommas and poppas at the

Arizona State University cap-and-gown ceremony, I opt to take the first nonstop flight to New York City.

I remember small travel escapades out of Arizona as a child. I know there were summers when my parents would take me to Coronado Island in California, but it is difficult to recount any intimate details like the feeling of the sand on my feet or the power of ocean waves or the look of the hotels. I can tell you this: getting out of Arizona was my plan since the day my mother died. That I can remember. I had escaped Tucson, and now it is time to leave Phoenix behind, too.

The only person I know in New York is my sorority sister Tina Mortney. She graduated a semester before me and is back in her hometown. She is going to pick me up at the John F. Kennedy airport. I am not sure exactly how this is going to work, but I play it off as if I do.

Descending the escalator toward baggage claim, I see a man dressed in a black suit and white tie. He looks to be New Yorker-ish and in his late sixties. He's holding a sign that says FERGUSON.

I look around at the crowd, thinking surely there has to be another Ferguson. The man approaches me and, looking me directly in the eye, says, "You must be Miss Ferguson." He smiles. "Miss Mortney said you'd be surprised."

"I am, I guess."

He looks at me from head to toe. "First time in New York?"

"Yep."

"Well, kid, welcome to the Big Apple. I'm Louie." He takes my bag.

"Nice to meet you, Louie. Call me Alice."

"I like that name. Had a pretty neighbor named Alice when I was growing up." He sounds the way I imagine a Mafia man would sound. "Okay, Alice, let's get your bags."

It's his turn to be surprised when, curbside at the car, I climb into the front seat. How was I supposed to know to get in the back?

Tina has given me a three-week window to stay with her at her parents' place. The idea is that this will give me enough time to find a job and a place of my own. I found out on the way here, after submitting over forty-six resumes, that I have landed a limited-income intern position at *Newsweek* magazine, so I can check that item off my list. With my journalism degree and an inherited gene to seek and tell about the injustices of the world, it seems a perfect fit for starting my career.

Miss Mortney, my weed-smoking buddy and former sorority sister, has gone to work at her father's biopharmaceutical company. It went public in the early eighties and made their family a small pile of cash. That small pile coupled with the massive pile the previous five generations had left meant she was rich, rich, rich. A rich I have never experienced. We could not be more opposite on the economy scale. She doesn't need to work and yet she has chosen to work for her dad. This is something I can't understand and have no intention of learning. She can do anything she wants. Why this?

She could be living her dream, whatever that is, but instead she's allowed her parents to groom her to take over the boring family business when she reaches the ripe age of thirty years old. She's in the lucky end of the sperm pool and she chooses to stand on the steps and barely dip her toes in the water! Why does she choose to wade when she could dive in the deep end and discover greatness and see where the tide takes her?

For now she is answering phones and learning the marketing with some creepy doctor who hits on her. It's beyond me. Her sheltered life irks the heck out of me. I mean, I like her—don't get me wrong. I just think all of it is soft and predictable.

Tina stands outside her building, smoking a clove cigarette

with her curbside doorman, as we pull up. "Welcome to Fantasy Island," she says with all of her size-zero, five-foot-three, designer-clad persona. She swings her shoulder-length, thick, dark hair around, which makes her six-stranded pearl-and-diamond Agatha jewelry jingle around her neck.

I get out of the car and give her an air kiss on each cheek. "Well, this sure isn't Arizona." I look at the buildings on Park Avenue and 53rd Street.

"Pete, will you grab her bags, please?"

"Sure thing, Miss Mortney." Pete tosses his cigarette into the gutter.

I turn around and look at Louie and Pete watching us go. No doubt checking out our young booties. "Hey, Louie—thanks for the ride."

He looks surprised that I've remembered his name. "Sure thing, kid."

I turn and catch up to Tina. "Miss Mortney, aren't you special?" I laugh as we walk into the lobby past security and into the elevator.

"Don't let the fourteen-karat bull fool you." She smirks. "But I do have good news. My *mother*"—she makes it sound regal—"has a friend who is a vice president or something for the Ford Modeling Agency and owns a bar called Live Bait downtown. It rocks. Anyway, they're opening a spin-off bar for the summer in Southampton, where we have a little vacation retreat—"

"Oh, I'm sure it's real little," I say sarcastically as we get into the elevator.

"Anyway, she totally hooked you up there to bartend, as they need hot chicks and I told her you were hot."

"So you lied."

"Sorta." She laughs.

I've been here two hours and I am already a publishing intern by day and a bartender by night. I have officially gotten the heck out of Arizona, and like Weezy on *The Jeffersons,* I'm movin' on up!

The elevator opens onto the swanky, palatial pad and gives me the view of their overtly opulent home. I am introduced to the full-time staff of dish, laundry, cooking, and cleaning fairies. The spread has a formal dining room, living room, media room, family room, huge kitchen, and at least six bedrooms. Four of which I never dare to enter. Their apartment takes up the entire sixth floor of the posh building. There are fancy paintings and marble statues of naked babies around every corner. Plush velvet sofas are particularly placed on large Oriental rugs. (They look soft but are itchy. I know this because, missing the familiarity of my torn La-Z-Boy, I sat down on one.) It's a little ornate for my taste.

As we relax on the balcony outside Tina's bedroom, listening to the horns honking and watching the people bustling on Park Avenue, we share a joint and smoke cigarettes. I think, *Self . . . let's be honest. I can understand why she would want to move home with her parents after college. I'm moving in with them for three weeks, but I wish it could be forever. I feel grateful. Grateful for the hospitality and grateful for a glimpse of a life I want.*

I had no idea that she, or anyone for that matter, really lived this beyond-measure way. I am in awe and work hard to keep my cool but, I will tell you, I have more in common with Maria, their sixty-five-year-old housekeeper, than anyone in Tina's family tree. I often find myself helping Maria fold towels and sheets in their laundry room. While I sit on top of the dryer, Maria tells me about life in Brooklyn with her husband. How she raised their children and they are off to college. How love and God and hard work are the keys to happiness—not fancy paintings in empty palaces. She always manages to smile at me when no one is looking at her. Or perhaps I am the only one looking. Yesterday she hugged me in the kitchen. I mean a big, long, clumsy squeeze—she said I needed it in her El Salvadorian accent.

Bartending at Live Bait is my first taste of real cash. I can easily rake in two hundred tax-free dollars on a good night. With my skintight, white, scoop-necked bodysuit, tight 501 button-fly jean cutoffs, Phoenix Cardinals ball cap, and cowboy boots, my nickname has quickly become *Arizona*.

A lot of B-list models are working at the bar for the summer in between gigs. I'm not the model type—I might be the only one there under five foot seven—and I'm further set apart from these uptown girls by my Western roots. The New Yorkers I meet are fascinated with the West. They see me as one of a bunch of cowgirls with fresh faces. I don't feel fresh and I'm certainly not ropin' calves in my free time. It couldn't be further from the truth, but once again I find myself morphing my brand to suit my audience in the skyscraper jungle. I become the tan, partying cowgirl from a small, dusty, desert town who is just trying to make her way in the Big Apple. Another character. Another storyline. With Tina and company, I'm like Charlie in *Charlie and the Chocolate Factory* holding my golden candy-bar wrapper. *Yee-haw! Let the games begin!*

Our entire bartending and waitressing team is made up of women. We attract waves of Wall Street types who, with their fancy suits and slicked-back hair, their beach houses and BMWs, indiscriminately throw twenty-dollar tips at us. It rains money in the bar just like it must rain money on the trading floor.

My after-work routine preys upon my customers' excesses. Most mornings around three o'clock I quietly walk the white sand along the Atlantic and sneak uninvited into a pool house on a not-so-secure compound on First Neck Lane and sleep on the couch. I refuse to put my hard-earned cash back into the already-bloated local economy, so I steal my shut-eye and a shower before my unwitting hosts get up. When I am done, I rearrange the pool towels, pillows, and rugs so that the maids won't suspect as much as a mouse has been there. Not that anyone with billions in their bras pays attention to their pool houses. When I am too tired to hunt down a crash pad, I go home with some preppy-type guy who shares a two-bedroom beach house with six other wannabe Gordon Gekkos for the summer months.

At dawn, there's always enough coke, pot, and various pill bottles left lying around that I help myself to a treat for later. It's all too easy.

I pull in a little extra cash bartending at the occasional high-dollar fund-raiser under big circus tents at the polo matches attended by the white-trouser-and-silly-pink-knit-top–clad, apple-martini–spilling native inhabitants of this exotic island.

Life in the Hamptons is ecstatic and blissful, but I am always aware I am not one of them. I am a grifter on the lam from my own life. I am the short con trying to go legit. I survive by sucking the fat off the meaty bones they carelessly dispose of and stashing hors d'oeuvres and white-chocolate-chip cookies in my backpack to eat at bedtime. There is such excess. Such waste. No worries. No cares. No bills. No death. No lies. No real pain.

A synthetic-laden, chemically induced jumpy house, it is perfect for my transitory existence. Nothing about this summer seems tangible, which makes it perfect.

My internship at *Newsweek* starts at nine o'clock. I am lucky to have it. The exposure to deadlines and people who care about world issues reignites the fire in my belly that my mother planted there long ago with a hairline fracture of heart faith. Another time capsule.

On weekend nights when I don't illegally crash in rich people's beach houses, I visit my apartment in Harlem. I pick up coffees at the diner on the corner for the third-generation, gray-haired dudes on my stoop. I love to listen to their old-school stories of Billie Holiday and Dizzy. They are like my secret backstage pass to history. The cup of Joe I bring them is the modest price of admission, even though they would probably tell me their stories for a smile.

My studio is on the top floor of a five-story dilapidated brownstone. There's a shower in my bathroom, which is located in the kitchen. The arrangement is convenient for washing Top Ramen out of coffee mugs while I shave my legs.

Memorial Day 1990: Opening weekend of beach season. Almost a year has passed of slaving and saving since I moved to New York. I have worked my butt off to pay for my apartment, and despite its being a world away from my first taste of the city in Tina's parents' home, I am more and more convinced that I will attain their lavishness and wealth and that this apartment, coupled with more hard work and the right connections, is just one step along the way. I am more determined than ever to become an active participant in their world, not an outlier who admires their Park Avenue lives with my nose pressed against the window glass.

The first time I see James in person is during this, my second summer in Southampton. His sun-kissed skin, short blond curls, and blue eyes catch my attention. I am dancing on the bar at Live Bait pouring shots into some drunken patron's overflowing mouth. I can tell James is trying very hard not to look directly at my breasts, which are confidently pushed up in a navy underwire bra and barely covered by a Pink Floyd T-shirt with the sleeves cut off.

"I think this is love at first sight," he says the next morning in between kisses. We are rolling on the sand as the sun comes up over the Atlantic.

But it isn't first sight. I know exactly who he is. I know that he has the perfect family, history, and bank account.

I knew who James was long before I poured him a Dewar's on the rocks. His father is the publisher at *Newsweek,* where I have been quickly promoted to an assistant copy desk editor after ten months of kissing butt and making binders. I know everything about their connections in the publishing world, which is where I believe I am destined to make my own fortune. I know they are Irish Catholics and still that doesn't shake me. I know they are my inroad to old New York money. They are a family of Irish immigrants who have made good. Really good. Their grandparents were what I am now: a dirty pebble tossed by the surf against the rocks over and over again, taunted by the shore of shiny emeralds just out of reach.

James, so I believe, is my future. He holds a front-of-the-line, lifetime ticket on the social roller coaster of upscale Manhattan. His glitter can fill in the cracks in my tarnished secondhand Ann Taylor armor. We mingle at parties at the Met and on the Upper East Side. We easily slide in the side doors and VIP entrances to restaurants that have no names. He has introduced me to the private lives of Manhattan's boldfaced names: John F. Kennedy Jr. and Daryl Hannah; Ralph Lauren's son Andrew; and Alexis Stewart, Martha's daughter. He knows the Trumps and Astors and Hiltons. He even knows Tina's family.

In September, James takes me to Flushing Meadows in Queens to sit center court, second row, and watch Stefan Edberg defeat Jim Courier in Edberg's first US Open title. I don't like tennis or understand it, but I did understand that it was special to be in those seats. Very, very special.

"You like the seats?" He smiles at me, clearly realizing I've never sat front row at anything other than the DMV.

I run my fingers through the hair on the back of his head and kiss him instead of answering. He seems satisfied with my response.

I meet James's father and mother at a private memorial for their friend Robert Maxwell. I get the sense that his parents' outspoken workingman views have intimidated James's previous crushes. Not shockingly then, his father likes me. "She's scrappy. A hard worker, I hear," he says with a wink for the forty-five seconds that James has captured his attention. "Not the spoiled, social-climbing debutantes that seem to be attracted to you like static electricity."

James squeezes my hand: he's proud of his father's appraisal of me but exasperated that his father is so dismissive of him.

Apparently their friend Maxwell, another international publishing billionaire, fell off his yacht and drowned. Funeral guests are gossiping: "Was it murder or suicide?" they say. "What *really* happened?" The questions remind me of my father, but the circumstances couldn't be more different. Why would a man with apparently everything that he or I could ever want volunteer to float like a champagne cork in the Atlantic? Ridiculous!

That night I watch James staring out his window onto Central Park. I know he is lost. The look in his eyes is the look of a jumper. I know it all too well.

"Hey," I whisper.

He turns around, unaware I am still awake. He just stands there. I wrap a sheet around my naked body and come up behind him, enclosing him in my white cotton cocoon. "Don't let it bother you."

"He's an idiot. He's been a dismissive idiot my whole life," he says.

"But you're not," I remind him.

"But I'm destined to be. I'm trapped by all of it."

"No, you're not," I say, wanting to share my hidden secrets on how to run—but maybe running is only for anonymous people, not people who grace the society pages. "You can be different. You are different."

"I wish that were true." He kisses me and walks away into his bathroom and I hear him call out, "You want something to help you sleep?"

Even the rich people medicate their problems away. Even the rich.

"Sure." Brokenness attracts brokenness.

Time is passing quickly since James and I kissed on that beach outside Southampton Beach Club. One year has turned into two and another summer has turned to fall.

November 1992: We are on our way back to the city from Bear Mountain. Our journey across the George Washington Bridge high above the Hudson River was my first road trip to the United States Military Academy in West Point. James has a cabin tucked deep in the thicket of yellow, orange, and red leaves dripping off aspens, oaks, and hickory trees behind Lookout Inn. The views are spectacular across all of Westchester County. It is a faraway scream from the overflowing polka-dot bikinis of Southampton and the hairy gorillas swinging from steel building to steel building in Manhattan.

It was a romantic, crazy, intoxicated weekend. James is as screwed up as I am. We are quite a fragmented pair drawn together trying to complete each other. When we fall short of being one another's glue, we put a line of blow or a bag of weed in our little seams so we're wasted enough not to notice.

Kate Bush's new album, *The Red Shoes,* is blasting from the

Blaupunkt in James's vintage 1966 cream Mercedes convertible with tan leather seats. The cool open air mixes with her classic soprano voice that can both lullaby you like a soft blanket and cut you like a sharp razor. As the scenery passes I listen to the lyrics . . .

I don't know if I'm closer to heaven but
It looks like hell down there.

The easiness of the weekend blends with the song lingering in my head as James and I make our bed in his apartment on 76th overlooking Central Park West. I've moved out of the Harlem walk-up and straight into my predetermined life plan. It is all coming to fruition, and it isn't until the chilling winds along the Hudson blow the last of the leaves off the Central Park tree branches to lie brown on the crisp ground that life begins to spiral very close to the edge. The orange, yellow, and red brilliance is wiped away by another color: blue.

The icy-cold blue of a positive cross on a home pregnancy test.

Wasn't this what I wanted? Living with James and carrying his child? I would be forever tethered to him and living the kind of life I dreamed of when I lived in a crummy apartment in Tucson. I'd have a private elevator to the executive floors at *Newsweek*. Why then does this baby-bomb scare me more than the serial killer running around Brooklyn?

A baby! A baby. A baby?

The cramping caused by the baby currently in my belly brings me out of my foggy New York nostalgia.

Pastor Tim's booming voice broadcasts to the room: "The second thing is, stop blaming yo' momma for yo' problems. You're a grown-up now. If yo' momma teaches you about faith in Jesus and you stop believing, whose fault is that? Sure ain't your momma's."

My mom had planted faith in me but life sucked most of it out. As for the faith that remained, I did everything I could to destroy it.

Easter 2005: I spend the day on the couch. Curled up on my left side, doctor's orders. So Burton and I have to miss out on Easter brunch with his family. I love that my unborn child is in cahoots with me already, conveniently helping me avoid unnecessary contact with my sister-in-law.

"Hey, how are you feeling?" Burton is in the kitchen following Dr. Schlossberg's orders and making us the worst-tasting food I've ever eaten. It turns out that without fat and salt, most things taste like cardboard. "I have something for you." He comes into the family room wearing big floppy rabbit ears.

There are at least seven cars at the bottom of Tim and LeChelle's driveway. I can only imagine what they've got cooking over there.

"Very nice." I can't help but smile at his attempt to make me feel happy. We have grown to be more than friends, or roommates, or engaged; we are clearly lovers and bordering on real intimacy. "Did I mention how happy I am *not* to be at brunch with your family? I am a mean-spirited old pregnant lady."

"Your honesty is one of your many charms." He squints at me. "Did I tell you how happy I am to have you as my excuse not to go?" He sits on the coffee table next to me and looks at my plate on a tray. "It's terrible, isn't it?"

"It's not terrible. It's just not fair. The rest of the world is eating chocolate bunnies and macaroni and cheese and honey-baked hams."

"You're so right," he commiserates. Then his face brightens. "Why do we both have to go without? I'll be right back; I'm going over to Tim's to steal some pie."

"That is so rude!"

Burton is funny, cute, and sexy. If I weren't so fat and in danger of crossing the line from high blood pressure to a full-blown stroke, I would order up some hot loving in appreciation of his little joke.

He pulls the table closer to the couch and puts the blood pressure sleeve on my arm. "Really, you okay?" His humorous boy-toy voice is gone. He's in serious doctor mode now. "Headache gone?"

I can't help but marvel at him. He's really concerned about me. Where does his genuineness come from? Maybe if I stare at him and his goodness long enough, I'll be able to see the answer.

The cuff finally stops squeezing and releases. "Normal," he says as his furrowed brow relaxes with relief.

"That's relative." I smirk.

"As your doctor, I am pleased to see that you have been a good girl. As a reward, I will go and get you one large bite of pun'kin pie."

"It's *pumpkin*," I correct him, carefully pronouncing the *m* and the second *p*.

"Not in the South it isn't. It's *pun'kin*, as in: 'Ooh-whee, sakes alive, you're one hot pun'kin.'" Burton leans down to kiss me. "One bite. Maybe. *If* you stay on this couch and *off* your computer. Do not let me catch you on your website. No working. Seriously."

Lying there I hear the door shut as Burton heads next door. When I'm alone again, my mind drifts to New York. It was the only other time that I had quit working. It was also the only other time that I had a baby in my belly.

December 1992: My poor New York publishing heir doesn't know I am plotting my exit strategy. James doesn't know about the four-week-old peanut growing inside of me. He doesn't know that I am about to destroy the beautiful something we have created together. He doesn't know that my hormones are chasing my fear around in my head like inline skaters during a never-ending race.

This whole unborn-baby thing is seriously freaking me out. But why is my freaking out different this time? Freaked-out chaos is my normal. I usually ride its choppy waves with ease. Why not now? I could stay here and he would never know. With the evidence destroyed, I am in the free and clear, but something has me itching to run.

I stand in our bathroom looking at my reflection, wanting to slap myself for being so stupid, so careless. I slide the palm of my hand over the smooth, cool granite countertop thinking it deserves to be here more than I do. I stare at myself knowing that at some point, after too much wine, too many truth-pills, I will tell James the truth. I will try to ease my own burden by pouring my pain into his cup and making him consume it with me.

I have no choice other than to leave. Leave before he kicks me to the curb. Leave before he sees through my facade. Leave before I make him an unwitting coconspirator.

As much as I love James's gold-and-silver-lined life of plenty, and our combined crazy, the thought of being stuck until I finally cave in is worse than walking—running—away. It is my punishment. I don't deserve any of this lavish life. I don't deserve him.

I'm a female Jason Bourne, constantly scanning the room for the exits. I'd rather risk the agony of drowning myself now than the pain I'd feel if he woke up one day, discovered the real me, and didn't like her. The version of me I have presented him with is so manufactured, so postured, I don't even know who the *me* is that he is in love with. I know my lies are going to catch up with me at some point, and I'd rather not be around for the meeting. This time, the consequences are just too great.

With my escape route documented and my parting words rehearsed, I slide into my getaway car—a taxi with ripped, leather, beer-scented seats—on 81st Street and put my plan into motion. It is time. There is no going back. All I can think is, *Please don't let some poor, pathetic, crying, regretful girl be in the waiting room with me.*

Step 1 is familiar. Today, as I had done back in Tucson with the remnants of my parents' apartment, I am getting rid of the evidence. Climbing out of the taxi, I hand the guy a twenty and tell him to keep the change. I tip him generously in return for his smile and no judgment.

The lobby of Manhattan Women's Clinic is filled with ladies from all walks of life. It seems there's a representative from every possible ethnicity and age filling out medical forms on clipboards. I try not to look any of them in the eye. The gum-chomping twenty-year-old behind the counter hands me a stack of paperwork and sends me to my seat.

Per the plan, I have a Vicodin in my pocket with me. I break it in half and chew one of the pieces, swallowing it with my saliva. It will help me deal with the benignity of the waiting room and will keep me unruffled and collected on my methodical walk to the locker-filled changing room.

Once my name is called and I am placed in an examination room, I hop up on the table and scoot into position. My bare bottom tugs at the paper covering the procedure table. The milquetoast doctor, who looks to be in his midsixties, is wearing a white lab coat and bifocals. He begins with a series of meaningless questions: "Other terminations?" "No." "Drug use?" "No"—of course I lie. "Pregnancy?" "About 4.5 weeks." He's done this over and over for at least three decades. I am no different from the girl before me and the girl who will follow me. I want to ask him if he delivers babies too but he doesn't seem one for small talk, and I'm not really in the mood for conversation so much as distraction. At this moment I need him and I'm happy to not be in some back alley with a coat hanger.

The nurse turns on a machine that makes a humming, sucking noise. My legs tighten nervously in response. Undeterred, the nurse pries my knees apart and places them in the cold metal stirrups. A sheet covers my belly and lower half.

I begin to sob.

I'm crying, not from pain, but from regret. The total shame that stinks on me like rotten milk. It is coursing through my veins and punching me in the gut.

Before the doctor begins the procedure, the nurse confirms with me: "Are you sure you want to do this?" I nod, unable to fully stop crying and speak the word. And then it occurs to me: I am the crying girl at the clinic today. I am *that* girl. How annoying and pathetic! My regret deepens.

I think I am so tough. That it is my right to choose. My body.

I am not ready to be a mother. I am barely hanging on to my sanity. Nobody wants a fat, pregnant lady behind the bar or, better yet, running a company. Once James finds out who I really am, I'll be kicked to the curb like a stray dog found in the pantry looking for scraps.

I am not going back to Safeway in some Arizona stinkhole. I have a career to conquer. I have big dreams, and having a child isn't a part of them no matter the surname that comes with it. I know where this road ends. I've seen it too many times.

In the recovery room, I'm given Valium. I take it along with the other half of the Vicodin that was still in my pocket from earlier. I have a heating pad on my pelvis, and I am impatiently waiting for the high to take away my feeling of being smashed in half. I have a vision of myself demolishing all of Moses' tablets. With "Thou shalt not kill" checked off the list, I realize I have broken the last commandment I had to break. Hurrah! It's a matching set!

James has gone to Paris with his father, so the fact that I spend the night on our couch in a fetal position goes unnoticed. I don't have the courage to sleep in our bed because of the betrayal that has taken place. There is no sidestepping that I have eliminated his child without ever giving him a vote.

I have chosen to destroy my own child. Our child. There is no way to ever tell him. Honestly, I don't even kill bugs on the sidewalk, I step over them. I'm not political and I've always advocated my womanly right to do whatever I want with my own body. But it wasn't my body.

Truthfully, I don't care about activists or rights or morality now. The cellular or embryonic debate of where and when life starts doesn't matter. All that I am acutely aware of in my own world is the consequence of my shame: I paid someone to execute my child and no one, no excuse, no bill, no social worker, no priest can make me clean from that feeling. According to my own heart, I have slaughtered a piece of me today. A piece of James. A piece of possibility that will never come to its potential, and there is no way to ever, ever tell the truth about it.

I am overwhelmed by a heartbreaking loneliness. It is par for the course with this type of life choice. My very own choice. I want to own it, I want to be strong, but for the second time in my life, I find myself calling out. I call out to my mother, to God, to whatever could pull me out of the guilt quicksand I have willingly jumped into. I sob and beg and cry out in true gut-wrenching sorrow and remorse. Sunken, I need a small ounce of security. Where life and promise had once grown within me, hurt and humiliation are now growing. I am sinking in my own doing!

Aching with wretchedness, I close my eyes and imagine warm arms around me, rocking me. I imagine them soothing me, rescuing me, and most of all, forgiving me.

And again, as it had in my mother's bedroom years before, It comes to me. It isn't my imagination: I am being held. Some invisible source of safety and love has come to envelop me and rock me, like a child, into a deep, deep sleep.

When I awake I realize that my plan is too far in motion to turn back. When I wake up the second morning in a row to dried tears on my cheeks, I do it. Once again, I run.

I decide immediately to abandon Step 2—which was to wait for James to come home from his trip and break up with him in person—in favor of running away without explanation. I see an open window and I go for it. This situation sucks enough already. I feel I owe him the respect to at least get out and not lie.

I can't shake running. I run because I am good at it. It is the only thing I am good at. I've been running since the day my mother died. I ran from the past; from myself; from Scott, my high-school love; and now I am running from James. Running from the truth.

James doesn't know me, he doesn't know my secrets, and this way, he never will. I flee New York just shy of three years after I got there.

I convince myself I am making a career move, that I won't be happy unless I make my own money and create my own security. I have been offered a job in Los Angeles. There is a new start waiting for me in sunny Southern California at the *National Celebrity News* magazine on Hollywood Boulevard.

If I stayed in New York, I would be anchored by a baby and tethered to James for support. I decide I cannot be dependent on anyone. A man will not be my answer: I am my own answer. The possibilities ahead of me are way better than the realities I am leaving behind.

* * *

"**I come bearing pun'kin pie!**" Tim is standing in front of me, proudly holding a tray with a plated piece of pie, a fork, and a napkin. Behind him, LeChelle and Burton, who is still wearing his bunny ears, head into Burton's home office. Was I asleep?

"Baby girl, you okay?" he asks quietly.

Just then I realize the memories of New York are streaming down my face. Embarrassed, I quickly wipe my tears away and straighten up. "I'm fine," I say. Remorse and regret are still churning around me.

"You ain't fine. You want me to get Burton"—he sets the tray down on the table—"because LeChelle's got him looking at a mole on her arm."

"Can I ask you a question?" I gesture for him to sit down on the table.

"Sure." He picks up the napkin and hands it to me as I pick up the fork. "Not too much, now. Doctor's orders."

"What if I don't have any faith left?" I look down. "I mean, there's so much stuff I've done . . ." I try to swallow the lump in my throat. "What if I am hopeless?"

He doesn't say anything, so I continue.

"How could God ever forgive me when I don't even forgive myself?"

And there it is.

I have chosen not to believe in God or live God's ways because I'm too far gone. I'm a lost cause. Why pursue something you know you can't have?

"The fact that you are in emotional pain means you know that sin, that stuff you think is so bad, brings pain. So let's start there," Tim says, speaking sympathetically and with certainty.

"Okay, yes. I accept that I feel guilty for stuff I've done." I sheepishly look at the pie, hoping that by averting my eyes, Tim won't be able to see my demons, skeletons, and other bad decisions.

"You *are* hopeless," he says, shocking me, "on your own."

Indignant, I wave my arm around the room, encircling my belly, a photo of Burton, the house, and him. "I'm clearly not alone," I snort.

"Are you willing to be open to the possibility that something outside of yourself can actually give you a different way forward? That just maybe doing it your way might not be the best way? Are you willing to consider that you could be wrong?"

I know my way isn't working. Look at me. I'm a hot mess full of intoxicated, wasted life choices. "Sure. I mean, I'm obviously not in the perfect condition to debate my circumstances. We both know how I got here. I'm just not sure I have the faith, or I believe—"

He shakes his head, saying, "Girl, you got plenty of faith. Faith isn't your issue. The object of faith is your issue. What you believe is how you live your life right now. How you been livin' your life. Make no mistakes, you have very strong faith. But what you have faith *in* has not helped you."

I'm not sure how to counter this. He's right. I want to argue and fight and take a stand on believing in what I have built myself, but he's right. Even with all the stuff I've done and the bravado I've accumulated, I'm still broken. I make James Frey's *A Million Little Pieces* look like an easy afternoon puzzle project.

"The God who made you took the punishment you deserve and put it on His Son, who was so undeserving of it. But He is willing to lift that pain and burden off of you, if you're just willing to be open. To turn to Him."

I realize that tears are again pouring down my cheeks. Freaking hormones. I take the pillow from beside me and begin to cry into it. What is wrong with me?

There is just silence in the room. A comforting silence behind the sobbing that I'm trying to drown in a down pillow.

"You ain't alone, baby girl. He loves you."

I pull the pillow from my face. I want so much to believe. But it's not that simple for people like me.

"'Have no other God above me'—it's one of the big ten rules. Commandments. Your pain, your money, and your job, even your past: they are like a god to you. They define you. You serve them. I'm not saying not to work hard. But all this stuff, you're letting it define you and it's not gonna help you. You keep trying to get *more,* and that only eventually brings this feeling of hopelessness. There's no finding peace. Or feeling truly satisfied. There's no real joy."

"Don't I look happy?" I try to deflect with fluid pouring from my nose and eyes.

"I'm not talking about happiness. I'm talking about joy. Look, you can't redo your past. But what you're feeling, that hopelessness and guilt and lack of self-forgiveness, is a life without God."

"You don't know." As I shake my head in denial, I choke up. "You don't know what I've done. To myself. To others. To—" I want to tell him about the baby but I can't. It's too dark.

"You're right, I don't. But I do know that you can't change that either. You can't change the world. But you *do* have the choice to continue to worship what you been worshipping, live the way you been livin', run from your own inadequacies, or at some point you can turn away and say, 'Maybe I'm wrong.'"

"I know I'm wrong about some stuff for sure," I say in between sobs and gulps, trying to catch my breath.

"You can live differently and not because of what you do, but because of what's already been done for you," Tim says.

"Jesus?"

"Yes, Jesus. All that stuff you've done; all those tears about your past—listen, He has already paid for the pain you think you deserve. He's already done it. Taken it. Served your time. I'm here to say no more tears, 'cause He came and took all the sin before you and to come after you. He takes it away from those who have faith in Him."

I kind of get that, but we're not doing a Bible study here.

"It takes humility to admit you're wrong, but the only thing harder than change is not changing and living the way you've been living."

"Humility?"

"Alice, you haven't seen real hopelessness yet—at least not on this side. There is still hope for you. The choices we make now, in the life we're all living, will affect our eternity. Right now we have an opportunity to see God and to turn to Him or from Him. But after death, when you leave this earth, there are no more chances."

"You're pretty convincing." I finally muster a smile and lift my fork. This time it is laden with a piece of pie.

"Baby girl"—as Tim says this, he looks at me with all the love in the world—"God loves you. I may not know all your stuff. But we all got a past. He knows and, believe it or not, He loves you anyway. He wants to know you, to help you, to love you. He's just waiting for you."

13

A Long Show

Without missing a beat from the pulpit, Tim wipes his glistening forehead with a white handkerchief. Even from my back-row point of view, I can see he is hot. Before he is finished wiping his nugget mop-job, I can see the work beads begin building anew. He's a sweaty preacher man! I wonder if he has a stock of clean undershirts and freshly pressed button-downs on hand so he can change his wardrobe in between performances.

Despite having to sit on this hard pew, I am enjoying watching him try to save the locals from the tribal squabbles. One thing in particular lingers in my head: God loves me.

Pastor Tim's preaching continues: "Again I'm gonna reiterate. Stop blaming yo' momma for yo' problems. You know what, just stop blaming everyone else."

Watching him up on his stage, I can't help but think that the arms around me on that lonely and painful night in New York might have been Jesus'. Who else would have been able to actually still love me after that day on the procedure table? God, with all His proposed grace and mercy, is perhaps the only one who can still love me.

Pastor Tim continues: "The third point is moving on from Momma, 'cause at some point, y'all got to." He mimics Martin Lawrence in his Big Momma voice as he bellows, "Get out of my house! You got to move on with your life." He smiles and continues speaking as Pastor Tim. "And I am not just talking about the building. I'm talking about moving on with your *life*. Letting go of your past and walking a new road."

Early summer 1993: Brown-taped boxes are still stacked six feet tall and pushed against the wall. I have yet to unpack them and I'm nearing my sixth month in Los Angeles. I live on Maple Drive north of Charleville and south of Wilshire Boulevard in a 1940s dilapidated yellow bungalow-style fourplex. It has a little grassy front yard. White and ruby impatiens grow along the sidewalk. I am the only resident under seventy years old in this place.

My new dwelling is a stone's throw away from my new office, or rather, cubicle, on the 15th floor of a high-rise off Wilshire. *National Celebrity News,* or *NCN,* as Hollywood insiders call us, is quickly becoming *the* weekly magazine. *NCN* distinguishes itself from tabloid competitors by featuring more provocative photos than *National Enquirer, Star,* or *Globe* would dare. We try to stay away from supernatural alien stories and focus on drunken shots of beautiful actresses brawling with other beautiful actresses in catfights over husband stealing while they're out of their minds on blow. We are a bloodless, photo-driven rag filled with tall tales of who is doing what, with whom, in what hotel, on what drug, and who got arrested (or should have).

NCN is a fantastic place to work for those bankrupt of conscience. There is no social, professional, personal, or media moral high ground or journalist's highbrow desire to tell the news in every story they report. My mother's epitomes of the open-minded and impartial media are quickly getting replaced with those that pander to America's insatiable appetite to devour what movie stars are wearing, eating, and—ultimately—throwing up.

The move from New York was smoother than I had anticipated. I successfully sealed the wormhole to the Big Apple; there's no going back. James is slowly getting the point that our relationship has died an unsavory, stumbling death. The long messages he left on my answering machine for the first four or five months were atrocious. I considered leaking them to *NCN;* they were *that* atrocious.

This morning as I sip my coffee in my kitchen and put ice in the bong and ignite the bowl, I fast-forward through James's earnest speech on the answering machine pleading and questioning and ultimately roaring and banging the receiver. I take a long inhale after an even longer week at the office and delete his emotional bargaining so it can't rip at my stomach lining anymore. I long to just kiss him one more time, but I will not even fantasize about a life that could have been. I learned early on in life that fantasizing about what could have been is a luxury not afforded to realists like me.

While I wake-and-bake the tears away, my doorbell rings. It scares the crud out of me. My first thought, as always, is *It's the cops!* My second thought is that it's the bonkers old lady who lives above me and thinks she's still a 1940s-era starlet. It's every bit as disturbing as *Sunset Boulevard.* Wait, maybe that *was* her. Nowadays, her former self would be disgusted by what she has become:

a cranky, complaining curmudgeon who is always banging her chair legs on my ceiling when my man Peter Gabriel is singing "In Your Eyes" too loud on my stereo. My third thought is . . . wait for it . . . Shoot! I forgot my third thought as the coughing from the smoke begins to eradicate my ability to think linearly. I'm whimsically numb. It's official.

The bell rings again. I get up while hacking out the last bit of smoke from my lungs. My eyes are watering. I open the door an inch with the chain lock still on. While I peek out, the aroma of weed pours out onto the porch.

"Lovely," says Amos, my new best friend from work, as I shut the door to get the chain unhooked.

"Bong hit?" I lure him by spinning around my glass one-footer Vanna White–style.

"Nahhh," he says, sounding way gayer than he does at the office.

I look in the mirror hanging above the antique green table where I throw my mail and keys and see twin trails of rejection on my cheeks. I try to wipe the mascara off quickly with the backs of my hands.

"You all right?" Amos asks. His thin, lanky six-foot-four frame towers over me. "More boy trouble from the homeland?"

"I am not purposely trying to hurt him," I explain when I really want to say that I have absolutely no idea how to deal with James's bewilderment, pain, and ultimate dismissal. Telling James the truth seems pointless and hurtful, and lying seems even more needless and a waste of time.

"He doesn't look like the one hurting, darling."

"I just feel bad for leaving so fast. It's been six months—you'd think he'd get over it. And for me, duty calls!" I muster a smile and hold up a copy of *NCN*. I will never divulge the nightmare of my visit to the clinic to anyone, "I will for the record say that I told him via an email that I have taken a job in Los Angeles, did not see a future in New York, and needed a fresh start and my own time."

"True. Chilly, but true," he says, putting on his sunglasses, signaling it's time to go. "More manly than me."

"I know he knows where I am from the endless hang-ups I get at various times of the night."

"Perhaps a little massage oil on the end of your club might be nice." Amos puckers his lips at me. "Ready to shop?"

"Yessss."

And with that, we are off like in a silly Hollywood romantic comedy from yesteryear. I'm Doris Day and he's Rock Hudson, except Amos isn't pretending he's hetero.

Arm in arm, we make our way down Melrose Avenue on a bustling Saturday afternoon. It is *the* shopping district and where I've spotted one of my celebrity crushes, Patrick Dempsey, from *Can't Buy Me Love*. He's skulking the streets with dirty curly hair, a vintage bowling shirt, unlaced Dr. Martens, and a Marlboro Red hanging from his mouth. Delectable.

I nudge Amos hard in the ribs as Lover Boy passes, whispering, "Mark my words: He will be mine. Oh, yes, he will be mine." I laugh dubiously.

Tucked among the traditional retailers like the Gap and Banana Republic is the Decades store. As we open the glass door, Whitney Houston's hit song insists we take a quick performance break. We toss back our heads and start belting along with her: "And I . . . ee-aye . . . will always love you-ooh-ooh-ooh-ooh-ooh . . ." We finish the song with Whitney and stare into each other's eyes longingly for a dramatic moment before bursting into laughter.

Seriously, I do love Amos because he's anodyne to me. There is nothing I need or want from him. There is nothing he wants or needs from me. We are just two companions who are cosmically connected. He's the thirty-five-year-old, tall, dark, and handsome version of me, with more money. We both like men.

Decades is my new favorite haunt. It is where rich Beverly Hills ladies send their maids to unload last season's designer suits, shoes, and jewelry. It is fabulous: my home away from home. At Decades, I have access to all the right labels so I can play the part of a successful, savvy businesswoman without having to actually lay out my hard-earned dollars. With Decades, I can fake it till I make it, and make it I will.

I am the best-dressed assistant editor at work, second only to Amos, who is a real editor with a corner office and who has a Mormon trust-fund bank account and a Range Rover. His trust fund is not real money. It's what he calls *fake money*, because he didn't earn it. "Pretty, fake money, honey," he quips. *Money is money*, I think to myself.

Last week I snuck onto the soundstage of the *Roseanne* show. She had filed for divorce from her husband, Tom Arnold, a few months back and we all thought it was a publicity stunt, but my boss wanted me to get to the bottom of it. Keep in mind this is the same Tom and Roseanne who mud-wrestled for the cover of *Vanity Fair* and delighted in mooning a World Series crowd. They sell magazines. As I stood looking nondescript in a catering jacket, re-filling the peanut bowl on the craft-service table, I watched the al-leged antics begin: a yelling and screaming match between the Arnolds turning from loud to in-stereo. The X-rated verbal sparring only got truly out of hand when their twentysomething assistant, Kim, who Roseanne insinuated was getting busy with her mister on the side, walked onto the set. I thought the big Mrs. Diva was going to jump her like a rabid lion ready to rip the haunches off an unsuspecting antelope. It was juicy, delicious cover material.

My used Prada loafers with silver buckles led me to just ex-actly what *NCN* wanted: an eyewitness account of the couple jawing at peak volume, utilizing every four-letter word not allowed in the dictionary.

For the first time in my life I feel powerful: I am making and breaking and remaking celebrities by wallpapering *NCN's* front covers with their follies and foibles. I am on my own, with the exception of Amos, who poses no threat; making my own way without the maddening necessity of having to depend on any other person. I am no longer a victim of circumstance or on the run from my past. I am in control of my destiny. I can do this. I don't feel like I'm standing on a block of melting ice anymore.

After a long day of shopping, we eat dinner at Marix Tex Mex on N. Flores Street in the heart of Boys Town and head home. "Marix has absolutely the besssssst tacos and margaritas in the city," I declare to no one in particular. I'm buzzed and bloated and I know I am slurring but I like the way I feel. I'm happy and safe and always comfortably numb in escapism.

Amos dutifully takes my party carcass home. He carries me up the steps, my body weight propped against him as he quietly turns the key, opens the door, and tiptoes into my bedroom, where he places me on my double bed, tucking the white cotton sheets in around me. He takes my latest bedside table read, *Men Are from Mars, Women Are from Venus,* off my nightstand and rolls his eyes at the title, and then uses it to prop open my heavy wood-framed window to let the California air blow into my room. "Sweet dreams," he says as he leaves as quietly and as gently as he came.

And dream I do. A half-baked, fully drunken, hazy dream of my mother. She and I are in our old house in Arizona watching Mr. Cronkite on the *CBS Evening News*. It makes me feel unabridged and peaceful.

Then a calliope-led swell of under-the-big-tent circus music ushers in the Beatles, happily singing "Octopus's Garden" in the background: "I'd like to be under the sea / in an octopus's garden in the shade."

This memory of a lullaby juxtaposed with vivid vignettes of media images on the television is the type of thing that has shaped my psyche. I am equal parts pigtails and hangnails in my own memory.

The song continues on . . .

A grainy color image of the White House and Jody Powell, the United States press secretary under President Carter, is on the TV. Powell is wearing a suit and tie behind his desk in his small office as the audio crew gets ready to interview him.

My mother shushes me. "He's so savvy," she reminds me from nowhere tangible.

"Momma?" *Momma, I am confused.*

Then I see another image on the small screen of my unconscious state. A mob of Islamic militants is taking over the American embassy in support of the Iranian revolution. My body twitches in frustration.

The Beatles are still singing as I watch the man recording Jody lean into his microphone while a large tape on a reel begins spinning in circles, capturing the audio. He starts speaking. "This is an interview with Jody Powell, press secretary, December 2, 1980, approximately 3:40 p.m., in his office in the West Wing of the White House."

The interviewer is David Alsobrook of the Presidential Papers staff. Mr. Powell, very clean-cut in a suit and tie, smokes as he listens. Mr. Alsobrook begins his line of questioning. "How do you feel television has changed press coverage of the presidency and the White House, say, over the last fifty years?"

Jody ponders before thoughtfully answering, "Well, I wasn't around before television so it's very difficult for me to contrast it to a situation that I never saw or experienced directly."

He smirks.

I smile, recognizing his cleverness.

After a drag on his cigarette, he continues, "But there is no doubt that it's had an immense impact, not just on the president but on America. Both the oversimplification of matters and that it tends to promote the extremes."

"The oversimplification of matters! You're all becoming dummies." My mother's voice booms in my head.

I look around for her. "Momma?" I call out but I can't see her.

Then something hits me like a cement block on my chest. Was she dead by that time? At the very least she had to be in a morphine-laced coma. I am savagely pushed to a heightened state of awareness. Not awake but no longer in the pitter-patter of my carnival subconscious.

"What are you doing in this place?" Her stern voice questions me. My peaceful dream has turned nightmarish.

Ringo Starr keeps on singing about boys and girls who are safe and happy under the sea.

Just then the music stops and out of nowhere, a lifeless woman drops into frame. She has a rope around her neck. She is dangling from a gangplank above icebergs and thrashing, freezing water. Dead. Is it me? Is it my mother?

The dead woman's hair blows as bright-white light engulfs me. I bolt upright in bed. I am drenched in sweat despite the sweet, cool night air. Was it a ghost from the past or a look into what was destined to become of me?

I can't shake the thought that I was meant to be more. To be a writer. To be a teacher. To be a journalist. To make a difference. To change the world for the better in my lifetime. To ask the tough questions and properly frame the hard answers. To raise the bar of American culture instead of being actively involved in lowering it.

I get out of bed. My head is pounding, my mouth is dry, and I am desperate for at least a gallon of Gatorade. I stumble down the hallway to the tiny bathroom. There, I rummage around clumsily until I paw a bottle of Xanax. I pop a pill in my mouth and run my tongue under the faucet in the darkness. I drink in the promise of manufactured relaxation. I lap up every last drop like a thirsty, orphaned kitten.

I tuck myself back into my cool T-shirt sheets and try to quiet my conscience. Try to quiet my passions of the past; to quiet the standard she planted in me. Before too long, my eyelids feel as heavy as wet pillows and my brain can no longer string together rational thoughts. I drift back into a medicated state of rest.

Reverberations of this moonlight memorific experience trace the words *my purpose, my purpose, my purpose* over and over on my heart. I swear I can feel her cursive script.

A month ago: I am eyeballing an invitation to the Rock the Cradle event benefiting Baptist Hospital's Neonatal ICU wing. We are attending for several reasons. The first is that, well, if we should need them, it's good to know they are there. Second and most obvious, because Burton is an employee of the hospital. Third is that the owner of the Titans, the team Burton stitches up, is getting the NICU wing named after him for his generous donation of something like ten million dollars.

The good news is the fund-raiser, unlike many of the swanky invites we receive, is casual attire. No black tie, no ball gown, no awful, binding pantyhose. Instead it is jeans and country chic. I've found a wonderful pair of A Pea in the Pod black corduroy pants and a shimmering gray flowing top. I am dangerously close to feeling pretty.

It is a small, very-high-dollar event in a posh barn behind the Loveless Cafe. Faith Hill and Martina McBride will be singing together. Between their highly anticipated sets, award-winning song-writers will perform and tell old-time stories about their music. The dance floor is primed and polished, ready for some high-end-hooch–inspired hoofing. Tasty-looking country cookin' is piled high on platters and being served up throughout the tents.

It's a rare occasion that I'm actually happy to be attending an event. After ten years of having to dress up and golf-clap every time a celebrity opened a tissue box in LA, I normally can't be paid enough to attend uppity fund-raising shindigs.

I'm starting to understand the culture of Tennessee as a whole, although I am not a part of it. There is exceeding wealth, but the families are more low-key and charitable when it comes to their money. There are old-school Southern families like the Ingrams. Martha Ingram is the patron of the family and is on the Forbes list of richest people. But she's more known in the social circles for her philanthropy than her two buh-billion dollars. Then there are the Frists. Mr. Frist and his children have an entire museum named after them. Some money is inherited, but most of it has been earned by the founders of FedEx, Dollar General, Holiday Inn, Krystal, and the heirs to the Coca-Cola fortune.

Nashville, unlike some other Southern towns, isn't a Podunk, country-bumpkin environment. People on the outside, like me, identify Nashville as the country-music capital of the world. What once was a little city rich in Civil War history has become a mecca for entertainment, good restaurants, theater, and professional and college sports. Burton has exposed me to a side of the city that stays hidden from outsiders, especially Yankee outsiders. It has a mini-cosmopolitan flair and remains unspoiled, unlike New York or Los Angeles. It has its share of poverty, sure, but there is a giving nature to the people here. It is as if it's not just their duty to give back to people in need, it's their responsibility and honor. And it is not the country, rock, pop, or gospel money that pumps kajillions of dollars into the inner city; the financial backbone comes from health care and publishing. (They are clearly printing a lot of the world's Bibles.) Entertainment finishes a distant third in terms of sheer dollars (even though the industry certainly ranks first in charitable visibility).

As we round a food station, we pass my doctor. Away from the hospital we refer to her as Nicole, but in the office, I call her *Madame Doctor*. As we head for the bar line she squints her mean face at Burton and says, "No salt for her. You hear me? No salt."

She keeps walking as I call after her, "Trust me, I have no desire to pee in a bucket again."

A woman helping herself to a piece of carrot cake can't help but scrunch her nose as she overhears me. My directness is a sharp stick in the eye to the polite Southern women and their parlor-appropriate conversations.

"Dance with me," Burton says with a squeeze of my hand. The dance floor is now full of people swaying to a slow country song. The crowd is illuminated by the twinkling lights strung overhead.

"I'm huge," I protest, not wanting to set foot on that sawdust floor for fear that I'll fall and spoil the sweetness of the scene.

"Come on." He pulls my hand firmly but gently. "You can do this," he says as he rocks back and forth like a fat swan stuck in deep mud, mimicking me.

"That's not cool."

"I want to dance with my fiancée." Burton knows just how to appeal to my junior-high-school need to be seen with the popular boy.

I don't want to do it. "Seriously?" My voice lowers.

"Yes. Seriously."

My shoulders droop in an unenthusiastic treaty.

He makes his way through the crowd, gently touching people on the shoulder to make room for his very pregnant date. I tuck behind him like a running back trying to get an extra five yards following the offensive lineman.

We find our spot on the floor and he whisks me into his arms with a little twirl. We are as close as we can get with our baby sandwiched between us. His left hand in my right hand, he leads me in a simple waltz. Here comes all of that Cary Grant style, charm, and grace. He grins at me just as the baby kicks, hard. Really hard. Hard enough for him to feel it on his body.

"Wow." He looks down.

I grimace a little and look deep into his eyes. "Yes, wow."

With his right hand, he strokes my belly where the baby just kicked, soothing us both. We continue to rock to the music, stepping back and forth.

"You look beautiful," he whispers in my ear.

I nuzzle his collarbone. "I'm dancing." I deflect his affection although I want to say something else. I want to say something meaningful like *I'm trying to love you*. Or *Thank you for loving me*. Or *I can't believe it, I actually feel happy!*

But I don't. I can't.

He lifts my chin, forcing me to meet his gaze. "Yes, we are. We are dancing." He stares right through me, reading my heart, knowing and sensing the emotions trapped, lumped in the bottom of my throat. We continue to dance and sway the night away, and I hope he can feel what I cannot say.

The next day I am making my way out of the Publix grocery store and the sweet-but-overly chatty bag boy insists on pushing my shopping buggy to my truck. He is adamant that I not lift a finger while he loads my bags into the back of the Navi. This is a Southern thing that I have had to get used to. The first time he did this, I thought he was a stalker and I had my finger on the trigger the whole time, ready to Mace him like a pesky swan. The second time he did it, I thought he just felt sorry for me in my fattened-up state. The third time I tried to tip him. He refused. In fact, they all refuse! This is what I do not understand: Why are they being so helpful and polite if not for the money? The answer is *good customer service,* something lost to me living in Los Angeles the last decade.

In exchange for my time and courtesy, I receive this hospitality, no questions asked. I learn to listen to my buggy boy's trials and tribulations and I alternate between raising an eyebrow and saying *Really?* or *Wow, you don't say,* before I thank him and head home.

I pull through the gate at Laurel Brooke, stop at the first corner, and see Tim sitting on the curb outside the clubhouse. For reasons beyond my comprehension, I do not slam my foot on the gas and make a sharp right toward Home Sweet Home. I have not seen him or LeChelle since my emotional Easter breakdown and I'm hoping to avoid them until some new lost soul wanders into their yard. But no. Heavenly intervention causes me to instead head straight for him, into the eye of the holy hurricane.

Sweat is pouring out of him and, even from afar, his shirt appears soaked. Drenched. He's breathing heavily and has the biggest smile on his face. He's watching Kyle, one of his twin sons, fly a kite on the big grassy field in front of the swing set and jungle gym on the playground. I assume his sweltering state is directly related to the barely blowing wind; he must have been running back and forth to help get that kite in the air.

I pull into the circular driveway and slow down next to him. As I roll down my window, the liquid version of my friend Tim rises up to greet me.

He leans in the window and says, "Girl, you been shoppin'?" I watch as he eyes my purchases. Oreos, Munchos, Combos, Cheetos, and Hawaiian Punch pour out of overflowing sacks.

"I know it's shocking, but I do make some of my own meals. There's some actual raw ingredients in there, too," I say, my defense mechanisms kicking in.

"You got something cold back there for a thirsty man?"

I sigh. Why did I drive over to him if not to visit? I put my truck in park, leave it running, and unbuckle the seat belt covering my huge belly while pressing the automatic hatch opener. I toddle around the back of the truck.

"You want Gatorade or water?"

"Water," he says, taking the bottle out of my hand, opening it, and downing the entire thing in one motion.

"Soooooo, nice kite," I say, nodding at Kyle, who is running toward the pool area trying to keep the kite airborne. It's not usually this hard for me to talk with Tim. What is going on?

Tim ignores me and leans his face near the air-conditioner vent on the driver's side of my Navi. I'm still standing at the back, mildly horrified that his presummertime Southern slime is now within dripping distance of my leather seat.

"I need to cool off."

Dang it! Just like the leather upholstery, he's soaking my seat with redeeming rain. With the push of a button, I close the trunk. Just then Kyle looks over at his dad. Tim waves at his little boy to signal that we aren't going anywhere.

I'm getting tired of standing outside my own vehicle. This can't take too long; surely he must know that I have ice cream, Skinny Cows, and Tofutti Cuties melting in my grocery sacks.

Or maybe not.

Tim purposely, almost in slow motion, adjusts the air vents until they are just right. He closes his eyes and absorbs the icy-cold blast on his face and says, "Man, I'm gettin' too old. But I do love a kite."

"Me too." I watch the kite sailing in the air. "Hi, Kyle."

"Hi, Miss Alice." He runs toward me, sending his kite soaring upward.

"Best entertainment two dollars and ninety-nine cents can buy," Tim says. He pauses, looks at me, and says, "How you doing?"

I play dumb. I don't want to *talk*-talk with him right now. I don't want to talk about Easter or my shame or my past. "Oh, I'm feeling good," I say as brightly as I can manage.

"Well, that's good to hear. But how you really doing? I mean with it all? The move, Burton, what we talked about last week? You thinking about building your new life here in Tennessee?"

"Oh, I wouldn't go that far. At some point I need to go back to my life. I had a career and my people. This life is temporary."

"Yes, it is." He never ceases to throw a double meaning at me.

"That's not what I meant."

"I know that, but you wait till that baby comes out. Life as you know it is O-V-E-R."

We both stand there, silent, watching the kite float in the breeze. I know Tim isn't moving away from the driver's side door until I throw him a connecting heart bone. He leans back and waits patiently for me to say something meaningful.

He is annoying.

"I've been thinking about what you said, and I sort of get it, but I will say, I miss working." There's my olive branch. That's pretty profound.

"You're a writer, right? A blogger or something?"

"Celebrity online news resource. I'm the publisher, if there is such a thing for electronic media."

"Catchy." I think he's mocking me as much as a preacher is allowed to mock.

"It's more gossip stories than news." I am not sure why I just admitted that outside of this four-door confessional.

"Writing's a gift," He shakes his head. "I can't do it."

"But don't you write your sermons every week?"

"Oh, no, the Lord does that. It just comes to me from Him and I scribble it down on my legal pad and piece it together. Seriously."

"Divine inspiration." I footnote his point. "My writing isn't so much divine as it is headlines and photos. But I do miss the writing."

"'Cause it's yo' gift."

"Oh, yeah, well, I think it's a little late for me to be writing the Holy Grail. I missed that window somewhere between George Clooney's latest breakup and coining names like *Brangelina*."

He's confused but counters, "I have faith that you'll get there."

"You just keep on believing that."

"See that kite?" His eyes squint at it.

"Yeah." I nod my head.

"What do you think would happen to that kite if the string broke?" Tim asks.

Oh, here we go! Somehow this just became about me—again. "Am I the string? I mean, I'm a little big to be the string. But I'm broken, right?" I try to finish his trivial string story safely on the surface when I know darn well Tim is going to twist it all around and make it mysterious and thought-provoking.

"No." His patience with me is pretty remarkable. "Just look at the kite. What if it didn't have a string? Or the string broke?"

The kite is bobbing around in the warm Southern winds. "It would get stuck in that tree," I say, pointing at a big oak behind the kids' jungle gym. "Or the electrical wire."

"Or it just may blow away. Gettin' tossed and turned by whatever is out there," he says.

We both sit there looking at the kite. He waves at his son, who waves back. Then there is another elongated pause. I stand, waiting for his concluding argument. I am learning that his pauses are expertly and purposely orchestrated.

"Fine! I give up!" I shout. "I've got raw chicken in the back that is probably getting salmonella poisoning from sitting in the car. What's it all mean?"

"You are not the string. You are the kite," he begins. "The string is God's purpose for your life—and He holds the string." He points upward on the *He*. "Without the purpose you're just getting tossed and turned. Doesn't mean you aren't flying. Doesn't mean it ain't fun up there. Just means at some point you're gonna get caught up in that wire or tree or on top of that roof."

I try to digest his little analogy.

"You got a gift, a purpose for your life, everyone does. Maybe you start working on that since you can't work on that tabloid of yours." And with that he puts his large, dark hand on the door handle and holds it wide open, signaling for me to get inside.

"I'm the kite?"

"Yes, you're the kite."

"Okay, then. Good seeing you!" I say with faux cheerfulness, raising my brow like he's crazy and none of that made sense to me, but it really did.

It's always been difficult to accept that my writing is a gift. If it's a gift, who is that gift from? And if indeed it is from a higher power, is it forcing me to explore the contours of that purpose?

I climb back in the car. "Bye, Kyle!"

"Bye, Miss Alice."

"Bless you." Tim smiles and shuts the door.

"Bless you too . . . preacher man," I say quickly.

Mining my history, I do know that writing has always been my dream. It has been planted there since childhood or, as Tim would have me believe, perhaps before. I lost the yearning to tell virtuous stories when I moved to Los Angeles or maybe it all died long, long ago. I had padlocked the hope chest on all my true aspirations and wholesaled them out to the very lowest bidder.

14

Stand to Your Feet

Back in church, Pastor Tim's voice softens to just above a whisper. "At what point are you gonna stop running from the past and have God heal your future?"

Ah, good question, preacher man. In the Gospel According to Alice, this query remains perpetually unresolved. When am I going to stop running? It is, after all, what I do.

"The Bible teaches us, 'Remember not the fooorrrrmer things, nor consider the things of *old*. But behold, I am doing a new thing; now it springs forth, do you not perceive it?'"

I perceive something about to spring forth all right: my baby. And she's got my ribs locked in a spasm.

"It's time to move the needle forward and stop listening to the same song over and over and let go of your shame, your guilt, your pain."

I object! It is all I can do to not throw up my hand and challenge this discussion. How is that even possible? When does it all really vanish and our pain get relinquished? We've covered so much ground these last few months, but we haven't covered this . . . yet.

As if Pastor Tim heard my internal question, he answers it. "If you would like to let go of your shame, your guilt, and your pain, all you need to do is confess your sins. That's it." He smiles triumphantly.

I'm not convinced.

"Pastor Bruce, will you bring me that target, please?" He looks up as he continues. "I promise y'all we're almost done, butchya'll gotta get this part, so I'm gonna make it real easy."

Pastor Bruce and an usher guy wheel out two bulky hay bales to the left of the stage. Attached to the front of the contraption is a huge target made up of black, white, blue, and red circles with a yellow bull's-eye dead center.

Tim walks out from behind the piano to reveal an archer's bow and arrows in a satchel. À la Robin Hood, he straps it on his enormous back, making him look more like Little John than Robin of Locksley. "Don't worry, y'all. During the nine a.m. service I only nicked one guy and he was sitting in the front row." Tim winks as he points a finger at a man in the first pew. The man in turn chuckles and feigns fear, holding his hands up and waving them.

Bow in hand, Tim approaches the giant target. "Living for Christ"—he raises his voice—"is the bull's-eye." He touches the yellow center with the tip of his bow. "Everything else," he says as he traces the other circles of colors, "is sin. You were created with many purposes in this life, but your main purpose is to live in here." Again he taps the yellow bull's-eye. "Once you're in here, the rest will come. This is a relationship with Him." Tim walks slowly to the right end of the stage. "Y'all with me?" At about forty feet, he stops.

Man, he is good! If he shoots those arrows and hits the target, never mind the bull's-eye, I'm seriously going to give birth right here.

"In the bull's-eye with Him, you have real love, joy, and peace and purpose." Tim pulls an arrow from the leather pouch. He places it in the bow and draws back the string. Cocking his head to get a good view, he squints his left eye. "But when you're living out here"—with a smooth *whoosh,* the arrow cuts a straight line through the air and lands on the black outer circle—"you're livin' in sin, you're lost, wandering. That black circle is your pride, your ego, your sense of entitlement. It keeps you far away from the goal."

He takes another arrow out, carefully resting it on the bow and then pulling back the string. He draws it back precisely and releases. *Whoosh.* The second arrow whaps the target, piercing the next smaller ring, the white circle.

"Next, you got the sin of your own desire. Human, fleshy desire: lust, greed, gossip, selfishness, immorality. All of it keeping you just out the reach of Him and your destiny, your purpose." Tim slides another arrow into the bow. He drops to one knee and shoots. *Bam!* This arrow hits the blue circle. Then, like a pool shark preparing to clear the table, he buries an arrow in each ring, inching closer to the center. Once he has landed one arrow in every circle but the bull's-eye, he stops and again addresses the congregation.

"And you just can't figure out why you're never satisfied. Why your prayers never get answered. 'Cause you ain't really living with Him. You're living outside of Him. You're tryin' your way. But you can't earn it. You might be close, but somewhere inside you're still wondering why you have that pain from your past, or why you're in that same bad relationship pattern, or your addiction or vices keep comin' back. Why you're fallin' just a little short every time you think you got it right.

"The only way you're gonna get what you really need, when you finally figure out your purpose in this life, is to stop trying to do it your way and start living His way." As he swings his bow back toward the target, the entire front row ducks in unison.

"Let in the One"—he pulls back one last arrow—"the One who came to rescue you from your own sin, who already took your sin on a cross at Calvary and paid the price for you . . ." He pauses without taking his eye off the target. "Can I get an amen?"

*Amen*s erupt from the crowd.

"Just let Him in." With a satisfying snap, he releases the arrow and it hits the bull's-eye.

He sets the bow and the now-empty bag down on top of the piano and walks back to the pulpit. "To live in the center with Him, all you gotta do is humble yourself."

My heart pounds at the possibility. At the archory session. At my baby wringing out my insides.

"And you don't have to do that for me, or for any religious church person for that matter. You just gotta look to God and tell 'im what He already knows."

Whoa. This takes my breath away. I exhale and my bravado deflates. He does know, doesn't He?

Tim looks down at his Bible. "First John says it plain and simple: 'If we confess our sins, He is faithful and just to forgive us our sins and to cleanse us from all unrighteousness.'" He closes his Good Book and it makes a satisfying *thunk*. "If you want a new beginning, if you want a new way, you got to release the ol' way and you got to get God's help. You got to get with Him. It's up to you. No one else is going to do it for you. It takes work to say, out loud, what you keep quiet. What you think is hidden. But the choice He has always given you is yours and yours alone. Only Jesus can re-move that guilt. When you just come to Him, talk to Him, confess to Him, He will heal your wounds."

Tim removes his glasses. He sets them next to his water glass on the pulpit as if to signal that we are coming to the finale. "And the truth"—he looks at the audience—"the truth will . . ." Tim ex-tends his hands toward all of us.

I don't know how, but even I know this one. I say the words along with the rest of the congregation: "Set you free."

The truth will set me free.

July 1994: In my first year with *National Celebrity News* I have learned there are partial truths in most of the entertainment busi-ness. This is particularly true with tabloid magazines. *NCN* is gossip news riding a galloping crack pipe, and it's been a very in-toxicating learning curve.

It's quarter past two in the morning and I'm standing on South Bundy Drive in Brentwood in front of Nicole Brown Simpson's condo. Ten days earlier, she and Ron Goldman were murdered here. My Nikon camera is slung over my shoulder and I'm wearing tight black jeans and a very sexy, fitted, low-cut black top with just enough cleavage showing to allure the police officer standing guard.

In the stagnant darkness of the early morning, I watch as Amos slips the cop a hundred-dollar bill. I smile as I pass him on the walkway.

Tangled oleander bushes grow thick and tall along the path-way. Traces of bloodstains and chalk marks are still visible on the tan and cream cobblestones. As I snap a few shots, an eerie sad-ness falls over me. It's as if I'm visiting two fresh, unmarked graves at the back of an old cemetery.

"Boo!" Amos grabs my waist from behind, sending me jumping two feet in the air.

"Creepy, right?" I take his hand in mine.

"More than creepy," he agrees. "Let's just hurry up."

"Okay, so Nicole was there." I point to a place on the ground with my flashlight where you can barely make out what might have been a body traced in chalk on the ground.

"Why again are we doing this?" Amos asks with obvious second thoughts.

I ignore him.

"You're so Morticia Addams. Let's get out of here."

"*Mon chéri,*" I say in my best French Morticia accent, "I want the cover. Okay, you be Goldman."

"Really. I'd rather not," he declares indignantly.

"Seriously. Do it."

"Umm, you work for me, Cagney. Get it?" he says with a very feisty inflection. "*Cagney and Lacey.*"

"So according to the cop, the killer—"

"O.J." Amos rolls his eyes.

"—swung at him," I continue, spinning around with my hand holding an imaginary knife. "Buuutttt I only get'cha a little on the neck." I whack him on the neck.

"Ow!" He touches his neck with his right hand and quickly examines his palm, looking for blood, surprised that I fake-slashed him.

"And then you come at me." I widen my stance, ready for a rumble.

Amos shakes his head at me. "I'm not doing this. It's morbid."

"Just pretend to fight." I hold up my fists in front of my face.

Amos starts prancing around like a boxer, partly to shut me up and mostly to make fun of me.

"Then *wham, wham, wham!* The killer slits him in the jugular." Just as I begin to feel something inside—empathy? remorse? sadness?—my ambitious inner voice dismisses the distraction and demands I stay focused. I look around on the ground. "There! Lie there." I point at a bush.

"I'm not lying down." He protectively pats his suit jacket. "This is Versace."

"Look, do you want a cover shot or not? Do you want to sell magazines? Buy a new Range Rover?"

"I already have a new Range Rover," he deadpans.

"Fine, but don't you want to buy *me* a Range Rover?"

"This is a new low in what you'll do for bonus money." He shakes his head at me in disgust.

Unfazed, I continue bullying Amos by pushing him down. "Just get on the ground. The killer had to be a lot bigger and stronger."

"And crazier." He pushes back. "O.J."

"Allegedly." I replay the crime scene in my head. "He said they fought. He was beaten pretty badly, something like five stabs to the neck, hand, thighs, and he ended up"—I point to the palm tree—"there!"

"No way." Amos's face changes. "I'm not doing it."

"Do it!"

"I'm not getting into the shrubbery."

"All I need is a shot of your hand in the dirt next to the bush."

"You have no ethical boundaries. I know we cross the line all the time, but this is out there, even for me. You realize their families will see this."

"So? Look, we are not leaving till I have the shot."

"You're going to hell for this. You know that, right?"

"Trust me, I'm fine with it."

Amos reluctantly lies down near where poor Ron Goldman must have suffered in agonizing pain on that horrific night and I *snap, snap, snap* a couple photos of Amos's hand near the bush.

Despite the illumination of my camera flash, neither of us sees what exactly jumps out of the bushes and pounces onto Amos's chest. He squeals like a girl and scares the crap out of me.

A cat. A black cat with a rhinestone-studded collar. It sits, relaxed, right in the middle of the walkway, mocking us both.

"That's it!" Amos says, getting to his knees as the cop from out front comes jogging toward us.

"Okay, you guys have to get out of here," the cop orders.

Our cover that week features a grainy black-and-white image of what appears to be Goldman's hand in the oleander. The caption reads: "What really happened to Ron Goldman? Exclusive photos from the crime scene."

Inside, I've written about how Ron had worked at Mezzaluna, a swanky eatery; driven Nicole's Ferrari; and frolicked with her children. But honestly it didn't matter what I wrote. The truth is beside the point in photo-driven tabloid media.

We at *NCN* are all about creating facts from fiction. Research and journalism have been replaced with gossip and posturing. I have quickly become the conqueror of getting it all because to me, it doesn't matter who it is or how much the story costs. Amos is right: I have no ethical boundaries, whether professional or personal.

"**Do you believe in God?**" Tim asks. It's April and I am standing on the sidewalk watching him pull weeds out of his front flower bed as LeChelle plants violets by the porch.

I take a swig from my water bottle while I formulate my answer. "I believe in something," I say, halfheartedly loosing weeds with the toe of my shoe. I thumb through yesterday's newspaper, which I've swiped off their deck.

"Something, huh?" He tosses the weeds in a big black Hefty bag.

"Why are you doing this? I mean, no disrespect, but you know there are gardeners who are just dying to pull the weeds in this neighborhood."

"I like doing it. So what's your 'something-God' like?"

"Different I guess from the God you're talking about all the time." I sit on the curb and pull the metro section out of the paper. "Look at this." I hold up a picture of an eight-year-old girl on the cover. "If there's a God, why is this girl dead? Why did someone feel the need to take her from her family's house, rape her, and kill her?" My voice goes up. "She was *eight*! Or for that matter, why bombings and wars and—"

"Bad stuff happens in this world because of sin, not because of God." The clarity in his voice is unmistakable. He looks up at me. "Can I get a little help here?"

I deadpan at him: "You want me to pull weeds?" I fold the paper. "Seriously?"

"Baby girl, it's good to get your hands in the dirt. Connects you with the planet. Get on down here." He moves the cushion he was kneeling on across the flower bed so I'll have a softer landing.

"I'm pregnant," I say. Not that if I weren't with child I would be weeding.

"So? I got two bad knees and no C5 or C6. Get on down here and give a man some help."

Reluctantly, I inch my very large butt over onto the cushion in the grass and cross my legs. Still, I'm watching, not pulling. What did he expect?

He starts again: "Sin is the result of the absence of God in whoever killed that little girl."

"But if God is all-powerful, all-knowing, all-loving, why doesn't He just wave his magic wand and stop it, and just make it better?

Make us better?" I lean back on my arms, tilt my head toward the sky, and close my eyes, enjoying the feeling of warm sun on my face.

"That would make us all a bunch of robots," Tim says. "You need to be leaning forward, not backward. Those there"—Tim swats my foot to get my attention and points at the weeds between the lilies—"aren't going to pick themselves."

"At least we'd be happy robots." I try to reposition my large self to be able to lean forward without squishing my baby.

"Put your hands in the dirt, like this." He grasps a weed at the root.

"I know how to pull a weed, thank you very much." I grab a weed near its flower and yank it. It tears in half but remains rooted. Clearly I don't.

Tim continues, "God gives us a choice to love Him or not. A true test of real love is making the choice. An example would be, say, if you choose to marry someone. As soon as you say yes in that church, you are saying no to everyone else who might be, hmmm, better lookin' or have more money. You're choosing that man 'cause you love him. It's a big choice. Now if you're just shackin' up—"

"Really?" I say sarcastically. "You're gonna go there?"

"No offense, I ain't talkin' about you and Burton specifically. But honestly, it isn't really a choice. You're just test-driving the relationship."

"So?"

"So in the beginning there was a *yes* tree and a *no* tree. God gave us a choice to do what we wanted."

"Wait, I thought there was just the forbidden-apple tree."

"There was the forbidden-apple tree, but it was in a garden and He gave them the whole dang thing full of *yes* trees. He said they could have it all if they followed His one rule, and that rule was: don't eat from this tree. There was only one *no* tree."

"This is all Adam's fault. Men." I chuckle a little.

"There was a spirit of temptation. We're always gonna be tempted by something we think might be better. But if you love God, if you love what that relationship with Him brings, you choose to be faithful. Just like in a marriage."

"Okay, but that doesn't explain the bad stuff."

"Sure it does. That guy who murdered that little girl, or the guy who stole a car, or the lady who cheated on her husband, or the lady who lied to her boss: They all got their own standard for right and wrong. Their own grading curves for good and evil." He looks at my half-pulled weed with shame. As he pulls it out from the top of the root, he does a measuring thing with his hands. "They're like, hey, you do what you think is right, and I'll do what I think is right. People be makin' their own moral choices. When mankind chooses to be its own god, they feel they got the right to do what they want."

"A 'life is short' attitude, so just be happy," I say.

"But here's the thing: most of them ain't happy and they got no idea why. Jeremiah 17:9 says that the heart of man is desperate, wicked. Which tells you something bad might happen when you're on your own, making your own rules. Living without Him. It's our human nature. Even at two years old it's our nature to defy authority. As a toddler we want it our way. We have to teach our babies to share, not to lie, to behave. They have to learn to follow the rules. But in the end, they choose to do it or not."

"I like the robot idea better." I have been playing with the dirt and my fingernails are black. I don't care. I like the way the soil feels cool in my hands.

"Most sin happens when people have no restraint. The lack of restraint, way back when, in the garden, and even now, with that"—his eyes drift back to the cover of the paper and that poor little girl's face—"has brought evil to the world. Sin is the absence of God in someone's heart."

I take a swig from my water bottle. I need water to help me swallow his theoretical God jibber-jabber.

"That's all fine, but it still doesn't explain why that innocent little girl and her parents got punished because of someone else's sin."

"Having Jesus in your life doesn't automatically put a bubble around your life, like you're gonna live in some pain-free incubator. Faith doesn't mean you won't suffer in this world, it just means you have hope beyond this world."

"If that was my baby, my child"—my eyes start to water at the thought—"what can anyone possibly say to stop me from getting my Glock nine millimeter, loading the clip, and finding that sick, twisted bastard, sorry"—I feel bad for my language—"and unloading it into the head of the person who killed her?"

He wipes his forehead with the back of his hand. "And that's exactly what the devil wants. He came for a two-for-one. If he can destroy the mother through that child, he will. He wants to steal her hope. Her possibility of healing. Her possibility of life. Her eternity."

"I'm still waving my gun over here." I hold up my hand, pretending to be cocking my thumb. "And the more I'm waving, the madder I'm getting at God if I'm that mom."

"The person who did this doesn't represent God. The person who took that child is evil. The God I know doesn't hurt people. I know this because He sent His own Son to die for us. If He wanted to hurt us, He would have killed us and let His Son live."

He holds out his hand as if asking me to surrender my invisible gun.

I squint at him.

He continues as if he's talking to the mother who lost her daughter. "I don't have all the answers—if I had all the answers it wouldn't be enough to bring your daughter back."

Or my mother, I think to myself.

"It will never be sufficient or good enough. What you need is hope. Hope to go on. Hope to have a purpose in this life. Hope to create a vision of living beyond this so it doesn't take your life as well as your precious baby."

I lower my invisible gun.

"But I promise you this," he says with conviction, "justice and righteousness are the foundation of His throne. That killer will be judged. *"We"*—he points at both of us—"will be judged. How did we respond in times of darkness? Did we trust? Did that mother honor her daughter's life by living it with the promises Jesus wants to give her? Faith in Christ gives us a chance to be healed and a hope beyond the pain of this world."

I hand him the gun.

Tim sees his opportunity to really push the verbal volley. "So how would you describe Him?" he asks.

"Who's to say it's a Him?" I rub my hand against the soft, wide lip of the white lily.

"God." He shakes his head. "How would you describe God?"

"I don't know." I turn my focus to the weed in front of me and vow silently not to leave this one with its tuchus still buried. I don't want it to pollute the beauty of the lily. "Maybe like a big, cosmic, universal power that is moving around in the wind and trees and earth and rivers. Like a life force, but I wouldn't say it's too concerned about the little stuff. I don't think it cares about the details in our lives."

"You don't think God cares about the little things in your life?" His face softens like he pities me.

"No. I don't," I say harshly.

"Why do you feel that way?" He sets down his digging spade.

"I think He, It, whatever, has a lot of bigger stuff to worry about besides whether Alice Ferguson is happy or not."

"How's your relationship with your father?" he asks, cutting through the clutter.

"What? You're a therapist now." I lean back, no longer interested in helping him with the weeds. My eyes are stuck on the lily.

"Sometimes I am. There's a good chance you developed your view of God from that relationship."

"He's dead." I am now starting to feel embarrassed, and hope the warning tone of my response will throw his chugging engine of analysis off its rails.

"Hypothetically speaking, even if your father, rest in peace, was a great man . . ."

I want to scream that he was a drunken piece of dung who open-handed slapped his daughter in alcohol-fueled rages only to pass out and puke on the carpet.

". . . and even if he was a good protector . . ."

Yeah, right. My eyes are locked on the lily so Tim won't see into my heart. Surely he must know that my dad was just the opposite of all of this, and his tactic is some reverse psychiatry ploy to break down my walls.

"Even if he was all that . . . God is a better Father." Tim gets to his knees and stands up. "God is the Father that we never had." He walks around the flower bed and offers an arm to help me get up. "He is a better protector, provider, comforter, and forgiver than any earthly man could be."

Suddenly I feel small and vulnerable. Before I can accept Tim's help, I look up at him and say, "Your father was pretty bad, wasn't he?"

Tim returns my gaze with honesty in his eyes. "Pretty bad indeed."

Then I accept his outstretched hand.

"But I had to have an open heart for my real Father to reveal who He is to me. Once I felt God the Father's love, oh, baby girl, it was the beginning of my way out of the darkness."

"You make it sound easy." I rock myself back and forth a couple of times to get on my knees and accept Tim's other hand in order to stand all the way up.

"What do think God expects from you?" He picks up his big bag of weeds and points at his gardening tools. "Grab those, I need to toss this."

I pick up the spade and three-pronged cultivator.

"I guess maybe like the Ten Commandments." I follow Tim as he walks along the side of his yard toward his house. As usual, I am the puppy following this spiritually superior family around, eagerly scooping up their emotional table leftovers.

"All He wants now is for you to respond to what He has done for you. He sent His Son for you. For you to be able to have a relationship with Him. That's all He wants."

"What's the catch?"

We make it to the top of the driveway. He looks me in the eye. "You meetin' His expectations?"

"Not very well."

"It's never too late to start." He punches the security code on the outside keypad, which makes one of his four garage doors open. "Do you believe in heaven?"

"I believe there's something after this, but I don't think it's all pearly gates."

"I don't know all that either. But I do know it's an eternal joy. It's a new heart. A new love and a new life." He lifts the lid to a blue can clearly designated for gardening rubbish. Their garage is so much neater than mine. Bikes hang on hooks. I see metal shelves with bins filled with sporting equipment, everything in its place and labeled.

"Does everybody go? Like all those people who don't chooooose the relationship?"

"Only God can judge that, but in the Word, in the Bible, it does say, 'Narrow is the gate that leads to light, and few find it.' Many are going to say, 'Lord, Lord,' but they never knew Him. Many folks are going to say they believe, but are they really living it?"

"Like all those religious hypocrites who walk around spewing hate in the name of God."

He takes the gardening tools from me and puts them in a green bin on the top shelf. "When I was playing football for the Steelers, I had done a Bible study the night before the game. There was this really funny, short little pastor from England leadin' the service. He was awesome. I'll never forget how he said, '*Gee-sus*' with his British accent. He prayed with me, called me before the game. He was a good man."

"Okay. So?" I sit on the back bumper of LeChelle's Escalade parked in the garage.

"So I'm taking this little Make-A-Wish boy, Tommy, onto the field with me during the pregame. We're comin' out the tunnel, and there's all these people behind the barricades yelling my name, and Tommy looks up at me and says, 'You know them folks?' And I say no and keep walking. But Tommy looks confused and says, 'But they're calling your name.' And they were. They thought they knew me, but I didn't know them." He sits down next to me on the bumper.

"Careful," I say, "this might not hold us both."

"But then I hear something from the crowd, a familiar voice. A voice I been with. I look back behind the barricade and it's that Englishman pastor. I look at Tommy and I say, 'Now, I know *that* man.' And I walk over to security and pull back the barricade and get my friend and bring him onto the field."

"So you're saying God needs to know you to let you in."

"Essentially, yes. That's what I've been saying. That is the start. All the voices don't mean anything unless you know Him."

"Greeeeaaattt. Now I'm picturing God's VIP lounge where all the good things happen, but I'm not getting in."

"Baby girl, you already got the key. It's in here." He touches his heart. "It isn't about money or good deeds or bad deeds or your past or your future, it all boils down to being humble. Humble enough to know that you started out a sinner but you're choosin' a different way. A way that God made for you when He sent Jesus to forgive you, save you, and set you free to be who you were made to be with Him."

As I lie in bed that night, listening to Burton's gentle snore, I wonder what it is that I have really chosen in my life. So much of my life has comprised random decisions of running and self-destruction built on a seemingly morally ambiguous pyramid with me perched at the top.

"Burton," I whisper, "are you awake?" I nudge him in the side. "Burton." Still nothing. "Are you awake?" I get him good on the upper-left rib cage with my elbow.

"Ow!" he cries out. "What's the . . ." He sits up in a drowsy, panicked fog. "Is it the baby? Is it time?" Eyes still closed, he tries to stand up and ends up falling off the bed and landing on the floor with a thud.

"No, no, I'm fine."

"Well, that makes one of us," he says, crawling back into bed. "I'm ready."

"Ready for what?" he says, turning on his bedside light. A soft glow fills our room.

"I'm ready to get married."

He sits up in bed and smiles. "Really?"

"Please don't look at me like that."

"Like what?" His overly sweet smile changes into a serious frown.

"And I'd like to do it this weekend."

"This weekend? Like in four days?"

"Yes."

"Okay. Anything else?"

"Yes, I'd like Pastor Tim to marry us."

"Should I invite my family?"

"Yes," I say matter-of-factly. "But just them. Not a big to-do. Just them and Tim and LeChelle."

"Do you want to call Amos?"

"Yes, I think I do."

"Is that it?"

I hear my clear, monotone voice but feel unsure it's actually me talking. Where did this sense of clarity come from? "You can turn off the light now. I'm really tired."

Burton leans over and looks at me in the face. "You sure you're okay?"

"Stop. I'm fine."

"And you're awake, right? This isn't some weird dream-talking thing."

"I'm awake, but I'd like to be asleep now."

He narrows his eyes at me for a second and I narrow mine back at him. Then he smiles and kisses my lips. I wrap my arms around his shoulders and our mouths melt into each other for a second longer than normal.

He rolls back over and turns off the light. We lie there in the darkness, both of us awake but neither speaking until finally . . .

"What?" I let out, exasperated, knowing he is more wide-awake than he ever has been in this bed at one in the morning.

"Why?" His voice sounds steady but curious. "Why now?"

"Because . . . because I don't want anyone else but you."

"You love me." He victoriously pumps his fist in the air. "Yes. I knew you did."

"Good night, Burton."

"Good night, Alice."

Almost two weeks later, Pastor Tim is signaling to his audience that he's on the last song before the encore. "Stand to your feet," he says.

Stand up, sit down, stand up. This place is killing me. Once again, I reach out and grasp the oak pew. It is getting harder and harder to hoist myself up. As I gain my footing, the most disgusting goop comes shooting out of me. It's as if a water balloon filled with liquid just exploded. In my underwear. Suddenly, my feet feel warm. And wet. I look down. I'm horrified to see my five-hundred-dollar Jimmy Choos covered with whatever just splashed and oozed its way out of me.

Ewww! I want to scream.

The eyes of the little girl next to me widen when she sees the puddle on the carpet and the tops of my feet glistening. The expression on her face is a mixture of confusion and disgust. She must think I just peed all over the place. She looks like she might throw up. She might as well. My shoes are already ruined.

Eyes still fixed on me, she tries to shield herself from the hot mess by stepping closer into her mother's body. My face turns from the girl to Tim.

His sermon rolls to a close. He proclaims, "The greatest thing that could have ever happened to you is happening right now!"

Duh. Something is happening, all right, but I am not sure it is the greatest thing ever. My baby is about to plop out of me onto the Christ carpet. In front of a bunch of holy-rolling strangers.

"Bow your heads and close your eyes," Tim continues.

The little girl is frantically trying to get her mom's attention by repeatedly hitting her leg and tugging on her arm.

"Lord, today, while all heads are bowed and eyes are closed, we have an opportunity to recognize the gift that has been given . . . *given* . . . to us. That gift is the gift of knowing You."

The only gift I need right now had better contain a towel, a washcloth, some soap, and an ambulance. And a new pair of shoes to replace the ones I just ruined.

"Maybe you have felt like you knew God, but you've missed His power and His purpose," says Tim. "You feel you've gotten away from Jesus or you're too broken, or you've sinned too much, that you're not good enough for His grace."

Okay, that last one applies to me but . . . *owww!* Now, that's pain.

"Or there are those here that may have had God on pause. Living your life your way while keeping Jesus on the back burner. Maybe your life has been about so many other things but it's never been enough, and today a revelation has come that you need more. You want more."

Another wave of pain hits me like a baseball bat at full swing in the cages at Dodger Stadium. My legs buckle below me. I am gripping the pew so hard that my knuckles are white and the veins in my fingers are bulging.

"Lord, I pray for these here today that have gotten separated from You. As You renew these people, their hearts, I pray that they would feel You, Lord—let them feel Your love, forgiveness, hope, and a future. Amen." Tim pauses and opens his eyes. "If you prayed this prayer and you want a new beginning, raise your hand, while all heads are bowed and eyes are closed."

It is all I can do to peel my fingers off the pew, one by one. I try to raise my hand all the way but I barely make it to my shoulder. My half-raised hand sums everything up, doesn't it? Once again my life is overtaking my ability to ask for help. *Owww.* More shooting pain.

The mother next to me still has her eyes closed and I want to shove her to the ground so I can get to the hospital. *Moooovvvvvve!*

Tim scans the crowd. "Okay, put your hands down. If you prayed that prayer, I want you to come on down. Come on down. Life-group leaders and ministry team, please come down here."

As instructed, a few people start to head down to the front.

"This moment is designed for you. For those who raised your hands, come on down."

You bet this is my moment, I think. People are moving. I'm moving. *I'm getting out of here. Get out of my way!*

The plan is to escape to the Baptist Hospital birthing center, but as I stumble into the aisle, they are all looking at me. The entire United Nations of believers is staring at me. I'm the only one. They are smiling and clapping for me. While the plan was to turn right and walk out the back door, I feel a pull toward the front of the church. Incredibly, despite my obvious need for immediate medical attention, people are encouraging me to go the wrong way.

Tim's face is filled with pride and hope and something I can't quite put my finger on.

When I find myself at the front, Tim walks off the stage, his eyes looking out at the crowd. He puts his hand on me. Then he gracefully wraps his entire strong arm around me. Another shooting pain drills into me. I scream as I drop to my knees.

A lady in the second row, prim and pretty in her hat and her Sunday dress, takes this for a call-and-response. "Yes, Lord!" she screams. "Yes, Lord."

I scream back: "I'm in *labor . . . Get me out of here!*"

The entire congregation goes silent.

15

Somethin' Ain't Right

Sitting in the passenger seat of Tim's black Range Rover, I can't help but notice how his giant hands are gripping the leather steering wheel.

LeChelle sits in the backseat. "Titans' security is getting a hold of Burton." She tries to sound like a woman with a plan.

I moan.

He's dodging cars on the freeway with the same intensity he must have used dodging offensive linemen when he was on the hunt to lay down their quarterback. He's precise, aggressive, determined, and speedy.

"How you doin', baby girl?" he asks.

"Well, let's see." I take a deep, labored—literally—breath. "I'm in labor in Nashville"—I shout the word *Nashville* for emphasis—"with a woman who might have to help me give birth to my baby in this car and as a bonus I've got a man driving who isn't my husband because *my* husband is at football practice. I'm alone and about to have a baby and, in just one Sunday service at your church, I've become acutely aware that I'm a completely screwed-up hot mess."

"That kinda hurts my feelings," he says, trying to make me feel better.

I snarl, banging my fist on the door.

"Easy on the Rover, the door hasn't done anything to you," he chides.

"You're next, preacher man!" I shriek. "Can't you drive this thing faster?"

He cuts off a "Got Milk?" tanker in the middle lane.

"This isn't funny!!!"

I place my right hand under my belly. I'm not sure if I should be trying to hold my baby in or pull my baby out. My hands are damp with sweat; I'm like a nervous teenage boy about to ask a girl to the prom. Gross. As I reach up to grip the doorframe in an attempt to find a more comfortable position—as if—something the color of port wine drips from my hand to my forearm.

"You're not *completely* screwed up and you know it," I can hear Tim say, but he sounds far away.

"You're not alone," LeChelle adds as my world begins to move in slow motion.

I feel dizzy and their words sound muffled. I suddenly have tunnel vision spattered with dark ink spots. I mumble, "Yeah, yeah, I know. I got you," as I realize my fingers are not soiled in port, but in blood. They were white and now they are red. Blood. It's blood. I'm nauseous and my eyelids are lead. I completely lose the ability to hold my head up, and I face-plant onto the side window despite still sitting upright and being buckled up for safety.

The last thing I remember is trying to say, "Something isn't right."

As I drift in and out of consciousness, I flash back to 2001.

Summer 2001: I am reminded of the potholders I used to make at summer camp as *NCN* headlines and covers frolic around my mind space. A-list divorces, crotch shots, studio implosions, and political image catastrophes: these stories formed the colorful backdrop of the late nineties when I antagonistically exploited every celebrity image catastrophic scandal in order to catapult myself into my own work sanctuary.

I stand in my corner office with my back to the picture window behind my desk, looking with pride at all of my framed covers lining the walls. Amos pours a glass of Cristal Rosé Champagne and we toast, plotting our exit strategy to launch Trashville.

"To Amy Fisher: a nice girl from Long Island who generously put a bullet into the skull of the wife of her Svengali boyfriend, Joey Buttafuoco, practically begging us to christen her 'Long Island Lolita.'" I motion to the cover story framed opposite my desk. We clink our glasses and drink.

The ironic tone of my truthful traipse down the golden-cover road could lead one to believe I might actually find humor in these overtly distorted tales of human woe. People who are clearly not living in the bull's-eye of good choices.

Amos shakes his head pitifully. "Sad, but seriously, what's he doing with the babysitter? Poor wife should have never answered the door that fateful day."

"To a decade of cheaters," I continue as we refill and hold up our glasses again. "And bad decision-makers.

"To the assistant coroner who agreed to cut off a John Doe's man snake for the bargain price of $2,500 so we could pretend it was John Wayne Bobbitt's soon-to-be-reattached organ."

"Oh, Lorena, thank you for doing a Belushi samurai chop on your husband's wiener." Amos pretends to sprinkle spices and follows it up with a karate chop.

"And we're just getting started!" I point to a cover of Nancy Kerrigan in a leg cast. "To the new stereo that I bought and installed in Tonya Harding's boyfriend's mother's minivan, in exchange for a juicy tell-all exclusive of why she and her accomplice thought Nancy Kerrigan deserved a clubbing."

"Alleged accomplice, darling. Alleged."

"Touché." I nod to Amos as I pour more bubbly into his glass.

"Ohhh, oh, oh! To Hugh Grant and his mug shot." My eyes direct Amos to a very sad cover of Hugh in the Los Angeles County lockup.

"Ahhh, and to my boy Tupac, who got shot in Vegas. A moment of silence, please," Amos says, as he grabs the framed cover of our magazine and clutches it to his chest. "Poetic genius. rest In peace."

To lighten the mood, I clap my hands and shout: "To Woody Allen, who married the girl he somewhat raised as his daughter, Soon-Yi. Thank you for this disgusting, stomach-turning cover shot of you two canoodling and holding hands in Europe."

We scream "Ewww!" in unison as we clink and drink and continue to roast pop culture.

"Oh, I got another one," says Amos, pointing at the funeral procession cover shot. "To Princess Diana allegedly being murdered by the monarchy. And, oh-you-betcha to the Minnesotans who elected former pro wrestler Jesse 'the Body' Ventura to be their governor!"

Amos's Fargo accent makes me laugh even harder. "But the mother lode on the road to our new enterprise has to be Jen and

Brad. Ahh, the breakup of the decade after I followed them in Cabo." I wink as I slurp down more.

Amos spits out his champagne, laughing. "You wore that green bikini and horrible sombrero and sat under a palm tree in the perfect position to capture shots of Jen weeping as Brad walked away. Brilliant. Just brilliant."

"Indeed I did, and I got a third-degree sunburn but soothed it away with shots of tequila and Vicodin."

"And, and, and . . . you were so right about Brad and his *Mrs. Smith* shacking up in his double-wide location trailer." Amos points at me in recognition of my sleuthing skills. He is Watson to my Sherlock Holmes.

"Without us, there would be no TomKat or Bennifer. We started a revolution with Brangelina." I gaze lovingly at our cover, the first of many, of Brad Pitt and Angelina Jolie. "America thought all there was to her was blood-drinking and brother-kissing, and then we flipped it upside down by plastering our pages with her humanitarian adopting, advocating, and testifying efforts for the United Nations."

Amos pauses in front of a framed cover of Angie in some jungle. "A modern-day Mother Teresa."

"I still have my *Team Jen* T-shirt." I plop down in my chair and spin.

"Frankly I'm still Team Angie." He fills his own glass to the rim.

Amos and I are hanging ten on the tsunami of a Jerry Springer–culture generation. Even our own president is embroiled in scandal, almost ousted from office after having an affair with an intern in the White House and lying his butt off about it, only to have his own DNA (which he deposited on her dress) become federal evidence and prove his pants were on fire.

It's these scrapings from the bottom of the barrel that fed the American tabloid-driven culture and launched Amos and me to the top of the money pile. I've received a good many promotions, but the thrill of such sophomoric motivation is gone. I'm ready to venture out on my own and the Internet has given us a plethora of new opportunities.

"And now, here's to Trashville," I say, raising my glass. "Where we aren't afraid to dig in your Dumpster." I giggle. "For money, the only true root of happiness."

"Watch out, Courtney Love! We'll find you in all of your lipstick-smudged teeth and popping-out-of-your-shredded-dress glory." Amos plops down on my cozy sofa. He's clearly getting buzzed.

"I will say this, I did like Matthew McConaughey. I thought he was pretty solid until—" I point to a cover showing Matthew playing his bongos naked at his house in Austin. "I didn't think we'd be writing a cover story about him. The bongos were one thing, but resisting arrest and disturbance of the peace while smoking cannabis. Nice." I wink at Amos. "Well played, Mr. M. I didn't think ya had it in ya."

Amos pipes in as his head tilts back against the wall with all my cover stories framed above him. "Subsequently *The Newton Boys* was also the movie set I visited where we broke the story of Uma Thurman hooking up with Ethan Hawke long before they were married."

"Ohhh, that's right! But my favorite girl so far is Cameron Diaz. After chilling with her on the set of *There's Something About Mary,* I decided she's my favorite straight-shooting actress. She curses like a sailor and throws a perfect spiral better than her day-part player, Green Bay quarterback Brett Favre."

"Cam, sweet Cam." Amos closes his eyes as he whispers softly, "We're sooooo not done with you yet."

I get up from my chair and go lie down next to him on the sofa. "Oh, Amos, why do you have to be gay? You're my perfect man."

"Alice, sweet pea, I may be perfect but I am not your man. He's coming, though, I promise." He kisses me on the top of my head.

The second week of September 2001: I am shacked up at the Ritz-Carlton in Pasadena with mogul Carl Angoli. Carl runs his very own cable conglomerate, which includes thirteen cable-television networks, countless radio stations, a pro hockey team, and several racehorses. He's got nice hair but is easily twenty-five years my senior. We met two months ago at a cable convention after-party that he hosted for A-list television stars. I was there doing what I do best.

He's a catch if you're fishing for billions. In the social skills department, however, he's a two or maybe a three. In the humor department, which is a must-have for me, he is better. He has a dry sense of humor and a weird, kinky way of looking at the world that I kind of dig. As far as looks go, I can't help but wonder how Carl would feel about a new wardrobe, new teeth, a personal trainer, and an overall grooming guru. I mean, I'm no ten (more like a strong seven), but I think everybody should strive to look as good as they possibly can, especially if they can afford the improvements. And Carl can.

Our enjoyment meter is usually dictated by my alcohol-intake meter. During my sober moments I try not to be shallow and to see past Carl's exterior and concentrate on the potential of the man I can make him into.

It's 6:46 a.m. I am pretending to be asleep so he won't try to kiss me good-bye. Squinting, I watch him skulk around, his shoulders shrugged. Financial magnitude definitely doesn't translate into stature: he has terrible posture.

Man, I need to be done with this one.

Finally, the light from the hallway is squeezed out as he shuts the door and heads to a breakfast meeting. Don't get me wrong: the island-hopping on his GIV jet and unlimited shopping sprees these last couple of months have been great, but I'm pretty sure that I couldn't sell out to life with a man who clearly doesn't fit me. Plus, he smells weird. And he either doesn't know it or tries to cover it—unsuccessfully—with cologne. If I had to describe his scent, I would call it l'eau de mildew. It's true. All the money and the success in the world can't wash the smell of mildew off Carl the Cable Billionaire. The smell follows him around Pig-Pen style, like a cloud of dust.

I get out of bed, rubbing my dry eyes, and head into the bathroom. My cell phone rings just as I sit down on the toilet. Annoying. I sit there feeling the fuzzy effects of too much red wine mixed with my last two Xanax.

I can hear the phone. Who in the hell is calling me this early?

As I wipe, flush, and get up to wash my hands, it's as if an aroma balloon full of Carl's mildewy cologne bursts in my face. I nearly gag as I realize the culprit of his mystery odor is here in the bathroom.

Carl's traveling kit is sitting next to the sink. I unzip it, hoping to find a prescription pain med to help take the hangover edge off. I hold my breath as I rifle through his little brown labeled bottles. Viagra (that explains a lot), high blood pressure and anxiety meds, something that I think is for male incontinence, and— bingo—a bottle of Vicodin. I exhale and empty five into my hand (gotta save a stash for later). I pop one in my mouth and tilt my head under the faucet to swallow my happy pill down, when another wave of that smell smacks me in the face.

My cell phone rings again from the bedroom. Really? Again? Don't they know I have to find the mother ship of the stink patrol first? In my lover's travel bag, I corner the culprit: a toothbrush container. I hold it up in the light, then pop open the top. I drop it. I feel like I just grabbed a beehive and the bees are attacking me.

He keeps his wet toothbrush tucked away in here where it collects bacteria, creates mildew, and is responsible for the nastiest odor I've had the displeasure of identifying in my life. I swear there is moss growing in that thing! How does this smart, successful man not know that smell is trapped in there, that it is on him and on his hands, neck, face, and everything around him? How does he put that toothbrush in his mouth? How did I let him put his mouth on me? What the presence of narcotics in one's body will let you do. Shame on me. Yuck, yuck, yuck.

I scrub my hands with the bar soap next to the sink and head back into the darker of the two rooms in our suite. Next to my underpants and bra on the floor, my phone is glowing. I pick it up. Two missed calls, both from Amos.

I pull on an oversize white Ritz robe, walk to the sliding doors of the balcony, and tug open the drapes about a foot to let in a little sunlight. Squinting, I make my way to the minibar. There, I shoot back a half bottle of orange juice in a miniature plastic container and refill it with Grey Goose Vodka left over from the night before. I shake it up and drink a morning cocktail to give my Vicodin a little jump start. Breakfast of tabloid champions.

Again my phone rings. I walk over to the bed, drop down, and flip it open. "What do you want?" My voice sounds raspier than normal. "Wh-wha-what?" I listen to Amos talk as my heart begins to palpitate. I feel a sickness in the lowest pit of my stomach and it is too soon to be a result of the feel-good cocktail I've just ingested. "Hold on!" I say as I dig around for the television remote control and turn the set on. The room starts spinning.

Amos is still on the line and I'm still holding the phone to my ear, but neither of us is talking. I sit on the end of the bed staring with sheer panic as an American Airlines jet beelines toward the World Trade Center.

I gasp into the phone as another plane hits the other tower. "Amos, is this live?"

I'm not sure how I feel other than overwhelmingly stunned. It doesn't look real. It looks like a movie set. A weird, end-of-the-world blockbuster starring Harrison Ford. "Is this footage authentic?" I whisper. I flip the channels: every station is covering the exact same thing.

Just then, the hotel suite door opens. Carl comes in. He's ghostly white.

"Where? Where else did planes crash besides New York?" I say in the phone.

"The Pentagon," Carl answers as he makes his way to me.

"I'll call you back. Wait—where are you? Stay there! I'll be there in an hour." And I flip my phone closed.

"I've got to get packed," Carl mumbles, moving toward his suitcase. "Come with me. I need to get to New York."

I spin around. "New York? No! It's not safe. Stay here." I tug him from behind.

Just then, I notice that he is more than just freaked out. He's trembling. "My . . . my daughter," he moans. He turns around to face me.

He's a shell of his slouched, smelly self, and that is saying something.

"She's in the North Tower."

I shake my head in disbelief. "Maybe, maybe she got out. She's safe."

"No. She called me."

He takes his phone and hands it to me. I'm confused. I don't know what he wants me to do.

"Do you want me to call her?" I don't know how to help. "I

could call her. I'll call my friends. They'll call her friends . . ." What am I saying? I don't know who to call.

He hits the voice mail and speakerphone buttons and I hear a young woman's breathy voice and an eerie stillness mixed with some static in the background. "Dad, I'm at work and, and a plane has hit our building." More heavy breathing. "I'm okay. But it's hit below our floor. I'm in my office." Her voice goes from a relaxed twentysomething executive to a little girl. "Daddy, I need you to come and get me." She sobs. "Daddy, I don't want to die. Please come help me. Daddy," she cries, "I'm afraid."

And then there is nothing. I look at him. His eyes are wide with fear and the conviction that somehow, someway, he can rescue his baby.

I watch his most primal instinct taking over and his deepest fatherly fear coming true. Someone, somewhere is hurting his baby and he is desperate to save her. Desperate to help her, to undo it all.

"She'll get out," I say, trying to sound convincing. "Come on, I'll help you."

I grab his suitcase out of the closet. I take everything on the bathroom counter and scrape it off the top and catch it in my robe that I'm using as a sling. I run from the bathroom to the bedroom and drop it all into his suitcase. I pull his underwear, T-shirts, and shorts out of the dresser, fling suits and shirts and ties into the bag, and zip it all up.

I want so much for him to save her. For him to be the one who does the impossible. For him to be able to hold her in his arms. I want it for them both.

He stands with his arms hanging limply at his sides, watching me hustle around the room until I shove his bag at him. "Go!" I say, heaving the bag at his chest.

He just stands there, traumatized, awkwardly clutching his suitcase.

"Go help your daughter!" I scream at him. "Go!"

He snaps out of his trance and heads for the door. He doesn't look back at me. He doesn't say anything. He just runs toward what matters most.

I sit on the end of the bed, alone and horrified as I watch the North Tower collapse. There is no safe place. No safe house. No safe relationship. No amount of safe money that can shield you from life. Her voice mail message plays over and over in my head. I know he is somewhere in his chauffeured Mercedes heading to the private airport and his pilot who is on standby. I know he is trying to rescue her and I know he is too late.

"Daddy, I'm afraid," I say out loud.

I get to Amos at the office two hours later. I am emotionless from the meds and mayhem. From the sadness and shock.

People in our office are glued to their computers and televisions. I jog to Amos's refuge. He stands up when he sees me. We fall into each other's arms and stand holding on to each other. We sit in his office all day watching the footage over and over.

I peer out of his 15th-floor corner office at the magic lights of Hollywood. From the outside, my life looks solidly and neatly put together like Legos. But in reality, I'm just a house of cards, capable of imploding with the slightest sneeze. This life I am leading seems so brutally vacuous and egocentric. I have everything I ever wanted and yet, I have nothing at all. What does it all mean? I fill my lungs with recycled air and put my forehead against the glass window, looking down at the people scurrying about. Remorse, or sorrow, fills me. I don't know what it is, but it is sharp and it cuts and it hurts. All those people, gone. Just like that. It doesn't make any sense. All those families, suffering. Confused. Stun-gunned by life. Just when I think the world can't touch me, it strikes me like a lightning bolt and tears my heart to shreds. There just aren't enough magazine cover stories in this world to wallpaper that type of pain in my heart away. Perhaps this is just who I am destined to be.

I wonder what my mother would think if she could see me now.

I can hear Tim on his cell phone, saying, "We're pulling up to the hospital now." He could be talking to my husband or Dr. Nicole.

The pain is winding around my back, across my stomach, and back again. I scream. The squeezing and cinching make me feel like a horse whose rider is tightening his saddle before a derby race.

The next thing I am aware of is Tim hoisting me up out of the truck and helping LeChelle put me in a wheelchair outside the emergency room. A nurse wearing scrubs the color of Pepto-Bismol is standing at the door, waiting for us.

I can see the veins bulging on the sides of Tim's face as we both notice the puddle of blood dripping from my skirt. My head continues to flop to the side as the nurse starts pushing me inside the hospital. I can see a trail of blood on the ground behind me.

"She's bleeding," Tim says calmly to the lady pushing me.

"I can see that," the woman says.

"*Aaaahh!*" I cry out in pain as another contraction grips my body, strangling me from the inside out. It jolts me up but I can't really hold my upper body straight. I feel hands lifting me. I am placed on a gurney of some sort.

"Her husband is Dr. Banister . . . We're taking her up," says a new nurse to the Pepto-Bismol pusher.

"I'll take it from here," I hear a young doctor say to the nurse. "Dr. Schlossberg told me to be ready for her."

Someone is taking my blood pressure and another nurse has

her hands on my belly. Someone is drawing blood from one side of me. Another nurse is putting in IVs; some lady is on the phone. Must not be a busy morning at Baptist Hospital, as it seems like every available medical professional is hovering over me.

The young doctor asks the nurse, "What do we have?"

A middle-aged nurse who could be my mother responds, "Her belly is rock hard. Call up to labor and delivery. Now! Tell them we are on our way."

I am whisked out of the room and back into the hallway. LeChelle and Tim are jogging next to the gurney. LeChelle says, "You're okay, sweet girl. Don't you worry."

I try to say, "I'm hot," but my tongue is swollen and my ears feel clogged. I try to pant like a dog.

She gets it. "You're hot?"

I roll my head around in agreement. Black spots are dancing in front of my eyes. Something is vibrating. I am moving fast but I am lying flat on my back. I think I am awake but when I move my lips, no sound comes out. I can't speak. The only sound I can make is when I scream in pain.

A stairwell door slams open. I can hear Dr. Nicole's voice but I can't see her. "Where are we, people?" she asks.

We've stopped outside the elevator. The young male doctor answers, "Her pulse is 120 and her blood pressure is dropping."

A new nurse has joined Team Save Alice. "Ninety over fifty," she says.

"It's an abruption. The placenta is separating from the wall of the uterus." Even in my distorted state, I admire the way Dr. Nicole is commanding the room. I'm withering under the heaving pain. I'm pretty sure someone is running over me with a small car. I'm crying but no one hears me.

Suddenly, I feel an arctic breeze. Goosebumps cover my body in response, trying to warm me up. I mumble, "I'mmmm freezing," as my head tilts to the left in slow motion. I'm trying to focus on anything other than the blurry walls running past me.

"Get me an OR team!" Dr. Nicole yells, "Now! I'm going to need a first assist and we need NICU. Let's roll her up."

Now we are in a small room. An elevator? Someone puts an oxygen mask over my nose and mouth. I can see Dr. Nicole with her Doppler on my belly. "Shut up," she snarls at the people around us. There's complete silence from inside the small ascending metal box. I hear rushing water in my head.

"Baby's alive." She moves to the end of the gurney and looks at the bottoms of my bloody feet as she rips off my underpants and pushes my legs up and gets between my legs.

Tim stands with his large hand on my head. I'm sure he's praying but I can't hear him. Dr. Nicole moves from between my legs to the side of the gurney as it's pushed out of the elevator. She's covered in blood up to her elbows.

In yet another hallway, Dr. Nicole says, "I need another IV, fluid going in wide." She looks at a nurse then barks at the other. "Tell them I need O negative blood *now*!"

I turn my head and see Tim. We are still moving. He's slow-jogging again next to my floating, moving bed.

"Hang in there," he says with a half smile. I can hear him praying under his breath. "Lord, protect and keep Alice safe."

My pain is turning into anxiety and fear. It is then that I realize I am dying. I feel like Carol Anne in *Poltergeist*. I'm trapped in the TV static and told to stay away from the light. It's creepy: I can hear everyone, I can't stay away from the light, and I have no idea how I am going to get out of here.

The woman in the Pepto-Bismol scrubs is mumbling something about blood clots. As if she didn't sound serious before, she sounds super serious now.

"This is Dr. Banister's wife." Another female voice.

Thanks to the fact that I am either having a near-death experience or am under the influence of some seriously powerful narcotic in my IV, I am now running alongside the gurney with the rest of them. I can look down at my big, bloated, bloody body. The sheet underneath me looks as if it has been tie-dyed red, with large, almost black clots clustered inside my legs, their inky tentacles clinging to the sheet.

"Move it!" a doctor yells at Tim after realizing I'm the wife of one of their own. Funny, no one knows me. No one knows Burton has a wife. I thought they did, but they don't.

But then I can feel both of Tim's hands on my head. "Lord, save your precious child and save this baby. In *Jesus'* name I pray."

My gurney flies through double doors and stalls in a sterile operating room. A shell of me stands with Tim and LeChelle. The double doors have shut us out. The chaos and movement continue inside, without us. I look at them but they can't see me. LeChelle's face is sunken. Tim looks at the ceiling, through the plaster and insulation and beyond, to the heavens. He prays, "Lord God, guide these doctors to save Alice's life."

LeChelle wraps her arms around him from behind as he turns to face her. They embrace. I smile.

"To save the life of her unborn baby, guide their hands," he continues.

"Yes, Lord," confirms LeChelle.

"Give them wisdom and all Your healing power," Tim says. "I pray in Jesus' name. Amen."

And then I am gone.

16

Death and Delivery

The operating room is bright with what appear to be flashbulbs ping-ponging off chrome machines. A kind man speaks with a calming tone as he caresses my head. "We're gonna lift you now. Ready?" Without waiting for my answer—perhaps knowing I can't answer—he and others lift me up and over to another table.

This table is cool on my bare bottom. It does nothing to ease the searing-hot pain that is shooting out of my pelvis. The man continues to coo soothing words as he places a mask over my head. "There, there. Now, now. That's good."

Until I feel nothing. Nothing at all.

Darkness surrounds me as I descend from pain to fearful to terrified. I am not sure if I am dead, but I am pretty sure this is not heaven. Where is my white light? Aren't my parents supposed to be here to greet me? Why am I lost in nothingness?

I am a grain of sand slipping through an hourglass, only I know the bottom can never be turned right side up. I'm done. This is it. But I'm not ready. It is not my time! In desperation, I claw at the walls, the sand, the edges of the hole to stop my descent, but I slip through the hole and fall into the pit.

Where am I? I am no longer a part of this world and it goes on without me. I can see nurses and doctors from all around, as if I am above, around, and beside them.

I am watching them from the darkness, almost as if the devil himself is teasing me, letting me view my own death. My child's death.

The pain that will ensue as a result of all this.

Like a choreographed dance troupe, Team Save Alice performs a remarkable operating-room routine. There's an underlying tone of urgency but no panic. Dr. Nicole is the director and star of the show. She has trained for years for moments like these. Rehearsal is over: this is opening night.

Pieces of purple hair escape from the sides of Dr. Nicole's Titans surgical cap as she ferociously scrubs her hands much more quickly than one would expect for someone about to operate. The nurses mirror her intensity; they are not painting but rather splashing Betadine on my bulging pregnant belly.

A nurse slips a catheter into my bladder. Another nurse straps down my legs before doing the same to my arms, creating an ER angel.

Another mask-wearing nurse comes into the room carrying blood. She's reading the label out loud to another nurse who is checking the hospital identification bracelet.

Wearing their nametags and NICU patches on their scrub pockets, a neonatal intensive-care doctor, two nurses, and a respiratory therapist are all in the room standing next to an infant warmer.

Dr. Nicole hurries in from the scrub room and rushes into her gown and gloves as the anesthesiologist inserts a plastic endotracheal tube in my mouth. As one of the scrub nurses hands Dr. Nicole a scalpel, the anesthesiologist looks up at Dr. Nicole and calmly says, "Go."

Without hesitation, as she's done thousands of times before, Dr. Nicole slices through the skin, fat, fascia, and abdominal muscles. She separates the muscles with her hands until she sees the huge, graying uterus. Looking at my unconscious face—now just her patient's face—she frowns. "Pale." Dr. Nicole says "Come on, Alice" as she makes another quick incision. Pushing with her two index fingers, she tears the uterus to make the opening big enough to get the baby out.

"There she is," she says under her mask. The baby is floating in the womb. Dr. Nicole touches the umbilical cord, which has prolapsed through the incision. "She is ashen but she has a pulse," she says loud enough for the NICU team to hear. "Let's keep her that way."

She lifts the baby out, milking the cord to squeeze every droplet of blood into the baby. When there is nothing left, the cord is clamped and cut. The silent, limp baby is handed off to the NICU nurse and the team immediately goes into action, placing her in the warmer and doing chest compressions. A tiny oxygen mask is placed over her precious face until finally, finally, a faint, muffled cry can be heard.

Dr. Nicole feverishly pulls the placenta out of the belly. "Barely attached," she notes to the nurse next to her as she tugs out shiny pink membranes. Large, dark blood clots follow it. Everything inside of the body cavity is pale.

"She's lost too much blood." Burton stands behind Dr. Nicole. He's wearing his scrubs, looking hopelessly at his lifeless, filleted wife.

"You shouldn't be in here!" Dr. Nicole barks. "Go be with your daughter. We need to get Alice closed so they can stabilize her. We're moving her up to ICU." She pulls the uterus out of the patient's abdomen. It's pinking up nicely thanks to the blood transfusion. A perfect flesh seamstress, Dr. Nicole begins to stitch up the incisions.

Burton walks over to his baby girl. "She's so little." He eyes the NICU nurse.

"Five pounds, nine ounces." The nurse's mask moves slightly and her eyes crinkle. "She's a fighter," she says with a smile.

With the uterus repaired and abdomen closed, the scrub nurse and Dr. Nicole begin to roll Alice to the ICU. Burton trails alongside the gurney. As they come through the doors, Tim and LeChelle stand up from their chairs. Burton nods at them to follow. "She's alive."

Dr. Nicole begins her debriefing. "My biggest fear is that she could go into DIC."

"What's DIC?" Tim asks, looking at Burton.

"Who the hell are you?" She looks at Tim and LeChelle.

"Our pastors."

"Sorry." She keeps walking.

"Disseminated intravascular coagulation." Burton clarifies, "It's when you bleed so much that your body uses up its clotting factors and you lose the ability to stop bleeding."

Dr. Klein, a middle-aged, solemn man with silver hair, greets Burton as they roll into the ICU. "We'll start giving her blood, fresh frozen plasma, and cryo to help her clot."

Nurses scurry around, hooking Alice up to machines and getting her ET tube attached to the ventilator. Alice is surrounded by eight people: three nurses, Dr. Klein, Dr. Nicole, Burton, Tim, and LeChelle. Team Save Alice is united.

Dr. Nicole turns and walks Burton to the back of the room. "You know she has lost a lot of blood, Burton." She is saying something more than those words. Words he's spoken before. Words that have many medical outcomes, most of them not good.

LeChelle takes Tim's hand. She's not steadying him as much as she is steadying herself.

"There is a chance she may not come out of it," Dr. Nicole says quietly.

Burton dismisses her slightly and walks back to the gurney. "I know."

"We just can't know now what kind of brain damage may have occurred."

Tim squeezes his wife's hand tighter. He places his other hand on Alice's foot over the blanket.

Burton tilts his head, looking past Alice's face and into her body, searching for signs and answers. "She loves me. She's not dying now. Huh, Alice? No checking out now."

I can no longer see any of them tending to my body. My soul is elsewhere.

I am standing in the middle of an icy lake. The ghostly bluish-white surface is cracking all around me and giving way. I try to run but slip and fall instead. The ice is replaced by a black water as my body slips into the bone-chilling abyss.

I weep as my eyes search for someone, anyone, but the dry, frozen bank is miles away. No one can hear my screams. No one is responding to my pleas for help. My prayers and my bargaining have lost their power.

I am alone.

With my last ounce of fight, I desperately try to pull myself up on top of the ice floes. But each time, just as I get an elbow up, the piece gives way and breaks. I am freezing; my clothes are heavy and soaked. My feet are lead blocks weighing me down.

Dread and anxiety creep over me like tiny ticks crawling on my skin, looking for a place to burrow. There is no escaping this frozen current. The terror paralyzes me. I panic as I realize I am being swallowed up and there is no escaping.

There is no redeeming me. I'm a goner. Hopeless.

I have been judged and I am serving my sentence, freezing in the still water. I am cognizant that I am eternally doomed. I'm drowning in all of my brokenness.

I let go of the ice, giving up, as there is nowhere to go and no way to hide from it. I succumb to my own demise. My lungs fill with immobilizing water, asphyxiating me. My limp, lifeless body is pulled toward the bottom of the black-and-purple terror of hopelessness.

As I sink, my past begins to swirl around me like a maelstrom, cutting me with sharp edges. Shrapnel of ugliness rips through me. I'm covered in bloodless gashes and painful scrapes. Dread rips and tears at my soul. It, which must be the great darkness, is more horrific than anything I could ever imagine. This is the descent to hell.

Shivering, I am again forced to watch more of my own demise. It is morning and the early sun shines on sparrows perched on the window ledge outside of the ICU waiting room. I'm aware of the surroundings, but I am not in them. It is a waiting game for more torture, I suppose. Where is my baby? Heaven, most likely. Another piece of me gone.

From where I am looking I cannot tell; I am simply part of the heavy emotion. Wearing the same clothes from the day before, Tim has bags under his eyes but a certainty in his step. He says hello to the male attendant as he passes the nursing station and heads into Alice's room. He hands Burton a Starbucks coffee.

Sadness and regret fill up my empty soul pockets as I watch the people I have lost. People who may have loved me.

"How you holding up, brother?" Tim asks, putting a hand on Burton's shoulder.

He turns to Tim. "She's come too far, you know?" He sounds frustrated and hopeful at the same time.

"Yes, she has. But you, my friend, you gotta keep the faith that God has a plan for her."

"I am."

"It may not look like our plan, but He has a plan."

"I know that." Burton sighs. "You know y'all have changed her, right?" he adds as if comforting Tim.

Tim looks down at Alice's motionless body kept alive by machines and medications. They stand in silence reflecting on a woman they have both grown to love.

"He"—Tim points up—"He changes us all. It's just a miracle to see Him work."

Dr. Nicole comes into the room and starts checking Alice. "Her wounds have stopped oozing." Dr. Nicole manages to make something distressing sound positive. She reseals a bandage on Alice's belly and continues her examination. "And her blood pressure has stabilized."

All of sudden I feel a dragging sensation, like I'm being pulled under again. Another yank toward hell. *Noooo!* I want to scream, but icy water fills my mouth, choking me.

Just as Dr. Nicole exhales her relief, Alice's legs start kicking violently. Dr. Nicole grabs one of her legs as an alarm sounds. The seizure moves to Alice's upper body. Her arms start flapping like a bird's wings. The bed shakes.

"What is going on?" Burton yells at Dr. Nicole. A nurse comes flying into the ICU stable, responding to the alarm.

"She's having an eclamptic seizure," Dr. Nicole says, trying to hold Alice still. Alice's face begins twitching. "Get her tongue!" Dr. Nicole barks. "She needs magnesium in her IV!"

"We don't have magnesium up here," the nurse answers with hopeless frustration.

Dr. Nicole is holding Alice's head and Burton and Tim each have a leg.

Dr. Klein hurries into the room and pushes past them all. "Valium. Give her Valium. *Stat.*"

Then Alice's body goes stiff. Dr. Nicole leans her head down and listens to her breathing. "Call down to labor and delivery and get the magnesium." She points at a nurse near the door. "You! Move!"

My mouth tastes bitter from what I have swallowed. I am separated from all that is good. Hope has been torn away from this unforgiving and dark place. Something merciless is mocking me and my fear. The same mocking tone I chanted making gossipy covers of my magazines at other people's expense is now turned back at me. No accountability. No remorse. No compassion. No truth. Only ugly perversions wallow in this place. Alternating cries of desperation and sobs of sorrow echo around me. The hatefulness and bigotry make me scream, but my voice is lost among the billions of other screams that swirl around me. A new, even more frigid wave overtakes me and I begin to shake uncontrollably. Then I become one with darkness under the deep, icy, beaten places of my soul and the lost souls of others.

I am certain that this is the final resting place for the tormented and the depraved. It is where corrupted souls go when they have run out of chances.

LeChelle sits next to Alice's bed. Otherwise the room is empty except for a nurse looking over numbers on the machines. The ventilator's *swoosh* sounds regularly. The low tones of the beeping heart monitors and the other machines that are keeping Alice alive provide orchestral background music. Placing her worn Bible on the bed, LeChelle scoots her chair closer to Alice.

"Baby girl, I know that you're resting, but you need to try and wake up." She rubs Alice's arm from wrist to bicep gently before opening her Bible to read out loud. "'He sent His Word, and healed them, and delivered them from their destructions.'"

LeChelle stands up next to the bed and places her hands on Alice's face. It's eerily similar to the way Alice's mother used to touch her as a child. "Father, I call You now for my precious friend. I believe it is through Your power that You can restore Alice. Take away anything that would hold her in darkness. You created everything in this child. Every hair, tooth, and nail. Every dream and hope. Every ounce of her heart belongs to You. You knew her steps before she could walk and only You can restore her to absolute health. Fulfill Your healing powers. We trust Your Word to be true, and the Word says, 'Then Your light will break forth like the dawn and healing shall spring up quickly.' Please, God, save my friend, save this mother, save this soul. I ask this through Christ our Lord. Amen."

* * *

LeChelle's humble prayers take me back to just a week ago. I'm sitting on the back porch in an oversize rocking chair at Tim and LeChelle's house after dinner. The warm summer sun has dropped below the horizon. The sky glows pale purple to the west and the stars glisten in the dark eastern sky. Fireflies are buzzing around, turning on and off, shooting nature's sparklers in the brush and foliage framing our backyards. LeChelle sits next to me in a glider.

I break the sound of crickets in the night air. "It looks like heaven."

"Heaven's going to be way nicer than this," Tim says, walking out onto the wood-framed porch.

"You think?" I look up.

"I know. I believe," he states.

"I believe, too." LeChelle leans into me. "Why do you like coming over here so much? I know my cookin' is good, but really, why?"

I stop rocking and just sit there. "You have something that I want." I start rocking again. "You have that peace. A love that I can see and feel and, when I am here, I can pretend I am a part of it." As I make my admission, my voice softens and my face drops. My longing for true happiness is exposed for all to see.

LeChelle gets out of her chair and kneels in front of me. With both hands, she gently lifts my face. Looking into my eyes, with all that warmth and love and security staring back at me, she says, "That ain't us, baby, that's Jesus in us."

Finally, something warm and positive is there with me. I feel a strange, deep sensation similar to salty tears coating my cheeks.

A Holy presence of hope bathes me in light. The hope that was ripped away by the darkness has been given back to me, even though I did nothing to earn it.

I cry out, "Mom! I'm afraid."

"Alliiice, where are you?" I hear her call out for me.

Where am I? Where am I?

Fear is giving way to promise. I am slowly starting to regain strength. The ugliness that gripped me an eternal moment ago has loosened its hold. It still feels very real, but I can breathe again. The damp coldness has been wrung out like a thawing towel left out all winter until the spring.

I have been raised from the sadness that came from a magnitude of loss, mourning, heartache, and decay. A sadness deeper than the deaths of my loved ones or the death of myself.

There's no sugarcoating what I just experienced: Wickedness. Pure evil. An evil with an intent to destroy, obliterate me by drowning me in all of my frozen brokenness.

It was just a moment. But it was also vast. Was it hell? Was it death? Was it truth? Did I just see the ugliness that is inside of me? Was that pitch-black icy well of sadness born of my inability to forgive? My bitterness toward my father or even my mother for leaving me, or God for not stopping it all? The shadows of my heart that I have been trying to run from and avoid all of my life?

"Allliiiiice," my mother calls out again. Her voice is my favorite melody.

I have no idea where I am now. I'm lost but I'm not looking anymore. I'm alone but I don't feel lonely. Here, wherever here is, is still and calm. A Holy presence is around me. It is the same teal-colored presence that filled my mother's room the night we buried her. Is it Jesus? Is it Mom? Is it an angel she sent to give me peace?

Humble tranquility engulfs my being and I understand my purpose and destiny. Peace and kindness live here. A sweet chorus of relief and adoration and worship reverberates from the gentle warmth that is present. Joy engulfs me as a flawless harmony bathes me, washing away my transgressions and making me pure again. Just like that.

Any awareness I may have had of longing, or being imperfect, is gone. In this place, I am made whole, completely refurbished, from inside out. There is nothing absent and I know I am no longer alone or damaged.

I hear Burton giving stern orders to a nurse standing in my room. "I want her baby near her."

My baby is alive! I fall on the ground realizing that she, like me, will now grow up motherless.

"You'll need to sign her out." The nurse sounds annoyed at Burton's lack of hospital protocol.

"Seriously, just get my baby up here. If they have a problem they can page me." He turns back to Alice, who is lying motionless on the bed. "I want my daughter and wife together. Life begets life. She needs to feel her baby in this room."

I want to feel her, to hold her, to love her, to raise her.

Dr. Nicole enters the room holding a chart. Her lips are drawn, her brow furrowed. She looks exhausted. "Okay, folks. Alice's labs are stable. We're taking her off the ventilator. She can breathe on her own now."

"Okay." It is all Burton can do to acknowledge the doctor's statement.

"After she finishes the last of her twenty-four hours of magnesium, we can take her for a head CT, but right now—"

Burton finishes her sentence and his voice cracks. "There's no way to tell if she'll ever walk or talk or hold our baby." He sighs and looks at Dr. Nicole. "I've said it a hundred times, but it's just so surreal to be on this side of the conversation."

She touches his arm. "I'm sorry, Burton. I really am."

"Me, too. Me, too."

In a heap of sorrow and complete honesty, I whisper with no one hearing me, pleading to Jesus, "Lord God—I'm sorry. I'm so sorry. Please, have mercy on me. Have mercy on my baby."

I'm in the calming yang to the horrific yin that must have been a quick, kaleidoscope view of hell. Now there is a supernatural tugging on my soul. I'm suddenly aware of what Tim meant when he talked about the battle of the darkness versus the light. Of evil versus good, and death versus life—in spiritual, supernatural, and metaphoric ways that are not of the known world.

I want to stay wrapped in this warm blanket of humility and grace. I feel relief as I hear my mother's voice calling out my name. I have an overwhelming desire to be with her again.

I crave moving from this place of peace to the next stage of what I recognize as bliss. I am conscious that it is as effortless as taking the invisible hand that is outstretched to me and moving on. It is a blink of reassurance. It is my choice.

Then I hear cries. At first I think they are my own cries from the overwhelming understanding, but I touch my face and my eyes are dry. I am not sad.

These cries are not the cries of death and fear. They are cries of life and boldness. They are cries from something that is a part of me but is now missing. Oh! It is the beauty of a baby crying. A newborn baby.

I am besieged with desire to comfort it. In all of its innocence it cries out and I am growing in my desire to ease it. I am acutely aware that I need to find this crying child and hold it. Rock it. Love it. Save it.

These are the most basic sounds searching for comfort and love to pacify its true inner desires. Wanting to be in the safe arms of its maker. To be reassured by the relationship with the omni-present, to know there is indeed something bigger. Something car-ing for it. Something in control and protecting it, like a father, a mother, or a God.

Suddenly, I realize I have been naive all along: I alone have the power to calm the crying. I have the power to soothe it.

And then, the epiphany.

This is how God feels about me. This is how He feels about each of His children. He walks our path from birth to death with every one of His children. He sends us to this world of choices. He lets us crawl, walk, and run. He watches us fall and wants to pull us up, wants to hold us, wants to provide us with the peace and comfort and safety that only a true parent can offer.

He sees how lost we are, He knows our fear. He can hear us crying out in desperation. We are humiliated: our naked, tender souls are exposed to a world that constantly pricks us with nee-dles. He wants to shield us. He wants a life of peace for us, but it's not a life that we can build alone, separate and away from Him.

He is the only real, loving parent who will never, ever fail us.

"Alice," a masculine voice finally says. "Alice, do you hear me?"

The baby is no longer crying. I am left to choose again. Only now, I get to choose knowing that our God wants to rescue me. I know now that He wants to rescue every one of His children, if only we will let Him in, and let Him be the parent that He was meant to be.

It is my choice and I make it. I choose to believe and I choose to live.

The baby cries and I try to say something, but my throat is dry and sore. I open my eyes and see Burton sitting next to me.

Burton: My good Southern man who is dedicated to helping

others. A man who did the right thing by marrying the woman who was pregnant with his child. Even though she was broken. Even though she was me. He could have run—heck, I would have run—but he didn't. He wanted to see this thing through.

And now I know that together, we will. I watch his worried, tired eyes boring holes in the machines. He lets out a deep sigh and turns toward me. He looks drained. Then his eyes meet mine and he springs back to life. "Alice! Alice! Can you see me?"

I can see him and I want to talk to him.

"Can you move anything? Move something if you recognize me." He searches my body for signs.

I'm too weak to move my limbs, but I have enough energy to activate the muscles in my face.

"You're smiling." His voice is filled with relief and elation. He leans down and kisses me. "You're smiling." His eyes are welling with tears. "Can you lift one finger?" He looks down at my hand.

I raise my pointer finger.

A baby cries from its hospital bassinet in the corner.

"Hey." A gravelly whisper escapes my sandpapered throat. I fight for every syllable. "My baby."

Burton brings her to me. She is peach fuzz and baldness with big dark eyes and wrapped tight in a pink blanket like a baby burrito. He puts her close to my face so I can smell her. I close my eyes and inhale the fragrance of her head. I try to nuzzle my face into her.

Her newness and the residual aroma of heaven is the last thing I remember before fading back to restful darkness.

My eyelids are heavy but I pry them open to see Tim rocking in a chair, holding a baby. My baby. Dr. Nicole is writing something on a chart at the end of my bed while a nurse attends to my machines.

I am in a different room now. This one has pictures of Bud Adams, the Tennessee Titans' owner, on the wall. Weird.

Tim stands up with the baby and walks over to me. He looks into my eyes and asks, "How do you feel?"

How do I feel? That's a loaded question. My voice sounds funny when I say, "I feel okay, I guess." I extend my arms, IV cords dangling, and reach out for my child, asking a question that I suddenly realize I have been waiting my whole life to ask: "Can I hold her?"

Tim looks at Dr. Nicole, who gives him a professional "Yes."

He gently lays her on my chest. A little pale-pink-and-blue cap is on her head. She's swaddled in a matching blanket.

She is so, so innocent. I've never seen anything more simple and perfect in my life.

"Feeling stronger?" Dr. Nicole looks deep in my eyes.

I nod yes. "Thank you—" I feel so indebted to her for so much. "Thank you, Nicole."

"All in a day's work." She rubs my leg.

"Or nine months," I add.

"Get some rest, lady." She hands a nearby nurse my chart and leaves.

Tim watches me as I look up at his face. "I saw things," I confess. "Things that—" I shake it off and stop, not wanting to sound crazy. "I want her to have a clean slate," I say, never taking my eyes off my little one. "I want her to have a sense of belonging to something bigger than me or this world or herself."

"You need to sleep, baby girl."

But I don't want to sleep. I can't sleep, so I just start rambling. "You need to understand. I don't want her life to be as hard as mine. I want her to know her worth and her value. I want her to be good and giving, and I want her to understand her purpose. I want her to have a foundation so she is not rocked when life comes at her with heartbreak and disappointment. I want her to feel the love. God's love. More than anything else, I want her to know that."

"You want her to be the woman in Proverbs 31:10–31." He chuckles. "Look it up. You'll have plenty of time to do it."

17

To Tell Them All

My daughter just face-planted into the cake on her high-chair tray. Her cheeks and chin are covered with vanilla icing, giving her a creamy sugar mustache and beard. She is wearing a birthday hat with a giant "1" on the top of it.

Burton has his arm wrapped around my waist, a waist that finally exists again. I have made the choice to stop my Alice in the Mad Hatter's crazy-making race and quit running. I'm not just choosing God but I'm choosing this man and this marriage. He pulls me close for a kiss, unashamed that Tim, LeChelle, their children, and Amos, who are all singing, "Happy birthday, dear Alleene, happy birthday to you," are watching his generous affection.

It seems fitting that we named our baby after my mother.

Little Allie squeals in delight, "Momma . . . Momma!" as she claps her hands, sending icing and sprinkles flying everywhere.

We all laugh as Burton grabs the paper towels to wipe us off.

Burton is quietly embracing and supporting my faith without forcing what he already knows on me. A believer in God, he is also learning new paths with me as I ask the questions that perhaps all people really want truthful answers to. It is nice to have that bond to connect us. That faith growing between us. I think he recognizes a slight shift in my attitude, awareness of others, and my genuine desire to be a better woman, wife, mother. This I hope makes him happy because it is working for me.

Tim and LeChelle and Burton and I have been doing what they call a *life group,* which meets once a week. Tim calls it my "hole-punching sessions."

But tomorrow is my day. Tomorrow, I join Pastor Tim and Opie on that great big stage at Bethel. Tomorrow is my day in the dunk tank.

It's taken me almost eighteen months since moving to the South to get here and not be embarrassed by the term *born again.* Truth be told I have been stigmatized with all of the negative stereotypes that go along with the Jesus train by a slew of my old business colleagues in Los Angeles—well, with the exception of Amos. I can't say I blame most of them. I would have totally thought the same of them if our roles were reversed. They knew me. They saw what I did. They heard my words and watched me spin out of control, fixated on being on the top, no matter what. I wouldn't have believed change is possible if I hadn't lived it. But someday, someday . . . they'll believe that it is possible, if even by just knowing me.

Also, I have learned that the easiest way to save the open seat next to me on the Southwest flight from Nashville to LA is to be reading a Bible as people walk past me. It's so funny. I could be holding a *Playgirl* and some dude would sit down, but a Bible is a surefire way to keep my middle seat sacred!

As I walk to the other room to get presents for Allie, Amos is on my heels. "You're sure about this?" he asks, picking up a manila envelope off my dresser.

"Yes," I say, scooping up birthday gifts wrapped in pink Barbie wrapping paper. "I've spent the last year growing spiritually as fast as Allie has been growing physically, and I'm ready to let go of the past."

He sits down on my bed and holds out the envelope.

I stand there looking at it. I set the presents back down on my bed and take the envelope and open it. After reading the contract, I look up at Amos.

"Never too late," he says. "Just tear it up."

"We really built something." I shake the paper. "But now, I'm just different. It's probably not the best idea for me to be digging in Dumpsters anymore, but I wouldn't trade one second of it. It made me who I was and got me to this place."

"Then why walk away?"

"It's not what I'm meant to do with my life."

"So you're just gonna throw it all away?"

"Amos, I'm not throwing it away. I'm making over two million dollars with stock options once we sell it. I wouldn't exactly say that's chucking it. I just don't want the day-to-day anymore."

"So this is it? Mommyville with a bunch of Bible-thumpers?"

"That's part of it."

"Part? I'd say you've strapped yourself into the Jesus dingy and gone over the falls with the rest of 'em."

"Look, I'm not saying I'm completely buying everything they are selling. And I'm not magically perfect. I have yet to completely clean up my sailor mouth; I still drop the occasional F-bomb. I still need to meet my Pinot Noir bottle for our six o'clock happy-hour date; I figure if Jesus turned water to wine it can't be that bad. If I were a street sign, I would be bright orange with black letters spelling out WORK IN PROGRESS.

"But it is true, I have gone from making fun of them to being one of them. But it's more than that. I know I have more to do with my life—"

He interrupts me. "So you know Christians hate gay people, right? Am I out now, too?"

"Amos, Jesus loves all people. Look at me."

I take the pen and sign the papers, put them back in the folder, and hand it back to him. With a smile.

"You do seem"—he stands up and back, as if to better assess me—"different."

"I do?"

"I've known you a long time, sweetie, and this is the first time I can say I've ever seen you happy."

"Something in me has changed. I can't really describe it. It's weird. It's like I'm not just living my life in the status quo of me anymore. I mean, I'm still sassy, it's just I have this . . . understanding. It's a peace that wasn't there before—or maybe it was, but I just never trusted it."

"Well, I like you now and I liked you before, too. You were always good . . . somewhere in there."

"I'm not ashamed anymore of who I was! I did the best I could with what I knew. If I didn't live the way I lived, I would have never been with Burton or gotten pregnant or met Tim and LeChelle or learned there is a different way for me to live my life," I say, smiling. "Sure, I still have shadows in my heart, but it's like a light is on now and I don't want to be that person anymore. I just don't."

"A God night-light?" He laughs, sounding like me over a year ago.

"Kinda," I say, shrugging my shoulders. "I've seen that no matter how broken we all are, there is hope, and true happiness is possible. There is meaning to all our madness."

"Really, now," Amos says with mock disbelief. "Can you tell me exactly what that is, please?"

I hug him one last time. "Amos, we all deserve love. But most importantly, none of us is beyond forgiveness. I think it all starts there."

He hugs me tight. "I love you, Alice Ferguson Bannister."

"I love you, too." I push back. "And more importantly, God loves us all."

"You think?" He's doubtful but then again, he hasn't had the year I've had.

"I do."

I often wonder why it happened to me. All of it. My mother dying. My dad's abuse. The truly morally bankrupt life that I lived while filled with so much hurt—most of it self-inflicted. Running. Always running. Why was I the one who got turned inside out? I look back now on those moments of true desperation and I see I was never alone. Maybe none of us are; we just don't know how to believe it.

Why did God pick me to see beyond what I thought to be the natural world? I think He picks us all. Maybe it took feeling all of my pain and discovering God's purpose for my life for me to be able to break down all my protective mechanisms and tell the story.

My mother had been right. I can make a difference with my life.

I sit down at my computer and begin to type:

> This is the story of an ordinary, broken woman who
> was given an extraordinary gift . . . one Sunday.

ONE SUNDAY
Reading Group Guide

Alice Ferguson is the definition of a self-made and morally ambiguous woman. She built a successful career as an assistant editor of a tabloid magazine; launched her own Hollywood gossip website, Trashville; and pulled herself single-handedly out of poverty and anonymity. But Alice's LA-centered world is turned upside down when a charming Southern gentleman not only gets her pregnant but dares to fall in love with her, too. Forced to move to Tennessee for her health and the health of her unborn child, Alice gets to know her African-American neighbors, Pastor Tim and his wife, LeChelle, who begin to open her heart and mind to the impossible idea that God may love her despite her painful, self-inflicted life choices. After years of hiding from her troubled and rocky past, Alice faces her demons, learning forgiveness and, ultimately, finding satisfaction and letting real love into her life.

Discussion Questions

1. "Once again, I was kinda listening, kinda not. Only this was my wedding, which should give an indication of my laissez-faire ideology regarding commitment" (page 2). How does this initial moment in the novel—Alice's wedding—depict her as a main character? Did you like her? If not, did you come to like her? In what ways does Alice change as the novel continues?

2. Do you think Alice was truly unhappy with the way she was living her life in Los Angeles? Do you believe that unhappy people can change and find joy with the help of God and Godly people?

3. The South—in particular, Nashville—is the main setting for this novel. Why do you think the author chose to set the novel in Tennessee?

4. Revisit the scene on page 44 when Alice recalls dancing with her parents in the kitchen. Why do you think Alice spent twenty-five years avoiding this happy memory?

5. Discuss Alice's collection of religious and spiritual paraphernalia. Why do you think she has amassed this collection? What does her interest in these items imply about her journey toward discovering Christianity?

6. In what way or ways does Alice's mother's illness affect her daughter? Do you think the early loss of her mother somehow led Alice to a career as a tabloid publisher? How is family—or a lack thereof—central to Alice's sense of self-worth?

7. In your opinion, why did Alice agree to marry Burton?

8. Why do you think the author chose to make Alice a Caucasian woman and the Jackson family African-Americans? Do you believe that true reconciliation can exist between races in the South?

9. Consider the figure of Alice's mother, who visits Alice shortly after her death. In what ways is "The Occurrence" an omen for what is to come in Alice's future? Turn to page 135 and discuss.

10. "At once, I understand. An understanding that I've never been more confident about, coming from a source not of this world. My tears stop. My sadness is wiped away by peace" (page 137). Do you think this is a definition of faith? If you were to define faith for yourself, how would you describe it? Is your definition similar to Alice's?

11. Discuss Tim and Alice's friendship. What does Tim symbolize for Alice? Does he fill a void for her? Do you believe Tim could be the spiritual father in place of her real father who died? If so, how?

12. Do you think Alice's transformation could have happened in California, or did the new landscape of Tennessee contribute to her change of perspective?

13. On page 195 Tim describes his son's kite with the following metaphor: "You are not the string. You are the kite. . . . The string is God's purpose for your life—and He holds the string."

Before meeting Tim, is Alice a kite without a string, "Gettin' tossed and turned" (page 194)? List with your group the ways in which Alice's life choices seem purposeless. In your opinion, what gives Alice a purpose, a direction?

14. A central theme of the novel is family and, in particular, parenthood. Discuss the ways in which parenthood and family affect Alice and the other characters. Consider Alice, Alice's parents, Burton, and the Jacksons in your response.

15. Is Alice's accepting of Christ's love a sudden awakening or a long-term process?

16. Do you believe that Alice's journey toward faith is a real yearning to belong to something greater than herself or just another passing religious fad for her?

17. Do you believe that faith and walking with God can heal wounds caused by death, abandonment, shame, or addiction? Have you endured any of these trials? If so, do you believe that God loves you?

18. Why do you think the author chose to make Bethel church a mixed-race congregation?

19. On page 250 Tim tells Alice that she ought to look up Proverbs 31:10–31, because that is the kind of woman Alice will want her daughter to become. Read the passage aloud to your group (you can find it at www.biblegateway.com).

   Why do you think Tim references this passage? Do you think Alice shares any characteristics with the woman described in the Bible? If yes, which? If no, do you believe that through Jesus Christ she can be like this woman?

20. In the end, how does Alice discover her happiness? What is her purpose? What purpose have you been called to fulfill?

21. Discuss the significance of the title. What happens "one Sunday" that so alters Alice's life? Consider the many layers of this title's symbolism in your response.

Additional Activities:
Ways of Enhancing Your Book Club

1. *One Sunday* is about the love and forgiveness of family, neighbor, oneself, and God. The Jackson family embodies these values, and, as a group, they practice what they preach. At Ava's birthday dinner, Alice is witness to the family tradition of "speaking life into someone" (page 28). Play this game with your book club. Have each member give a "one-line affirmation" (page 28) to the other members. Afterward, discuss how this felt. Why do you think this tradition is called "speaking life into someone"?

2. Alice's transformation took place largely because of her relationship with Pastor Tim and his family. Read aloud the prayer Tim gave to Alice—A Prayer for Hope—on pages 65–66. Discuss the importance of the prayer and why you believe it touched Alice so deeply. Did you feel similarly? Share any favorite prayers, spiritual practices, or poignant life moments with your group.

3. Alice finds joy in the comfort of Southern food throughout the course of the novel. Have a dinner night with your book club. Over traditional Southern comfort food, such as fried okra, mashed potatoes, ribs, and peach cobbler, discuss with your group the ways in which sharing a meal is a form of God's love. Why do you think Alice loves to eat with the Jackson family so much?

Questions for Carrie Gerlach Cecil

1. **In the epigraph you write, "Although this novel is fiction, I believe we write what we know." How much of this story is fiction and how much is true? Would you classify this story as fiction based on personal experiences, or personal experiences peppered with fiction?**

   I wouldn't classify this book as either fiction or nonfiction, as it is both. Honestly there is a lot of Alice's emotion in my soul, but unlike Alice, both my parents are very much still alive and well. I write of familiar places and people that have come across my path, and I try to create characters that embody a motley crew of real people in real circumstances. I tried to take levels of joy, pain, laughter, and shame that all people share, me included, and pump it up to extreme levels to make it compelling. I want to change lives; otherwise, what's the point?

2. **Why did you decide to write this story? Describe the journey from conception to publication.**

   In 2005, I was in my house in Los Angeles. I was relatively new to the Christian faith but was on fire for Jesus. I was praying and meditating, waiting for a sign or a moment of clarity before deciding what to do for my next project. I literally felt God in my heart say, "Write the book."

It wasn't that moment in *Field of Dreams,* when Kevin Costner hears the voice, "If you build it, they will come." But it was my own private version of that. The problem was I didn't know what book to write and I was fearful to write this one. But over time God opened my heart and put people into my life to help encourage me to pull this story out and put it on the page.

3. **Were any of the characters based on people you have known in your life? Or yourself? Do you relate most to Alice? Why or why not?**

Alice is a grittier, more morally bankrupt version of myself. Although I wouldn't make a lot of the choices she made, there were plenty she did make that came from things I did, so she is closest to my spirit. The other two main characters, Tim and LeChelle, are based on my friendship with Pastor Tim Johnson and his wife, Le'Chelle. They are my spiritual parents. Everything that is kind and accepting and gentle in Burton is pulled from my husband. There are others, but I'll keep them a secret!

4. **What would you name as the major theme(s) of the novel? What do you hope readers will take away from the story?**

The major theme of this book is HOPE. Thematically, the book is about change, reconciliation, forgiveness, and redemption through the love of Jesus Christ. I want people to take away from this book that you are never too broken, tarnished, or sinful to turn to God and have Him forgive you, accept you, love you, and make you new!

5. **Discuss the significance of setting in the novel.**

Setting the novel in the South was premeditated. I believe it is a wonderful part of the country, rich in history and diverse people. I wanted to showcase a region historically filled with racial tension and demonstrate that African-American and Caucasian people had differences, but we are united in our love of Christ and humanity. I love showing God's colorful tapestry of people.

6. **Who is your favorite author and why?**

My favorites are Anne Lamott and Stormie Omartian, as they both keep faith real to me. They are unabashedly honest and inspiring in their writing.

7. **How did you come to be a writer? Like Alice, do you feel inspired by God to write?**

I started writing in the sixth grade as an outlet for my emotions. My teacher, Mr. Eisenfield, recognized my gift and put me in an advanced creative writing class—and I've never looked back. God gave me the gift of writing, but I did not realize that until about six years ago, when I had the epiphany that my purpose in life was to use that gift to reach others and help them to love themselves and to love God.

8. **What does Alice's baby girl symbolize?**

The birth of Alice's daughter prefigures Alice's rebirth as a Christian. She is a clean slate with new hope and new life and endless joy.

9. **How did the experience of writing this book differ from your first book, *Emily's Reasons Why Not*? How was it similar?**

Emily's Reasons Why Not was a fun chick-lit book without a true purpose. I loved writing Emily because she made me laugh out loud, and women in the dating world could relate to her. *One Sunday* is more meaningful and soulful to me. I felt led by something greater to write it, and it has more layers and ideally evokes change in people.

10. **At what point in your writing career did you decide to write about faith and God?**

I decided to write about faith when I realized God is real. When I knew I was changed and couldn't put into words what exactly had changed me. As a writer, I found it daunting and exciting to try to tell a version of that story. In the beginning, I was afraid to write about real faith that exists in damaged people. I thought faithful people had to be perfect. Perfectly behaved, perfectly dressed, and perfectly mannered. I suppose I had more of a *religious* viewpoint than a Christian outlook. It wasn't until I had actually been saved from my pain that I realized the best stories of redemption come from the darkest places—and I knew I could articulate that in this story. People want to debate religion all the time, but what they cannot debate is a human heart change. My heart is changed.

11. What is next for you as a writer? Will Alice be making a comeback in any future novels?

I am working on two nonfiction books and a television show at the moment and want to get them to the marketplace, but Alice is haunting me. So many Christians come to know the Lord but do not get the support and foundation and teachings to keep moving forward on their walk. They end up back where they started. I'd like to show Alice at the next stage of her faith, facing the obstacles thrown at her as a new believer. Tests that will shake her belief, friends who will doubt her sincerity, the love that will sustain her on the journey. . . . Alice is ready to hit the page. I'm just letting her enjoy the moment for now.